THE BETTER SISTER

THE
BETTER
SISTER

A NOVEL

ALAFAIR BURKE

HARPER

An Imprint of HarperCollins*Publishers*

HarperCollins books may be purchased for educational, business, or sales promotional use. For information, please email the Special Markets Department at SPsales@harpercollins.com.

FIRST EDITION

Photograph by Skylines/Shutterstock, Inc.

Library of Congress Cataloging-in-Publication Data

Names: Burke, Alafair, author.
Title: The better sister : a novel / Alafair Burke.
Description: New York, NY : Harper, [2019]
Identifiers: LCCN 2018051071 (print) | LCCN 2018057887 (ebook) | ISBN 9780062853356 (E-book) | ISBN 9780062853370 (hardback) | ISBN 9780062887955 (large print)
Subjects: LCSH: Sisters—Fiction. | Murder—Fiction. | Family secrets. | Domestic fiction. | Man-woman relationships—Fiction. | False arrest. | Criminal defense lawyers. | New York (N.Y.)—Fiction. | BISAC: FICTION / Suspense. | FICTION / Crime.
Classification: LCC PS3602.U755 (ebook) | LCC PS3602.U755 B48 2019 (print) | DDC 813/.6—dc23
LC record available at https://lccn.loc.gov/2018051071

ISBN 978-0-06-285337-0

ISBN 978-0-06-289492-2 (International Edition)

19 20 21 22 23   LSC   10 9 8 7 6 5 4 3 2 1

For Jennifer Barth
editor in title, sister in spirit

THE BETTER SISTER

Fourteen Years Earlier

I BETRAYED MY sister while standing on the main stairs of the Metropolitan Museum of Art in a beaded Versace gown (borrowed) and five-inch stiletto heels (never worn again).

At the time, I never could have scored an invitation—or been able to afford a ticket—to the Met Gala in my own right. I was the guest of my boss, Catherine Lancaster, the editor in chief of *City Woman* magazine. She wasn't even my boss. She was my boss's boss's boss. And somehow she personally invited me.

Well, not personally. She had her assistant swing by my cubicle to deliver the message, which turned out to be a good thing, because my immediate RSVP was laughter. Not even a normal-person laugh. More like a snort. Even back then, the so-called Party of the Year was paparazzi porn, a celebrity-soaked, fashion-focused spectacle. The idea of me—the bookish new member of the writing staff—hobnobbing with rock stars, Oscar winners, and supermodels was ridiculous. So I snort-laughed.

The assistant hid neither her disapproval nor her eye roll, but I assured her that I was honored to accept. Then, after pulling up photos of last year's event from the magazine archives, I went about begging my friend Kate, who worked at *Cosmo*, to smuggle out a suitable dress for me to borrow. Fake it till you make it, as they say.

She was downright gleeful when she handed me the garment bag. "It's Versace. And it has pockets!"

Catherine even offered to have her driver pick me up at my apartment prior to the event. If she had been a man, I would have been worried about what I'd gotten myself into. Instead, I felt like Cinderella going to the ball. Because she was a woman, I trusted her.

She validated that instinct when she joined me in the back seat of the car outside her Upper East Side town house and told me she had invited me because she was impressed by a sidebar I had written about Take Back the Night events on college campuses. The main piece was about two child actresses—famous twins—starting their college careers at NYU. But when I heard that one of the sisters was active in organizing NYU's annual event for survivors of sexual abuse, I pitched the idea to *City Woman*.

Catherine told me I had "a smart gut," and that the best advice she could give me was to learn to trust it. Times were changing. "People think we're watching *Sex and the City* for the clothes and the orgasm banter, but it's feminism disguised as dramedy. Another wave is building. It's just a matter of time before the floodgates break, and women like you will be the ones to write the stories."

Way better than Cinderella. All she got out of the night was a prince. I was going to have a career.

When we arrived, not even Catherine merited the attention of the photographers snapping away on the front steps. But once we were inside, a voice called out, "Oh, Catherine, perfect timing. Join us for the step-and-repeat."

As she jumped into her spot before the backdrop banner for official event photos, she thrust her purse at me, silently mouthing a "Thanks, can you find the bar?" before she left me on my own. The bag was a sequined clutch emblazoned with a Venus symbol, which *City Woman* used as the O in our magazine title. It was a clever accessory for the evening, but I allowed myself a beat of pride that my borrowed dress had pockets big enough for a lipstick, cash, and my company-issued cell phone. No bag necessary.

I found the bar as instructed and then realized I had no idea what Catherine would want to drink. In light of her *Sex and the City* reference in the car, I ordered two cosmos, tucked her clutch between my waist and elbow, and managed to teeter my way back to the step-and-repeat. By the time she finally extricated herself from the photography session, I was done with my drink and ready to start on hers. When she rejoined me, she grabbed the drink, but not her purse.

"Catherine . . ." I held up the sequined clutch.

She was hugging a fashion designer.

"Do you need . . ."

Then the mayor.

I ended up following her around with that stupid purse all night long, leaving only to get drinks, which I decided to vary wildly as the night went on. If she noticed, she didn't say anything—and Catherine Lancaster would definitely speak up if she disapproved.

These days, if I treated an assistant that way, I'd worry they'd take to Twitter or call in a blind item to Page Six. But in the early aughts, a young writer like me considered it a privilege to do the grunt work for those who had earned their spot at the top of the masthead. I was the designated silent purse-holder.

The first call to the phone stashed in the very expensive pocket of my designer dress came as dinner was being served. My parents. I let it go to voice mail. Stupidly, I actually assumed they were calling because they were proud to have a daughter at such a lavish event. They had never heard of it, of course, but I tried to explain to them when I first got the invitation that it was highly unusual for someone at my level to be included. But when they called five minutes later, and then again an hour after that, I knew it wouldn't be about me at all.

I had two options: leave while Catherine was holding court at the *City Woman* table, or let it all flow into voice mail. It was possible something was wrong with Mom or Dad, but in my gut, I knew it was probably something with Nicky. It was always Nicky. I stayed put in my seat.

When another call came in during dessert, I snuck a peek at the tiny screen of my Nokia. This time it was from Nicky's house. Yep, as suspected, it was my sister's drama once again, perfectly timed with one of the most important opportunities I'd been given since moving to New York City to pursue a writing career. This time, I turned off the phone before stashing it in my pocket.

Catherine glanced at me as she rose from the table, which I interpreted as an invitation to follow. When she broke off for the ladies' room after what I deemed to be an uncharacteristic smoke break outside the tent, I finally powered up my phone to check my messages. Three from my mom: "Call me," a hang-up, and "Damn it, she's still not answering."

That left the most recent call—the one from Nicky. It was just like her to pick this night to implode.

When I pressed 1 to listen, it wasn't Nicky's voice that I heard. It was her husband, Adam.

This wasn't the first time Adam had reached out to me about my sister, but this one was different. I'd never heard this kind of emotion before in his voice—anger, mixed with exhaustion and fear. The message itself was short. "Call me when you can, okay? It's important." He left me the number of the cell phone he used for work. I repeated it over and over again in my head until I dialed it.

When he picked up after two rings, he laid out the facts like a lawyer, not a husband. Nicky was at the Cleveland Clinic. As he spoke— while A-list actors and socialites mingled around me—I pictured my sister. Her long, honey-brown hair plastered against her shoulder blades. Pool-soaked clothing clinging to her thin frame. And the baby—I still called him a baby, at least—spitting up chlorinated water from his tiny lungs.

"I can't keep going through this with her, Chloe. Not with a child in the picture. She could have really hurt him. If I hadn't walked outside . . ."

I started to protest that Nicky would never hurt her son, but realized I had no way of knowing if that were true. Nicky would never intentionally harm anyone, but she had a way of damaging everyone who entered her orbit. She always had.

"Just tell me, Adam. Tell me why you're really calling."

"I need your help."

How many times had I noticed that Adam had more in common with me than with his own wife? How many times had I held my tongue, not wanting to be accused of sabotaging the only (sort of) healthy relationship my sister had ever had? Now here we were, five hundred miles apart, connected only by a cell phone signal, and it was clear whose side I would take. Adam needed me.

Our story—independent of Nicky—would develop later, but you could say that night marked the story's beginning. It was the moment I chose Ethan over the rest of my family, which meant I was choosing Adam.

I had no idea that four years later, I'd become the second Mrs. Adam Macintosh, or that ten years after that, I'd be the one to find his dead body.

PART I

ADAM

1

Fourteen Years Later

THE BACK OF Café Loup was dark and cool, so every time the restaurant door opened to the sun and humidity outside, I found myself craning my neck to look for Adam. He hadn't promised to join us, but I knew that the entertainment reporter conducting the interview was "dying to meet the man behind the woman."

Unfortunately, I had made the mistake of telling Adam about her expectations. If I had kept that piece of information to myself, I could have lied and told her that my husband had a scheduling conflict and couldn't make it. But instead I had set myself up for uncertainty and therefore disappointment, and was now waiting anxiously to see if he would put in an appearance.

I forced myself to focus my attention where it belonged.

The interviewer was named Colby and was probably twenty-five years old, around the same age I was when I first landed a journalism job in New York City. The landscape had changed dramatically in the interim. When I started at *City Woman*, we boasted an average monthly

circulation of nearly three hundred thousand copies, and a staff that occupied a full floor of a prestigious midtown high-rise. *Eve* was one of
the last women's magazines standing, but we were struggling to crack
a hundred thousand print readers a month.

These days, most publishers were putting the "free" in "freelance."
Given the changes in the market, my guess is that young, eager Colby
had twice the résumé I'd compiled at her age, yet was happy to have
landed her full-time gig with a web-only e-zine aimed at millennial
women.

We were finished with introductions, and I could tell when she looked
down at her notes that we were moving on to her prepared questions.

"By the time you were named editor in chief at *Eve*, the industry
had all but written the magazine's obituary. But you worked a complete
turnaround—ramping up online readership, adding more politics and
less fluff—and now *Eve* is one of the last remaining successful feminist-
oriented magazines in the country. Now you're on the eve—no pun
intended—of receiving the vaunted Press for the People Award for
your influential Them Too series. Does this moment feel like the culmination of your entire life's work?"

I knew my answer would make me sound sad and tired to Colby
and her peers, but I told myself that at least it was authentic. "The
culmination of my life's work? I certainly hope not. That kind of talk
makes me feel like I'm being put out to pasture."

She hit the pause button on her iPhone and began apologizing pro-
fusely. "Oh my god, I'm so sorry. You're like my idol. That's not what
I meant at all."

I hit the record button again and told her that she should never
apologize for a question, and then gave her a sound-bite she could use.

"I feel guilty taking credit for any of it," I said. "The real heroes
are the women who told their own stories first. The Me Too movement
made women begin to feel safe speaking out. We all knew such conduct
was repugnant—and rampant—but we were always taught to tough

it out. Don't rock the boat. Smile and make it to the next day. But then women found power in the collective, and powerful men learned that there could be consequences to their actions, even if delayed, even without police and courtrooms. That was the starting point for everything, so, really, my work was just following the lead of all those other women, and the journalists who helped tell their stories."

The work she was asking me about was a series of features covering an initiative I launched at *Eve*. On the heels of the Me Too movement, I wrote an opinion piece exploring my concern that the movement's seismic cultural shift would be confined to high-profile, celebrity-driven workplaces. After the initial takedowns of predators who had committed heinous acts for years, the movement's influence had seeped into a discussion of lesser offenses by other famous men. But would it affect the workplaces of women employed by bosses we had never heard of? What about the women who worked in factories and on sales floors? What about waitresses and bartenders who were beholden to managers for the busiest shifts, and to customers for tips? To help spotlight their stories, I paired "everyday" women suffering sexual abuse and harassment in the workplace with a better-known Me Too groundbreaker. I personally wrote the articles tracing the commonalities in their stories and the impact of the resulting friendships. In a twist on the now-famous hashtag, I had dubbed the effort Them Too.

What I began as an experiment blossomed in ways I never predicted. An A-list actress who was among the first to come forward about an abusive director brought her "them-too sister" as her date to the Academy Awards. The host of one of the network morning shows was now godmother to her match's newborn daughter. And, most important to me, seven Fortune 500 corporations had fired high-level executives and implemented corporate-wide policy changes as a result of the series, all because women had used their celebrity—and I had used my magazine—as a way to bring attention to the narratives of women who believed they had no voice.

Although I tried to focus on the women who had participated in the series, Colby of course wanted to hear all the crap I had put up with over the course of my own career.

We were on the topic of the second man who had offered me a job in exchange for sex when the restaurant door opened again. By then, I was deep into the story and had assumed that Colby and I would be alone for the rest of our meeting. Adam was well past the bar, almost to our table, by the time I spotted him in my periphery.

"Oh my goodness, what a surprise," I said, rising to greet him with a hug. "I can't remember the last time we were together before five o'clock on a weekday."

I noticed Colby sizing him up, surprised at his youthful appearance, as many people were when first meeting him. Adam was six years older than I am, making him forty-seven, but I joked that he'd stopped aging about a decade ago. He was seemingly genetically incapable of either hair loss or weight gain.

Phillip, our waiter, appeared instantly. "Oh, there he is. The handsome husband I was hoping to see." Our apartment was three blocks from Café Loup. We'd been regulars for years.

As Adam ordered a slightly dirty martini, Colby asked me if I was used to Adam being welcomed so enthusiastically. "So annoying," I said with mock resentment. "I kid you not: there's not a person on this planet who would say a bad word about him."

"Tell that to Tommy Farber," Adam said, reaching for my wineglass. He took a sip of my cabernet, wrinkled his nose, and handed the glass back to me. "Kid beat my ass every Friday afternoon for two years. I think I still have creases on my forehead from the locker door."

"How'd the two of you meet?" Colby asked.

I hated that question, but had the usual highly edited response ready to roll. "We knew each other back in Cleveland where we grew up, but reconnected when he moved to New York for work."

I was relieved when Colby seemed satisfied with the answer and went on to ask Adam what it was like to be a successful man married to an even more successful woman. I found myself envying—and resenting—the complete absence of discomfort or apology in her question. She wasn't in the habit (yet, at least) of protecting a man's ego.

As Adam spoke, I enjoyed playing a role I rarely got to occupy. I beamed as he told Colby how proud he had been of my every achievement: starting out as an assistant and then making it as a writer for *City Woman*, editor in chief at that little downtown-focused rag, my first essay in the *New Yorker*, my photo shoot three years before for *Cosmo*'s "40 Under 40" feature.

I grew up with parents who didn't even notice when I earned a blue ribbon in . . . anything. It was so like Adam to have a running list of my achievements at his fingertips. How many times had I been told how lucky I was to have a husband who was so unabashedly proud of his wife? As if there was something unnatural about it.

WE HELD HANDS AS WE made the short walk back to our apartment on Twelfth Street. "Thank you so much for doing that, Adam. If Colby has a boyfriend, I have a feeling he's going to be a little confused about why she seems so disappointed in him tonight. You were absolutely charming."

He looked at me out of the corner of his eye and winked.

At home, I automatically found myself rewarding him for supporting me, pouring a shot of sambuca from the bar cart in the living room.

He downed the drink in one gulp and grabbed my hands as I was wrapping them around his waist. "Were you happy with the interview?" He entwined his fingers in mine before placing my hands at the base of his neck and looking into my eyes. Then he was kissing that spot beneath my right ear, his go-to move when he had other plans for us. "I swear, that interviewer looked at you like you were Gandhi."

Adam and I hadn't been intimate in weeks. We'd both been so

busy. All I wanted was to crawl into bed with a novel. "Did you really just say Gandhi to try to get me hot?"

He stopped. "What's wrong?" he asked. Note to self: the least sexy phrase in the English language is "What's wrong?"

Back when I was still writing articles aimed at the sexed-up-wife crowd, I actually said that the key to saving your marriage was to fool around at least two times a week. "It's a lot easier to put up with each other's shit when you're putting your parts together." The advice wasn't exactly progressive, but at core, there was some truth in it. I closed my eyes and tried to match his earlier mood.

"Nothing's wrong. Sorry, I was just joking." When he started to kiss me again, I whispered "Please, don't stop." Did you know that in survey after survey conducted by women's magazines, those three words were the ones that men most wanted to hear in bed? *Please. Don't. Stop.*

I felt my breath quicken as his mouth paused at my clavicle and began moving toward the belly that I could have described as "a six-pack" just a few years earlier. I stepped out of my slingbacks, and, just like that, I was eager to finish what he had started.

As they say, fake it until you make it.

WHEN WE WERE FINISHED—both of us—I tucked myself into the crook of Adam's arm, the way we always used to sleep for the entire night before we bought the king bed. "That was amazing. Again, thank you so much for doing that stupid interview."

"Why would you call it stupid?"

"You know. Just cheesy. I'm not used to being the center of attention that way."

He looked at me for a full five seconds, studying my face. "But it's what you've always dreamed of, isn't it? And now you have it."

The words themselves were unobjectionable, even congratulatory.

But for some reason, they stung. I tried to tell myself I was being paranoid, feeling guilty about dragging him into that interview, where it was all me-me-me.

When he rotated 180 degrees and turned his back to me, my fears were momentarily confirmed. Then he reached for my top arm and draped it around him, pulling me into a spoon position. He kissed my hands and let out a satisfied sigh. Our cat, Panda, suddenly appeared from nowhere—the only way he knows how to make an appearance.

"Greedy Guy?" Adam's eyes were closed, but he had felt the nineteen-pound fur ball pounce on the mattress. When we first got married, we let six-year-old Ethan name our new kitten. He opted for Greedy Panda for reasons we still didn't understand, and ten years later, the name had taken on various iterations.

"Hmm-hmm." I smiled as Panda snuggled into the small of my back. I felt happy and relaxed.

When I heard the front door of the apartment open, I wasn't sure if I'd fallen asleep or if I'd only been resting my eyes. I glanced at the clock. It wasn't even ten. Ethan had made curfew with a full hour to spare.

"I should make sure he ate," I said.

"He's sixteen years old. He's probably had three dinners by now. You deserve to sleep. You have a big day tomorrow."

We both knew I'd be tossing and turning all night. I always felt confident with the written word, but I would need to stand up before hundreds of people at the awards ceremony to deliver my speech. I'd been preparing for the last week.

"I still can't believe all of this is happening," I whispered.

He pulled me closer, placing his top hand on my bare hip. It felt good.

"Hey, about that, I didn't have a chance to tell you earlier. Something came up with work, and I may be late tomorrow night."

I was glad he couldn't see my face. The news, delivered so casually, felt like a slap. I kept my voice level, not wanting to give him the ex-pected reaction.

"Well, what is it? Maybe I can talk to Bill." The head partner at Adam's firm was *Eve*'s lawyer and also a close friend.

"No, it's a client. It's Gentry."

I knew he was under pressure at the firm to bring in business, and that his biggest client, the Gentry Group, was an important part of the picture. "So . . . how late do you think you'll be?"

"Maybe not at all, but they're flying in from London, and I'm sup-posed to meet them at some conference room near JFK. I'm pretty much at their whim."

"But you'll definitely be there?"

"I just don't know, babe. I'll try, though. You know how proud I am of you, right?"

He kissed my hand, reached for the nightstand, and turned off the light. I listened to his slow, relaxed breaths as I rehearsed my speech in the dark.

2

ALL MY LIFE, I have been a creature of habit. In college, when other students scoured the catalog for afternoon classes to accommodate their idiosyncratic sleep schedules, I was the one who set the alarm for seven so I could hit the gym and the commons before a 9:00 a.m. lecture. I handled bills on the sixth of the month, did laundry on Saturdays, and grocery shopped on Sundays. Even now, I almost always ordered the same two things for lunch—Greek salad with salmon and roast beef on rye—from the deli beneath my office, and rarely ate out unless it was at one of my five regular restaurants, where I sit at my regular tables and order my regular meals. No chaos, no drama. Boring? To some people, sure. But I was convinced that routines and rituals were the key to both my happiness and my productivity, which—let's face it—were interrelated.

No surprise, then, that I followed a routine when it came to my work, too. Rare was the day when I wasn't at my desk by eight thirty.

But the day I would be honored by Press for the People was, in fact, a rare day. That night would be a celebration of a free press and the First Amendment more generally. Thrown at the Natural History Museum and less fashion-centric than the *Vogue* party at the Met, it was informally known as the Geek Gala. I knew that if I went into the *Eve* offices, staff would be popping in all day with congratulations—some out of sincerity, plenty out of sycophancy. Plus I'd have to leave early in any event to get ready, so I decided to work from home.

Now here's the thing about people who swear by routines. When they decide to break from the usual, they go big. The Greek salad is replaced by a large pepperoni pizza. The skipped day at the gym becomes a month of couch-potatoing. And working a half day from home meant that I was still lying in bed in my PJs at one o'clock, my legs pinned beneath the comforter by a nineteen-pound purring machine named Panda.

But my laptop was on lap duty, and I was getting more work done than if I'd suited up for the office. I had edited one article about the implications of recent health-care policy changes on birth-control access, and had moved on to a feature we were running on a female candidate who had recently become the youngest person ever elected to Congress. She had rocked the political establishment by dethroning a senior member of the Republican Party's leadership during the primaries. Her opponent was so certain of his continued tenure that he had refused to debate her and, in fact, never spoke her name until she knocked him out of the race with a double-digit lead at the polls. Perhaps most shockingly, she won a heavily Republican district with a platform that patched together centrist economic policies, inclusive social views, and a full-throated attack on the influence of corporate money on the electoral process. In the aftermath of her shocking win, pundits were calling for both parties to revise their allegiance to tribal partisan dogma. Even a skeptic like me found myself hopeful as I read the feature. Maybe the next generation would find a way to unite a divided country.

My warm fuzzies were quickly drenched when I clicked on the Dropbox link from the photographer we'd hired for the photo shoot. Where was the candidate who had worn her hair in a ponytail at the base of her neck? What had become of the jeans and brightly colored sweaters she'd donned for knocking doors? This, after all, was a woman who had gone viral by retweeting and mocking every single sexist insult she had received after showing up at a town fair meet-and-greet without makeup. And now she filled my screen in over-the-top glamour shots. More than a hundred of them, all the same. Oscar-ready hair, smoky eyes, and glossy lips. I didn't even want to ask where the clothes had come from. I recognized one of the jackets from this year's Prada collection.

I could already picture the calls for a boycott of *Eve*. Canceled subscriptions. Tweets bemoaning the demise of one of the last feminist magazines still in print. Someone funnier than I was would start a meme satirizing the front cover of the magazine.

Each shot was more nauseating than the last. I stifled a scream when I got to the photo of her dressed like a sexy librarian in thick glasses. What the hell was the photographer thinking, and why had a congresswoman agreed to participate?

I clicked out of the photo editor and drafted an email message to Maggie Hart, the writer who had been assigned to the profile. Hey Maggie. I'm reviewing the photos of Sienna Hartley. Did you attend the shoot? The looks are problematic, no? Please see if the photog has other shots we can use. Thx.-CAT

Chloe Anna Taylor. The staff at the magazine was so familiar with the initials that concluded my nonstop emails that they referred to me as "Cat" when I wasn't around.

I knew I should walk away from the computer while I waited for a reply, but I couldn't help myself. After forty years of nursing primarily good habits, I had managed to develop an extremely bad habit as of late. As I did almost every day—multiple times a day, usually—I clicked over to Safari and looked at my mentions on Twitter. Just one little @ typed before my user name, and total strangers could get my attention.

In theory, I'd started using the site to interact directly with *Eve* readers. In today's climate, a print monthly can't survive on paper content alone. Our digital marketing department now made up 30 percent of the staff, and every single *Eve* employee was expected to build and maintain an online presence consistent with the magazine's branding efforts.

I clicked on the heart image for all the supportive posts, indicating that I had read and liked them. Thank you @EveEIC. U helped me find courage to call out my boss last night. Scared the shit out of him! #Themtoo #Metoo

@EveEIC. Felt like one of the thems, but now I'm a me too. Went to HR last week. Harassing coworker fired today! Time's up! Followed by three applause-hand emoticons.

I retweeted the post with my own comment: We're changing the world with our stories! Keep it up. Power in numbers. #Themtoo #Eve

But for every five atta-girls came one of the trolls.

@EveEIC Your just mad cuz your old vag is 2 dried up for any man to want it.

Can you imagine being married to @EveEIC? What a man-hating cunt.

My favorites were the ones who tried to pretend as if they knew something about me personally. @EveEIC You act like you don't need a man, but I bet you let that cuck of a husband treat you like a dog at home.

But mostly they liked to tell me I'd be less of a feminist if I were hotter. @EveEIC You could stand to lose a few. Quit your job and go running.

That one got a reply from another user: She's a little thick, but, man, I'd hate-fuck the shit out of that.

Then another, and another, and another. I'd seen it before. Once the nasty comments hit a tipping point, the thread transformed into a contest of sorts: Who could be the very worst human in 140 characters?

I want @EveEIC to have a daughter so I can rape both of them.

Ding, ding, ding. I had found the winner. I hit retweet and typed
This kind of comment is how we know we're winning the war. #Runningscared
#snowflake

I knew that my 320,000-odd followers would go to town on the guy (at least, I assumed it was a guy) until he deleted his account, but I went ahead and reported his tweet as abuse anyway.

Adam had warned me to ignore the threatening comments that came with being a woman on the internet. I had the option, for example, of ignoring all my mentions or filtering out people I didn't know personally. But that would defeat the purpose of engaging directly with *Eve*'s readers.

Besides, I wasn't going to let a handful of cowards hiding behind the anonymity of a website silence me. As my Twitter bio said, "Nobody puts baby in a corner."

Having scratched the itch, I found that I couldn't stop. I closed Twitter and opened Poppit, an anything-goes message board that allowed users to post anonymously without even a registration process. A quick search of my name filled my screen with hateful rants. When they weren't calling me a dried-up, bitter old hag, they were labeling me a skank and a whore who had slept her way to her position—even though I had gotten married at the age of thirty-one, when I was already a features editor at *City Woman* and months away from becoming editor in chief of a downtown cultural paper. Plus, my husband was a lawyer who had nothing whatsoever to do with the publishing industry. If anything, I had been the one to help his career. But of course none of these strangers who hated me for trying to make the world a little more fair to women knew anything about that.

I was about to close my browser when I saw a new post appear at the top of the thread, under the user name KurtLoMein. She's a hypocrite. Full of tough talk about the world needing to change the way it treats women, but she's a coward in her own life. Cares more about her picture-perfect image than actual reality.

My fingers lingered over the keyboard, knowing I shouldn't respond, and not knowing what to write if I did. The *ping* of an incoming email pulled me out of the social-media sinkhole. It was Maggie, getting back to me about the photo shoot.

Hi Chloe. You don't like the pictures? Oh no! It was Sienna's idea to blow up the traditional, ridiculous glamour shoot. She was totally psyched about it, but I can ask her for some images from the campaign if you really hate it. Let me know? Maggie

A second message quickly followed.

I just called your office so we could chat directly, but Tom says you're out today. I feel terrible now. I should have asked the photog for some other looks as well, but got infected by Sienna's enthusiasm for irony. How can I make this better? Maggie

P.S. Congrats again on the P for the P Award! Hope the gala is amazing!

I clicked back to the photographs and saw them in a completely different light. I felt like one of those people who gets outraged about an email, only to be told that it should have been written in a nonexistent sarcasm font. I was that nerd who didn't get the joke. I was barely into my forties, and I felt . . . old.

No worries, I typed. Just wanted to make sure Sienna was 100% okay with the look. CAT

I reread my original email, making sure I hadn't said anything inconsistent with this one. As I hit send, I found myself thinking about that final, scathing Poppit message. Did I really care more about my image than reality?

A few minutes later, our landline rang. It was Les, the afternoon doorman, letting me know that Valerie was here. She was the woman I had hired to do my hair and makeup for the gala. Two hours and $500 from now, I'd look like an older version of the woman in the ironic photo shoot my magazine would be running next month. I tried not to wonder what Maggie Hart would say about that.

"WHAT DO YOU THINK?" VALERIE asked. I'd been perched on the foot of the bed so long that my legs hurt when I stood.

Looking in the mirror, I barely recognized myself. My normally straight shoulder-length dark brown hair had been shaped into a perfect wave of spiral curls tumbling from a deep side part. My skin looked natural, but dewy and flawless. She had used light blush and a nude gloss, and given me dark, smoky eyes. My heart-shaped face had previously unknown contours.

"You're a miracle worker, Valerie." We had first met when one of our usual makeup artists was hit with a stomach flu and sent a friend to replace her. When I set eyes on Valerie's hot-pink Mohawk and array of facial piercings, I wasn't sure she was the right person for the job. But she was proof that some people simply choose to march to their own beat, even if they can keep perfect time with the rest of the band.

"Do you want to get dressed before I do one final blast of hairspray?"

"My gown feels like a sausage casing. I want to wait until the very last minute."

"All right. Just be careful. The makeup will rub off. And your lips are so perfect right now. Try not to mess with them, but if you need a touch-up, I'm leaving you both the liner and the gloss. And use this brush for the gloss, not the applicator that comes with the tube."

"Message received, Michelangelo. I won't destroy the artwork."

"You sure you don't need help with a zipper or anything? I can wait if you want."

I declined the offer, saying that Adam would be back in time if I needed a hand, even though I hadn't heard anything from him since the previous night. He'd left early in the morning, before I woke up.

Valerie was shellacking my carefully positioned waves with spray when I heard the creak of the apartment door. We'd had a Post-it note on the refrigerator to remind one of us either to call the handyman or pick up some WD-40 for at least three weeks. I longed for the days when a to-do sticker never lingered for more than forty-eight hours in our home. We had both gotten so busy.

"See?" I said, feeling my own smile. "That's probably him now."

We followed the sounds into the kitchen. Instead of Adam, Ethan stood in front of the open refrigerator, his eyes searching for something that obviously wasn't there.

"Oh. Hey, Valerie." His voice had probably dropped an octave since he'd seen Valerie last winter during the holiday party season. He immediately straightened up, pushing the refrigerator door shut behind him.

I watched with profound discomfort as Valerie offered him a generous hug and a kiss on the cheek, seemingly oblivious to the effect she had on my teenage son. Ethan had never expressed an interest in dating, but I had seen the change in him over the last year and had spoken to a couple of the better teachers at his school. The good news (in my view) was that he had been late to shift his interests from video games and don't-try-this-nonsense-at-home YouTube videos to actual human girls. The bad news was that he hadn't quite figured out how to be comfortable around members of the opposite sex.

"Okay, Valerie," I said, tapping her shoulder to pull her attention from Ethan. "Thanks again for dolling me up. You really are an artist."

As I walked Valerie to the door, I could feel Ethan's eyes following her. It would be weeks before I asked myself whether that was yet another sign that something was deeply wrong with my son.

3

D ESPITE ITS POPULIST-SOUNDING name, the Press for the People gala was a veritable who's who of what most of the country would call the "media elite." But as was typical with the New York City social scene, not all levels of elite were equal. Even with a starting ticket price of $500, the reminders of the night's hierarchy began at check-in. As the recipient of the night's major award, I learned that my family and I were seated at Table 2. I took small (and admittedly petty) satisfaction when I overheard a former employee of mine who had left for a minor promotion at a competitor magazine being informed that he'd be enjoying the program from Table 132 on the balcony above the stage.

"And am I checking in all three in your party, Ms. Taylor?" the young woman asked with a smile. She was not much older than Ethan, probably the daughter of a board member who had volunteered in exchange for another entry on her college applications.

"My dad's not coming," Ethan said. "So we'll have an extra seat. You know, just in case you need to rest or something."

The volunteer's stylus paused over her electronic tablet, and her eyes shifted from Ethan to me. Her smile grew nervous.

"My husband's just running late," I assured her. "Adam Macintosh."

"Certainly. I'll leave him unchecked then."

As we walked away from the table, Ethan groaned in embarrassment. "Oh my god, what was that? I sounded like a total chode." It was his new favorite word for someone who was a jerk. I had to look it up in the Urban Dictionary.

Adam had been the one to suggest that I ask if we could bring our son to the banquet. I had done so reluctantly, foreseeing the battle of wills that would erupt when it came time to go. Ethan, in my view, was a normal kid, which meant that a night in a monkey suit with fourteen hundred adults celebrating the value of the First Amendment to a free democracy ranked only slightly above being poked in the eye for three hours straight. Adam, on the other hand, was determined to force Ethan to be some other version of himself. More like Adam, I supposed.

But now here we were. Ethan had come home on his own, put on the tux we'd bought him last month, and let me help him with his tie without a single grimace. He had even rushed to the car waiting for us at the curb to get the door for me. And his father was still nowhere to be seen.

Jenna Masters, the board member in charge of the gala committee, spotted me at the tail end of the bar line and rushed over, a seemingly impossible feat in four-inch stilettos. "We need you at the step-and-repeat. Tell me what you need, and I'll have someone bring it to you."

I asked for champagne if they had it, and Ethan said he'd "do" a Coke, and then added a "Please" when I shot him a corrective Mom look.

The smile plastered on my face felt like someone else's by the time Jenna finally told me I was finished with my photo duties for the night. Her brow remained impressively uncreased as her gaze dropped to her iPhone screen, right thumb tapping and swiping furiously. "I'm sending you this great shot of you and Darren, if you wouldn't mind posting to your social. Remember, we're hashtagging Press for the People, Not the Enemy."

"Darren" was Darren Pinker, the multiple Academy Award–winning actor who was serving as honorary cochair of tonight's gala. He was also a fierce First Amendment advocate and a hero to wishful liberals, who were trying to recruit him to run for president.

Ethan held out a hand toward me. "Want me to do it?" he offered. "It takes my mom, like, five minutes just to do a tweet."

I turned over my phone so he could do his handiwork. He had just finished up when I heard a friendly voice from beneath one of the dinosaurs in the main hall. "There's our star client!"

I turned to see Bill Braddock holding up one arm to get my attention. As Ethan and I wove our way through the crowd toward him, I saw that he was standing with four other attorneys from his law firm.

"Bill, I didn't expect to see you here," I said, leaning in to exchange dual pecks on the cheeks.

"Now how could I let you get this kind of an honor without your octogenarian boyfriend in the house? We've got a whole table, in fact. Number seventeen. Not too shabby for a bunch of egghead lawyers."

When Bill celebrated his eightieth birthday the summer before, I had adjusted his title as my septuagenarian boyfriend accordingly. Bill was what some people his age—even liberals—called a "confirmed bachelor." He was also one of the preeminent First Amendment lawyers in the country, having argued more than a dozen constitutional cases before the Supreme Court. He served as counsel for some of the biggest publishing outlets in the world and even a few smaller ones he enjoyed, such as my little magazine. I had first met him through Catherine Lancaster, but he had become my friend as well.

I didn't know the names of all of the lawyers around him, but I did extend my hand toward Jake Summer, one of the partners who was closer to my own age. As I watched one of the female attorneys welcome Ethan with a big hug and a remark that he looked like "a grown-ass man," I realized I needed to make more of an effort to get to know the other lawyers at the firm. After all, they had made Adam a partner nearly two years earlier, in large part because of the push I had made on his behalf with Bill.

"Where's your lucky husband?" Bill said, scanning the crowd.

"He's running late from work," I said. "His firm's a total sweat-shop," I added dramatically.

"I popped into his office to see if he wanted to leave with us, but he wasn't around."

The comment, from the woman who had been so friendly with Ethan, had a couple of the lawyers exchanging awkward glances. I offered her my hand. "Hi, I'm Chloe. I'm not sure we've met."

She told me her name was Laurie Connor and that she was an associate in the litigation group.

"It's the Gentry Group thing," I assured them. "He was meeting them near JFK."

"I'm not familiar," Bill said.

I'd been under the impression that Gentry was a major client. I tried to tell myself that Bill was kidding, but I was beginning to worry that his age was taking a toll.

I noticed another set of attorney eyes shift toward Jake. Adam was the one who'd brought the Gentry Group on board as a Rives & Braddock client, but I knew for a fact that Jake was working on some complex issues that had come up with regard to the federal government's jurisdiction over some of their international dealings. I found myself wondering why Jake wouldn't also be with the client today, if it was really so important.

Bill smiled and placed a reassuring hand on my shoulder. "Adam will be here. This is a big night for you, after all."

"Of course he will." I managed to sound like I believed it.

"And if he doesn't show, you know where to find me. I may be eighty, but I'm meaner than him. I'll kick his ass."

———

I SMILED TO MYSELF AS I caught sight of Ethan lingering near the
entrance to the ballroom, the clutch purse he had offered to hold when
he saw me struggling with it between sips and handshakes still tucked
awkwardly into his underarm. He looked relieved when I began heading his way.

"You're my knight in shining armor tonight, Ethan." I tried to
plant a kiss on the top of his head, the way I used to when I was taller
than him, but it landed on his temple instead.

He feigned repulsion. "How much champagne have you had?"

"Mom Juice doesn't count." I wasn't a super heavy drinker, but the
family joke was that I had an extra liver when it came to Veuve Clicquot.

"I've got to admit, it *would* be seriously funny if you got up on
the stage totally hammered." He recited a sentence straight from my
prepared remarks, slurring his speech and swaying slightly during the
delivery.

"You know my speech?"

"How could I not? You practiced it, like, a hundred times Tuesday
night in the kitchen."

He'd had his Beats headphones on in the living room. There was
no way he could have heard me unless he'd wanted to. He was actually
proud of me.

"You're such a good kid." I felt my eyes begin to water.

"Oh my god, you are drunk," he said with a smile.

"Should I see if I can get us into the banquet room a little early? I
want to look at my speech one last time before the program begins."

"That'd be good. Maybe we can sober you up, ya big lush."

THE PRESIDENT OF THE FOUNDATION took the stage, explaining that the award was to honor a journalist whose work had changed

the lives of ordinary people. "To introduce this year's honoree, it's *my* honor to introduce the editor we all know as the quintessential 'City Woman': Catherine Lancaster."

I let out a little gasp and joined in the applause. Catherine had told me she needed to be in Los Angeles tonight and wouldn't be able to make it. Next to me, Ethan was grinning knowingly.

"You were in on this, weren't you?"

Catherine had turned seventy-three in March but could easily pass for fifty. Her gown was a peacock-blue shirtdress style with a big, dramatic pointed collar. Her bright orange hair was pulled up, wrapped in one of her signature turbans, and her makeup was minimal with the exception of dark brick-red lipstick.

She began by telling the audience that I'd had no idea she was going to be at the gala that night. "If I had told her, she would have felt obligated to write my remarks for me—a side effect of the deep and abiding fear that resides within all of my former employees—for reasons I cannot fathom, of course."

I never guessed when I began working at *City Woman* that Catherine would become not only my mentor but also one of my closest friends. But hearing *her* marvel at *my* accomplishments was utterly surreal. "I told Chloe early in her career, 'You've got a smart gut; just learn how to trust it.' But, watching her over the years, I've realized she has raw gut instincts, yes, but she also has an enormous heart filled with passion and empathy. And it's that combination that makes her so exciting as a writer and publisher. I have never told Chloe this, but she has far surpassed any work I even *dreamed* of doing at her age. Or at *this* age, in fact—the tender age of thirty-five." She paused for the laughter. "So it is my honor tonight to introduce my dear friend—a talented and gutsy warrior: Chloe Taylor."

Even though I had memorized my speech, I could feel my eyes darting to my notes on the podium—better than the alternative of staring into the sea of glaring lights. I couldn't make out any faces in the audience. And I had to trust on blind faith that the tech people were displaying the photographs on the huge screen above my head as I had requested. They were pictures of the women whose stories I had published. It seemed fitting to keep the focus on them tonight. No one needed a close-up of me at the podium.

When I was finished, I heard applause break out immediately, along with the sound of chairs scooting as people rose to their feet for a standing ovation. A loud wolf whistle caught my attention as I edged toward the stairs at the side of the stage. It was from Table 2. Ethan held one fist above his head. "Yeah, Mom!"

Next to him came another loud whistle. Adam was there, his pinkies pressed into his mouth.

Of course he was there. When push came to shove, he always came through.

4

I HAD TO admit, Nicky did call it.

When Adam got the court's permission to move to New York two years after he left Nicky, my mom phoned me and made me promise that I wasn't "messing around" with him.

"Ew, he's my brother-in-law. No."

"*Former* brother-in-law," she reminded me. "Nicky's convinced that's why he's moving there—to be with you."

"Nicky's paranoid," I said. "He has a good job here, Mom. Like, *really* good. And, besides, I have a boyfriend. Matt, remember?"

Nicky was wrong about anything going on between Adam and me back then, but I wasn't wholly uninvolved in Adam's move to the city. He had been trying to make things work as a divorced dad in Cleveland, downsizing to an apartment and finding a day care two blocks from the courthouse that a lot of the female prosecutors relied on. My mom and dad even pitched in sometimes, since Adam's parents had both passed away while he was still in college, not that he would have wanted them around his son in any event.

But Nicky was still a problem. A couple of cops had mentioned seeing her acting sloppy in the usual haunts, and she had shown up twice at day care without permission—both times acting intoxicated. It had gotten to the point that Adam had to tell the day care and babysitters to call 911 if they received any contact from her. He'd never really be able to protect Ethan while he was still in Cleveland.

I was the one who slipped his résumé to a friend who worked in the US Attorney's Office. Apparently the hiring team thought they could use some lawyers who didn't go to the same five law schools, and they were also touched by Adam's personal story. He had needed a judge's permission to move, but the combination of Nicky's bad behavior and an offer to be a federal prosecutor in the most prestigious district in the country had done the trick.

I helped him find an apartment in Tribeca. It wasn't exactly Brooklyn Heights, but it was kid-friendly by Manhattan standards, and not too far from his office. It was also a straight shot to my place in Chelsea. I became his regular Wednesday-night babysitter. The highlight of my week was seeing Ethan's chubby little face light up when he saw his aunt "Glow-y." He hadn't spoken until he was nearly four, even with the work of speech therapists, so every word—however imperfect—was exciting to hear.

At the time, my only goal in life as far as kids were concerned was to be the beloved aunt. Even though women weren't supposed to say this, I never particularly liked babies or little kids. You hear people say that one of the greatest rewards of parenthood is seeing your children develop into adults, but with my parents and Nicky, I'd seen the downside of that equation as well. I knew at some cognitive level that my parents were proud of me, and took some amount of responsibility for the fact that I'd turned out pretty well by most measures. But was it worth all the heartache they'd suffered because of their children overall?

As far as motherhood was concerned, I could leave it just as well as take it.

Some weeks, Adam didn't have a need for my sitting services, so we'd hang out instead, ordering takeout and playing with Ethan. I could see how hard it was for him to adjust to Manhattan. He was a nice, good-looking thirty-five-year-old man with a cool job in a fun neighborhood. In theory, he could be out with models every night. But he also had Ethan, and he was too solid of a guy to be serious with any woman who didn't take an interest in his son.

For more than a year, we were just buddies. Then my birthday happened.

I had sent out invitations to four other couples, a month in advance, for a dinner party at my apartment. I'd need to rent an extra table, and borrow a taxi-trunk full of folding chairs from the office, but I was thrilled to be able to host a bona fide adult dinner party. I was turning twenty-nine. I was done drinking from red Solo cups. I scoured *Food & Wine* for the perfect menu, something impressive, but still manageable on my own. When I didn't have a pot large enough to hold the braised short ribs I wanted, I bought one. When Matt asked me what I wanted for my birthday, I snipped a page from the Williams Sonoma catalog and asked him for a white serving platter, and could I please have it the day before the party, just in case something was wrong and I needed to exchange it?

I never did get the platter. Four days before my birthday, Matt dumped me. He said he was young and still having fun, and that my birthday had him realizing that his friends had been right about me all along.

"I thought your friends liked me."

"They do. But you're . . . *a lot*, Chloe. I can't do this with you."

"Do *what*?"

"Be that couple. With the parties and the platters and the Sunday Styles wedding announcement."

"*Wedding*? I never said anything about getting married."

"You didn't have to. You plan every single thing, and then you're miserable once it's over and go looking for the next thing to worry about. I guarantee you, the second this party's over, you'll be pressing me about Christmas. And New Year's. And then an engagement ring on Valentine's Day."

I gave Adam the abbreviated version the following night during our regular Wednesday hangout. We were sitting on the floor, putting more effort into the Legos than Ethan was.

"You know what's really embarrassing? I actually asked him if he could go to the dinner on Saturday anyway."

"Oof."

"I know. But now I'm going to be the ninth wheel at my own party. Is it too late to cancel?"

"Do *not* cancel. Being with your friends will cheer you up. Besides . . ." He reached over and touched my ankle. "You're smart and successful and pretty nice to look at. You'd have no problems finding another plus-one, if that's what you wanted."

The moment sat in the air. His hand felt warm against my skin. I honestly don't believe I'd ever thought about the possibility before then, but it was there now. I waited for him to say more. To *do* more, but he went back to fiddling with the castle he was building.

"The last thing I need right now is to grovel for a date," I said. "Maybe I'll just leave the empty chair next to me and let my friends nominate potential candidates."

He showed up at my apartment at six o'clock, because after a year in New York, he knew no one ever started a party before six. He had a gift box from Williams Sonoma. It was the platter I wanted, even though I'd never told him that part.

Nothing happened that night, but we were definitely different than we were before. He wasn't Nicky's ex, or Ethan's dad. He was there for me. It was like we had a pact. It was going to happen. It was inevitable.

5

WHEN MY EYES opened the morning after the gala, I saw the crystal typewriter with my name etched into it, next to a tumbler of water and a container of melatonin from Vitamin Shoppe. Last night, I had won a prize. Before I registered anything else, I recognized Adam's scent, a mix of grocery store soap and something like salt. My right leg was hitched over his thigh, and my face was pressed against his chest. I felt a dribble of spit as I lifted my head.

Adam was already awake. He was holding an iPad above his face, reading the news. The image on his screen was a photograph of me standing next to Darren Pinker.

"Hey, I know that lady," I said, planting a peck on his sternum.

He tilted the screen in my direction. "Should I be jealous?"

Apparently Darren, the honorary gala host, and I had landed a spot on the front page of the *New York Times'* Arts section.

"Pretty boy's not my type," I said, stretching my arms above my head.

"Sweet of you to say, but he'd be exactly your type if he ran for president. First Lady Chloe? Can you imagine?" I felt his chest sway slightly as he sang an old Nas song that featured Lauryn Hill. "'If I ruled the world, I'd rule all of the things.'"

"You know those aren't the words, right?" I thought I detected an edge to his compliments. I had always been successful in my field, but in the past year, I had been on a professional elevator that seemed to be missing a down button. On the heels of the #ThemToo series, I had signed a multimillion-dollar publishing deal for two books: a behind-the-scenes detailing of the series, plus a memoir-slash-advice-for-the-savvy-career-woman kind of thing. My general profile had risen, too. I'd been stopped for autographs more than once, and even had a GIF on Twitter from when I danced with Ellen. Apparently people were surprised that I had "money moves."

With the big shifts in my career, Adam and I were now one of the roughly 25 percent of heterosexual married couples in which the woman outearned the man. I wish I could say we followed all the advice we'd published in *Eve*—"healthy steps" for couples when the "traditional financial script gets flipped." Maintaining the balance of the marriage, both emotionally and practically. Adjusting the roles each person plays in the relationship as necessary. And most of all, communicating openly about the dynamics that inevitably change when money threatens masculinity. If we took one of those questionnaires that were so popular with readers, our score would be in the red zone: danger.

The one time I confronted him about the prospect that he might resent my success—just the month before—he had been vehement in his denial, insisting that he was "insulted" that I'd even raised the possibility.

To Adam's credit, I was certain that any bitterness he held was subconscious and not even related to money. He had never been one to chase riches or keep up with the Joneses. When he graduated from law school, he probably could have landed a job at a decent-sized firm in Cleveland, earning a six-figure salary, but he wanted to be a prosecutor. Being on the side of justice was part of Adam's identity. He told me once that it was his way of assuring himself he was nothing like his father, who had gone to prison a few times, but not for the crimes he was committing against his own wife and son when he wasn't locked up.

After I introduced Adam to the head of the criminal division of the US Attorney's Office for the Southern District of New York—who was dating the head of publicity at *City Woman* when I was on the editorial staff—he went from being a county prosecutor to being an assistant US attorney for the most prestigious federal prosecutors' office in the country. His Ohio State education and rough-and-tumble county-court trial experience stood him apart from the former appellate court clerks whose office walls were lined with degrees from Harvard, Yale, and Stanford. But Adam quickly earned a reputation for bringing a gut instinct to his cases, intuiting precisely how jurors would react to certain facts. And he was absolutely fearless in the courtroom.

It had been nearly three years since his last big win at trial . . . as a prosecutor, at least. The chief had encouraged him to take a plea on a human trafficking case against a supposed nail salon owner who had been using his chain of shops as a cover for horrific abuses against the scores of young immigrant women he employed. Adam convinced his boss to let him take the case to trial, where he prevailed. The defendant was sentenced to thirty-seven years, meaning he'd likely die in prison.

The *New York Times* had published a front-page article using the case to expose a pattern of abuse that was often just beneath a couple coats of polish on a discount mani-pedi. As I reread the article while drifting in and out of sleep, I told him again how proud I was of him. The way I remembered it, he pulled me into the crook of his arm and said something about those kinds of cases making it all worthwhile. He asked me whether it bothered me that he was still working for a government salary, when many of his colleagues had upgraded their lifestyles in the private sector.

And the way I remember it, I told him that of course I wasn't bothered. I said something like, "I mean, you could always do the partnership thing at a big law firm if you wanted to, but you love your job. It's what you do."

My response was "so Chloe," he said. When I asked him why, he quoted my words back to me. "'You can always do the partnership thing,' like it's a given. And of course it would be for you . . . if you were a lawyer, because you're Chloe. I love it that you have that kind of faith in me." I remember he kissed me, in a sweet way, not sexy. On top of my head.

I told him it wasn't about faith. It was simply a fact. I said he was the best lawyer in the Southern District, which made him one of the best lawyers in the world. I told him that any law firm would be thrilled to have him.

And then he told me all the reasons it would never be that simple, because the world wasn't as fair as I thought it was. That, with my prodding, he may have talked his way into the US Attorney's Office by pulling at a hiring committee's guilt about always hiring from the same pedigree pool, but he'd never be good enough for the white-shoe law firm crowd. "They let guys like me do the public service work. We don't get to be partners in big law."

Not wanting to hear him run himself down that way, I said something like, "Wanna bet? Just make a few calls." And the next day, I made one of the calls for him—to my friend and lawyer, Bill Braddock.

That's the way I remembered it happening, at least.

I hadn't realized until the month before—when I finally asked Adam if he felt any resentment about the way my career was blowing up—that he recalled the conversation and what happened afterward differently. He had never been the one who cared about money, he reminded me. It was me who had pressured him to leave a job he had loved, all "to fit some idea of who your husband is supposed to be."

He had "sold out to the man," as he called it, by joining Rives & Braddock. And he hated it. Every day, I could see how much he hated answering to a client. He wanted to be one of the good guys again. But instead, he hated his job, and he blamed me for it. And despite the compromise he had made, I still managed to earn more money than he did.

Now, as I lifted my leg from Adam's thigh and prepared to slip out of bed, I replayed that history in the face of Adam's comment about my wanting to be first lady. The last thing I wanted was to start another round of backhanded resentment bingo.

"I don't think we need another celebrity running for president, thank you very much. On another note, thank you again for making it in time for my speech. It wouldn't have been the same without you there."

"I think I nearly gave the driver a stroke on the way in from JFK, bird-dogging for any empty pockets on the LIE." I always teased Adam that he drove like a bank robber. "Hopefully the tip I gave him will keep him from destroying my Uber rating."

"Speaking of the LIE," I said, "what time do you think you can leave today?"

We hadn't been to the house in East Hampton for three full weeks, and the weather forecast looked glorious—almost as warm as summer, without the post–Memorial Day crowds. I even had our pool opened early for the occasion.

"Bad news. Part of the reason I was able to make it last night was that the Gentry people decided we had more work to do and decided to stay over another day. I have to go back to their hotel in an hour. I'll just get a car from there when I free up, and you and Ethan can head out without me."

"What's up with them staying near the airport? I got the impression these were high roller clients."

We had met Gentry's in-house counsel and his wife at a summer garden party four years earlier. After Adam made the transition from the US Attorney's Office to law firm life and was being pressured to bring in additional clients of his own, I cajoled him to join me when I flew to London for a publishing conference. Once he agreed, I pulled up the wife's contact information and scheduled a dinner. It was a big deal at Rives & Braddock when Adam announced he was pulling some of Gentry's business into the firm. The law firm press release that followed described the London-based Gentry Group as a "global powerhouse" in the industry, energy, and health-care sectors.

"Maybe they want to be able to fly out to a nonextraditing country in case of emergency."

I searched his face for some kind of a smile as I crawled out of bed, but found none. He didn't even bother to hide his disdain for his job and his clients anymore.

I pulled off the Blondie T-shirt that had doubled as last night's pajamas. "I'll send your regrets to Catherine?"

It hadn't been enough for Catherine to give that gracious introduction at last night's gala. She was also hosting a little party at her house in Sag Harbor to get some of the old gang from *City Woman* back together for a celebration.

Now Adam was smiling. He had the best smile—sweet but a tiny bit naughty. "I wouldn't exactly call it regrets." Catherine was a little too much for Adam to handle. She was too much for most people.

I was tugging a sports bra over my head when he pulled me toward the bed and kissed me above my belly button. "I've got an hour."

I glanced at the clock. "I don't. Pilates. If I miss it, Jenny charges me."

"That woman's a Nazi."

"And my abs love her for it," I said, giving him a quick kiss on the lips before yanking on my workout tights. "I'll see you tonight. And tell those Gentry people to pay for a proper car for you."

That was the last time I saw my husband alive. At least, that's what I told the police, but I could tell they didn't believe me.

6

I HAD NO idea how long I had been at the police station. It could have been twenty minutes or three hours. It was as if time had stopped the moment I found Adam, his legs splayed unnaturally, his heather-gray T-shirt and white jersey pajama bottoms soaked with blood.

I answered every question they asked, even as my mind was fighting to accept the reality that Adam was gone, and I had no idea what life would look like without him. Then I answered them again and again, doing my best not to appear impatient or defensive.

And I could tell they didn't believe me.

I hadn't caught the name of every person I'd spoken to, but I had the detectives straight. Bowen and Guidry. B and G, like boy and girl. Bowen was male; Guidry was female. It's how I remembered.

Bowen, the guy, said, "We need to call his mother." He was tall and slender, with dark, wavy hair and angular features. His skin was pasty.

I could only imagine the look I gave him. A photographer from Cornell's alumni magazine once told me that my natural expression made me seem "intimidating and inaccessible." I wore my friendliest smile as I responded that I had no problem with either of those impressions.

But now I wasn't posing for a picture. I was in a windowless room with cinder-block walls and blue linoleum floors and a door that probably used to be white—a door that I heard lock behind us after I followed the two detectives into the room. I noticed a camera hanging from the corner of the ceiling and wondered if it was on.

I wasn't stupid, after all. The last thing I'd ever been was stupid. Despite the kind gestures—the bottled water, the coffee, the offer to help with any calls that needed to be made—I knew the police had a job to do. And testing me was part of it.

As I walked them through every horrible step—driving home from Catherine's party, slipping keys in the door to enter a dark, silent house, finding the bedroom empty, and then circling back to the living room, seeing Adam there, on the floor, with so much blood—another part of my brain was somewhere else entirely. My words were all about that night, but the movie playing on a screen in my head was *The Story of Adam and Chloe*. Seeing him at the mall when I was a little kid. Meeting him again when he picked up Nicky. The first time he had called me, instead of Mom, when there was a problem. The move to New York. Playing on the floor of his apartment with little Ethan. The first forbidden kiss. Our feet in the sand as we exchanged rings at sunset on Main Beach. I could see all of it, vividly in bright, intense Technicolor.

The divided halves of my brain finally reconciled when an image of my hand checking Adam's neck for a pulse managed to break through. I remembered thinking at the time that it was the same spot on his neck that I would press my cheek against when he was on top, making love to me. I could still feel his blood, dried and crusty on my black jersey jumpsuit. I could still taste the vomit that had finally come as a police officer walked me across the lawn to his car after the ambulance departed.

"Would someone have expected you and your husband to be at your house tonight?" Detective Guidry asked. She had long ash-blond hair, tied into a messy knot that seemed too playful for her profession. "We get a lot of break-ins at the part-time properties. People assume they're empty."

I shrugged. How was I supposed to know what a burglar would expect? "We come out every two or three weekends off-season. Sometimes more. Sometimes less. No real schedule."

I felt them judging me. They had to, right? They'd seen the house. Not huge, compared to other homes on the block, but surely more luxurious than what police were used to. And here I was, admitting how rarely we used the place beyond the summer months.

"Flip side of the coin," Bowen said. "Did anyone know for certain that you and your husband *would* be there?"

"I told you before: I can't imagine anyone wanting to kill Adam."

Bowen told me he understood, but then asked the question again anyway.

"I guess. I mean, I told my assistant when I left a little early today that I was trying to beat traffic. A friend wanted to have brunch in the city on Sunday, but I told her we'd be out here. And the people at the party I was at tonight—I told them that Adam was on his way out, so they might have assumed the house was empty. But obviously they were all at the party with me, and none of them would do something like—" I couldn't bring myself to use the words to accurately describe what was happening.

"You told your friends he was 'on his way,' but wasn't he actually already at your house fairly early on during the party?" Guidry's expression was blank, but the tone of her voice made it clear she thought she'd caught me in some kind of lie.

"Easier on my friends' feelings than explaining he wasn't exactly a fan of their company." I managed a dry smile, but neither detective seemed to appreciate the humor.

"It's just a little unusual for one half of a couple to attend a party while the other one's home," Guidry said. "The two of you weren't arguing or something like that?"

"You can check our texts if you'd like." I reached into my purse for my cell, pulled up our most recent exchange of messages, and placed the phone in front of her. She glanced down at it.

7:02 pm

Heading to Catherine's soon. ETA?

7:58 pm

Sorry, fell asleep in the car. Driver actually had to wake me up! Finally here though. Having fun? Where's Ethan?

8:12 pm

Went to movies with Kevin. Told him he could spend the night, so you're solo. And, yes, fun here. Bill is telling that story about hooking up with a stranger at Studio 54 before finally realizing it was . . .

8:13 pm

Has anyone guessed right yet?

8:14 pm

Everyone here has heard it before. I give it three more tries before someone finally says the name.

And BOOM, there it is. Better go. Catherine's glaring at my phone. Think she's about to herd us into the dining room. Not too late to join;-)

8:16 pm

Um, yeah, no. Plus ZZZZ. Pro tip: Water down Catherine's vino when she's not looking.

8:17 pm

😈 🖤

Jesus. My last communication with my husband was a fucking emoji.

Guidry managed a friendly nod as she slid the phone back to me. "Your husband probably told others he was heading out here tonight?"

"I guess," I said with a shrug.

"Such as?" Bowen had his pen ready above his notebook, prepared to jot down names.

"I have no idea." Instinctively, I reached for my phone to text Adam, then shook my head. "People at work, I guess. The clients he met with today, maybe."

We were interrupted by a knock on the door. A uniformed officer whispered something to the detectives, and Bowen followed him out of the room.

Guidry shifted her chair toward the center of her side of the table so we were seated directly across from each other. "There's another possibility I think we should discuss, Mrs. Taylor. Do you think there's a chance someone went to the house looking to target you?"

I opened my mouth to tell her I had no enemies, but no words came out. I couldn't begin to calculate the number of hours I had spent reading online posts about myself in recent months. I woke up at least once a week from a nightmare built upon the words that had become a familiar part of my daily routine—*die, rape, bitch,* every possible description of my breasts and genitalia. But at some level, I must never have believed that I was in actual danger. Otherwise, Guidry's question wouldn't have caught me so off guard. Can you have enemies if you don't know who they are?

I swallowed before answering. "A lot of nasty comments on social media and that kind of thing. But nothing physical."

"What kind of nasty comments?"

I reached again for my phone, pulled up my Twitter mentions, and handed it to her. Her eyes widened and then widened again as she read.

"Pardon me for asking, Mrs. Taylor, but with these kinds of threats, why wasn't the alarm set?"

"The alarm?"

"At your house. You said when you got home, you entered with a key and that you didn't need to disarm the security system. And obviously the motion detectors we saw inside the house didn't activate an alarm after the break-in occurred. But your husband was in his pajamas, and you said it looked like he had been in the bed before getting up— probably because he heard someone in the house. You're getting these kinds of threats, and he didn't set the alarm before going to sleep?"

"You sound like you're blaming Adam for what happened to him."

She sat back and let out a puff of air. "Not at all, ma'am." *Ma'am?* She looked like she was older than I was. "I'm just trying to get the best sense possible of what happened tonight."

"What happened tonight is someone murdered my husband. And we never really use the alarm when we're at the house. I use it at night if I'm out here alone—which is rare—but otherwise it's more for when we're in the city. Like you said, burglars target the part-time houses."

I imagined some amorphous figure peeking through the back window, deciding no one was home.

"And these threats," she said, handing me my phone, "all of it was online? No letters or packages? Anyone following you home or something like that?"

I shook my head.

"We'll take a look into it," Bowen assured me. "We'll be looking into everything."

I MANAGED TO KEEP MY cool through all of it, which is absolutely what Adam would have expected of me. The police seemed satisfied. Or at least they were doing a good job of faking it.

But then I mentioned Ethan. "At least Ethan wasn't home," I muttered. He had gone to see the latest Marvel movie with his friend Kevin Dunham and spent the night at his house. My son was safe. At least I could hold on to that. "I need to find him. I don't want him to hear about this when he wakes up."

"We'll need to call his mother," Bowen had said.

I must have looked so confused. And irritated. And dismayed by his stupidity. Adam calls it—*called* it—my "not having it" face.

"I'm not having Kevin's mother tell him about this. I barely know the woman."

"Not Kevin's mother. Your *stepson's*."

Ethan started calling me Mama around the time he was five, after I was seeing Adam regularly, but before we got married. I corrected him at first, feeling guilty about taking the title from Nicky, not to mention missing the sound of his little voice saying "Glow-y." But Adam convinced me that it was a sign Ethan missed having a maternal figure in his life.

And somehow the police already knew that I wasn't actually my son's mother.

The satisfaction they must have taken as they saw my face move from fatigue to offense and finally to realization. I pictured them googling Adam. Finding our wedding announcement in the Sunday Styles section. "The groom has a son from a prior marriage."

The police needed to call Ethan's mother. My husband, Adam, was dead, and now his son—my son, or so it had seemed for nearly a decade—would need his mother.

I recited her home phone number from memory. It was the same number I'd had for the first eighteen years of my life. When she asked for a second number, I had to look up the mobile information in my contacts. "Her name is Nicky Macintosh. And she's my sister."

7

I STARED AT the Dunhams' house from the passenger seat of Detective Guidry's car. My right index finger was fixated on a small tear in the upholstery beneath my thigh. I felt something hard and forced my thumb into the hole to get a grip on it.

Guidry shook her head when I held up a bullet-shaped piece of bright yellow candy. I was pretty sure it was a Mike and Ike.

"Sorry about that," she said softly. "Detective Bowen has a weird sense of humor."

"Uh-huh." I went back to looking across the street. It was past first light but not quite sunup. Early enough to see that most of the house was still dark except for a small window to the left of the front door. I'd only been inside once a few months before, when Ethan had taken forever to come outside despite my many texts telling him I was waiting. The lit window belonged to the kitchen, I thought. Probably Kevin's mom—was her name Andrea?—waiting for my arrival.

I had called Ethan's cell before Guidry and I left the police station. It took two more tries before he answered, so he knew something was up. All I told him was that I was going to be picking him up early.

"How early?" Like I was torturing him.

"Like, now. In fifteen minutes."

"Moooooom. I'm tired. I'm just sleeping, I promise."

What did he assume I thought he was doing? If I had to guess, he and Kevin had stayed up all night playing video games.

"I'm sorry, kiddo. I'll see you in fifteen minutes, okay?" He didn't say anything, which meant he'd be complying. Ethan has a way of letting you know when he's got other ideas. "I love you," I added, wondering how he was going to go on without his father.

"Fine," was all he said before hanging up.

We were halfway to the house when my cell rang. I didn't recognize the number, but it was the 631 area code. From the East End, not the city. I picked up. It was Kevin's mom, whose name I'd already forgotten. Apparently Ethan had been his usual loud self taking the stairs from the bedroom, waking her up. When Ethan told her I was suddenly picking him up, she decided to call me to make sure everything was all right.

"Is there some reason you don't want him here?" she had asked.

I made the mistake one time of telling Ethan that I thought Kevin's parents weren't the best role models for their son, and it obviously had worked its way back to the mom, because she always seemed to think I was judging her.

Honestly, I didn't trust the woman to keep whatever I said to herself, so I lied. I told her that I needed to get back to the city as soon as possible for a work emergency. I had hoped the story would convince her it was okay for the rest of the house to go back to sleep, but she told me she'd see me in a few minutes and hoped I could come inside for coffee.

Now we were here, and I had to go inside.

"You sure you want me to go with you?" Guidry asked.

I nodded before stepping out of the car.

———

BEFORE ADAM, THE ONLY PEOPLE close to me who had died were
my parents. The first to go was my father, five years earlier. It was
only the third time he had ever visited me in New York City, and it
wasn't wholly voluntary. He had been diagnosed with prostate cancer,
and according to my father, his doctor in Cleveland had told him to
"ignore it."

That was my father's way of summing up the doctor's assessment
that, at my father's age of seventy-one, the risk-benefit calculation
weighed against intervention. Put another way, the doctor thought my
father would die of something else before the cancer caught up to him.

I nagged Dad to see someone in New York.

Dad resisted, telling me that Dr. Millerton was a "good man" who
went to "good schools." I had no doubt that both things were true. But
few in the country could match Sloan Kettering, and one of Adam's
coworkers at the US Attorney's Office was the brother of the chairman
of the surgery department. He could get in right away. They'd even
accept his insurance. "It's all about specialization," I told him. "I guarantee you they see a hundred times the number of patients with exactly
your condition compared to Dr. Millerton."

I flooded him with rankings of hospitals and physicians, studies
of successful outcomes at the best facilities, and summaries of all the
treatment options available to him. I got the impression he didn't read
a word of it. The Taylor family—myself excepted—had a tendency to
act on impulse, not facts.

Mom seemed to resent my efforts. "You made it very clear you
wanted to get as far away from this house as you possibly could, but
now suddenly you care," she said. "Maybe it was only me you hated."

Of course I wanted to get out of that house. According to the outline of the memoir my publisher bought, my life story included an entire chapter dedicated solely to the violence I saw my father heap upon
my mother, who refused to do anything to stop it. But I never stopped
loving my parents, not even my father. To my mom, though, getting

Dad to see a "fancy doctor" was just another way of reminding them that I thought I was better than the rest of the family.

I was so proud of myself when I managed to change his mind. I looked up the football schedule and found a home game where the Giants were playing the Browns. I pressured Adam to make sure he could get good seats from one of his friends who'd sold out to law firm life, which came with perks like season tickets in the suite level.

Who needed all those medical statistics when I had my father's love of football? Dad finally caved.

I made sure to book him on a flight that landed in Newark. Adam picked him up, and they headed straight to Giants Stadium. My job would come on Monday, when I had him lined up with doctor appointments.

He texted me the view from Adam's friend's law firm's corporate box, with the caption "Worth getting cancer for." He even added a smiley face, followed by a crying face, followed by a purple devil. I had no idea until that moment that my father knew about emojis.

When I saw the final score pop up on Facebook—Browns 24, Giants 10—I pictured Dad going home and telling Mom and Nicky what a terrific time he had in New York.

But that conversation never happened.

Forty-five minutes after I saw the score, I got a phone call from Adam. Dad was on his way to New York-Presbyterian Hospital. He was in an ambulance. He'd been complaining about acid reflux as they left the stadium, but had chalked it up to all the greasy food he'd binged on during the game. By the time it became clear that it wasn't merely a stomachache, Adam was stuck in standstill traffic at the Holland Tunnel. He held my father's hand while waiting for an ambulance to clear a path to them.

I knew he was dead before the doctors ever told me. I managed to beat the ambulance to the hospital. When I told the lady at the emergency room window that I was there to see Danny Taylor, brought there by ambulance with a suspected heart attack, she didn't even make eye contact while tapping away at her keyboard and telling me I must have the wrong hospital. I explained that my husband had just called from the ambulance and was certain my father was on his way. She made a phone call that confirmed her suspicions: no new ambulance arrivals. She told me to go ahead and wait, if that's what I wanted to do.

And then a few minutes later, I heard the phone next to her ring, and I watched her answer it. And I heard her say "Uh-huh" and "I see." And then she got up from her desk, walked around the front counter—outside the bubble of her little window—and headed straight for me.

"We did just have a new case arrive by ambulance." Both her face and voice were kind, and she placed a gentle hand on my shoulder. "It'll be a few minutes, but I can take you in the back to wait for Dr. Tan."

I knew right then that she had already been told the news. Fate found a way of proving that Dr. Millerton—the doctor who was a good man who went to good schools—had been right all along.

I listened stoically as Dr. Tan gave me the details. My father didn't respond to the EMT's efforts to revive him. His death was officially called upon his arrival to the hospital. An autopsy would be performed pursuant to New York City's usual procedures, unless the next of kin objected. He speculated that it was sudden cardiac arrest. "It would have been like the lights just turned out."

Except that Dad felt something wrong when he was leaving the stadium, I thought. If I had been there, I would have taken him inside to make sure the pain subsided, wouldn't I? Of course I would have—to make sure nothing was wrong before he got into the car. The stadium would have had defibrillators on hand. But it was too late, so I said nothing.

Adam waited until the doctor had left the room to join me. "I'm so sorry." He put his arms around me while I cried. "I thought it was best for you to hear it from the doctor directly—in case you had questions."

I nodded through my tears, agreeing he had made the right decision. Five minutes later, I found Dr. Tan, gave him my mother's number, and asked him to tell her precisely what he had told me.

So how do you tell a sixteen-year-old boy that his father has died? If you're me, you don't. You have Guidry do it.

I WAS RIGHT ABOUT KEVIN'S mom being the one in the kitchen with the lights on. Her name was Andrea, and she had gotten up to wait. The coffee she offered us was weak, but it was hot and desperately needed.

Ethan was initially annoyed that I'd accepted Andrea's invitation to come inside. He'd been ready at the door, shoes already on. I knew that kid like the back of my hand. If he absolutely had to get up at the crack of dawn on a Saturday, he wanted to make it quick so he could return to bed as soon as possible.

Ethan's irritation shifted to worry when a woman he didn't recognize followed me in.

Once we were all gathered in the kitchen, coffees poured, I introduced the stranger with me as Detective Guidry from the Suffolk County Police Department.

Andrea placed a worried hand to her mouth, and her eyes immediately drifted to the staircase beyond the kitchen, and then to Ethan.

"It's nothing the kids did," I assured her. "It's—something happened at the house. The police responded." I asked her if she could give us a moment alone. She nodded and left, but not before giving my shoulder a quick squeeze. I wondered if she could already guess the news that was about to be delivered. Maybe my decision to come inside for coffee was as telling as that hospital nurse's sudden kindness.

Looking at Guidry, I guessed that she was in her late forties. She seemed prettier, and more feminine than I would have expected of a person in her role, but I was going by stereotypes. I realized that I had also been operating on stereotypes when I asked her, specifically, if she would come with me to deliver the news to my son. Her partner, Bowen, had stayed at the station to work.

Once Andrea was gone, I gestured to Ethan to sit down at the kitchen table. He did so, and then crossed his arms in front of him and rephrased my previous assertion as a question. "Something happened at the house?"

"There was a break-in," I said, but then looked to Guidry to elaborate.

"We think your father interrupted an intruder," she said. "A bedroom window at the back of the house was broken. There was an assault inside the home."

Ethan flinched.

"Your father was badly wounded. I'm sorry, but he did not survive."

Ethan stared at the white tile of the tabletop and began working his thumbnail against a section of stained grout. "Did you catch someone?"

"Not yet. It's still early."

He nodded. "So, like, what happened? You said there was an assault. But how exactly did he die?"

I swallowed, no longer caring about all the logical reasons I had for involving Guidry. "The person who broke in stabbed him," I said. Five times. The doctor told me it was five times. "Your father was so brave. He fought back. He was doing his best to defend himself. They think he would have made it except one of the wounds was to an aorta in his abdomen." I was parroting what the doctor had told me at the hospital, and hoped it was close enough to be accurate. "It collapses the circulatory system. Even though paramedics got there fast, it was still too late." I had tried and tried to find a pulse, but there was nothing. The doctor told me there would be an autopsy, and then I would need to decide where to have his body moved from there. That's all he was now. A body.

Ethan nodded again. His arms were still folded, but when he finally looked up, he looked directly at me. I saw a flash of heat on his face that I couldn't read. Before I could put my finger on it—was it anger?—his expression fell flat again. "So now what happens?"

Guidry shifted. Both literally and figuratively. She had been leaning forward, her body language as open and giving as Ethan's was closed and withdrawn. But now she moved slightly back in her chair. She had only come here out of a sense of obligation, helping out a family during a time of tragedy. But suddenly, she seemed . . . curious.

I didn't like the feeling of a detective being curious about us right now.

"Well, the medical examiner will follow up with your stepmother about making arrangements," she said. "And we, of course, investigate."

"To me," Ethan said. "What happens to me? Where will I live? Do I stay in New York or go back to Nicky?"

Guidry looked at me. We had already talked about my sister at the police station, but a final decision hadn't been made yet about contacting her.

"Do you mind if I talk to Ethan alone for a second?" she asked.

"Why is that necessary?" I replied.

"You had asked us for an accommodation for your family. He seems capable of having input on that decision."

"Oh my god," Ethan muttered. "My dad's dead, and you're talking about me in code. I'm sitting right here. Yes, I'm perfectly capable of speaking for myself."

The rational side of my brain was telling me not to leave him alone with a police detective, under any circumstances, ever. I had seen the way something in Guidry had shifted, and I knew that she and her partner had been treating me as a suspect for hours, whether they meant for me to feel that way or not.

But the other side of my brain was asking the same question as Ethan: What was going to happen to him next? I didn't want them to call Nicky. Not yet. I had given them an abbreviated summary of the history there. All I wanted was to wait a day. One day for Ethan and me to deal with losing Adam on our own. But I understood why Guidry would want to hear it from Ethan directly.

I told them I'd wait outside by the car.

8

Poppit

Thread: Chloe Taylor/People for the Press Award

Posted by BilboB

Making sure everyone saw the video of our favorite feminazi getting yet another honor this week. Can't the libs find someone else to slobber over for a while?

Posted by SoxSuck92

Can barely recognize her with all that makeup and ten layers of Spanx. I wonder if she called the cops on anyone with XY chromosomes who paid her a compliment.

Posted by FireStarter

These cunts won't be happy until it's illegal for men to speak before spoken to.

Posted by JustTheTip

She cleans up OK. I'd do her. It'd be a hate-fuck, but just sayin'.

Posted by IncelMRA

Went down the rabbit hole reconning this bitch last month. She's married to her sister's ex.

Posted by Bighead

@IncelMRA WTF? Seriously?

Posted by FireStarter

Where's @KurtLoMein? He always acts like he knows her IRL. Dude, is that true? She's married to her brother-in-law? Do you know the sister? We need deets.

Posted by JustTheTip

Is it bad to say I'd fuck the sister too? Just doing my part for the cause. LOL.

9

I SAT NEXT to Ethan in the back seat on the way home. He let me put my arm around him, and eventually rested his head on my shoulder and shut his eyes. I noticed Guidry glancing at us periodically in the rearview mirror.

When Guidry took the fork onto Ocean Avenue, Ethan sat up. It was Saturday, the rare day when not even our entitled neighbors would dare think of having the landscaping done. He opened the car door to the sounds of birds waking and ocean waves high enough to hear from four blocks away.

I counted a total of five police cars in the driveway and against the curb outside, three marked, two unmarked. Guidry had already warned me that it might be days before we could get back into the house. I wasn't sure I ever wanted to walk inside again.

"We can be out of the way in the pool house," I said as Ethan took in the unfamiliar sight of so many cars in front of our property. I'd gotten the all-clear to come and go there, since it wasn't considered part of the crime scene. "We can ask them for anything we need from your room."

He nodded. I let him step out first and then asked Guidry in a low voice, "So we're okay on my sister?"

Adam was awarded sole custody of Ethan when he was two years old, but Nicky's rights were never fully terminated. The arrangement was put to Nicky as a compromise, but Adam's own lawyers had told him that a judge was unlikely to extinguish her parental rights, even with the evidence he had. Then, after we got married, we wrote a will that named me as Ethan's guardian in the event of Adam's death. But the lawyer had warned us that the provision wouldn't be binding in a family court. If Nicky sought custody, the judge would have to look at Ethan's best interests to determine who would finish raising him. On the one hand, I'd been with him nearly every day since he was four years old, and Adam obviously wanted him to stay with me. On the other, Nicky was his biological mother and wasn't quite the train wreck she'd been fourteen years before, at least not on paper.

I was still trying to process the reality that my husband was dead, and was already wondering if I'd have to wage a legal battle to keep Ethan.

Guidry nodded. "I'll wait until the end of the day."

"Thank you." I was about to get out of the car when I stopped. "Hey, is there a way to confirm that Nicky was actually in Cleveland last night? You know, before you involve her in all this?"

"Wow, that's quite a loaded question, Mrs. Taylor."

"Can you please call me Chloe? Every time you say Mrs. Taylor, I wonder who you're talking to."

"Of course. Chloe it is. Do you really think your sister might be responsible for your husband's death, Chloe?"

Did I? Of course not. But then why had I asked the question? "No. We just have a complicated history, is all. She's basically been out of the picture since Ethan was a baby. To be honest, I'm not looking forward to whatever the next steps will be once she's notified. And I'd feel better if I'm a hundred percent certain, just in case."

"Fair enough. You're sure you don't want to be the one to call her? She is your sister."

I was sure.

———

THE STRUCTURE WE CALLED THE pool house was actually a small cottage that happened to sit on the opposite side of the pool from the main house. Adam thought I was crazy when I decided two years earlier to add what was essentially a second house next to the three-bedroom, three-bath carriage house that was already our secondary home. "How are we going to keep the guests away?" he joked.

I told him that we'd need it someday when Ethan was older and wanted to visit with college friends and eventually his own wife and children.

What I didn't tell Adam was that I wanted—no, I needed—a place to work that was more than a hallway's skip from him and Ethan. As a partner at a law firm, Adam worked hard, but it wasn't the kind of work that seemed to call for deep concentration. He was one of those men who was constantly fiddling with his phone, answering emails between holes on the golf course and returning calls between courses of a meal. He strategized and filed lengthy legal briefings with the court, but managed a small pack of younger lawyers who did the actual research and writing. Adam's final role in the work product would be a quick line edit, often on the sofa as he watched the news.

I, on the other hand, wrote essays, articles, and, so far, two books from whole cloth. Even my work as editor in chief of *Eve* required me to absorb every square inch of an entire magazine edition, with a close review of copy, layout, and content. In my office at work in the city, I keep the door closed, instructing my assistant to block all calls and visitors for hour-long blocks or more, knowing that I work best when I am assured there will be no interruptions.

So what was I thinking when I was the one to suggest buying a house in East Hampton? I knew what I was thinking: I did it for Ethan and for Adam. I wanted Ethan to know some place other than New York City. I wanted him to have fresh air and the ability to ride a bike around the neighborhood without getting sideswiped by a bus. And I knew that Adam had never really come to love Manhattan. No matter how many years went by, he still flinched at the blaring sounds of sirens and needed a drink to calm his nerves after a crowded ride on the subway. A house outside of the city, near the beach, would be a paradise for them.

But I should have realized that paradise meant I wouldn't be able to get an inch of work done. For a wife and a mother, there's apparently no such thing as a "home office." Home meant Adam and Ethan wandering in whenever they couldn't find something, had a question, or stumbled upon a movie on cable they thought I'd be interested in. It wasn't until I tried to do my job under a shared roof with my family that I realized that neither Ethan nor even Adam truly understood that my job involved actual work.

And so then came the "pool house." By the summer before, it had become evident that my intention all along was to have the essential Room of One's Own. Once, when I disappeared into what was now my working space over a holiday weekend, I returned to the main house to find Adam brooding in the kitchen. "I wish you'd at least tell me when you plan to ignore me all weekend. I wouldn't have bothered coming out."

I'd never need to worry about creating space between us again.

I HUGGED ETHAN AS SOON as we were inside with the door closed.

"Are you okay?" he asked.

For the first time since I had left the hospital with the police, I almost lost it all over again. He had just learned that his father had been killed, and he was worried about me.

"Numb," I said. "Scared."

"Scared that they could come back?" His eyes searched mine for an explanation. "Whoever did it, I mean."

I held him tighter, not knowing what to say. "The police will be patrolling the area, keeping an eye on us. We have the security alarm, too." I thought again about Guidry asking me why Adam hadn't set the alarm. I had given her a possible explanation, but I was wondering the same thing. We always set it before going to sleep. I tried to remember the few times I got back to the house after Adam had turned in for the evening, and could picture myself disarming and then resetting the alarm. But was I certain? Of course not. I knew how fragile memory can be, especially for those kinds of inconsequential details. And even if I was right, every routine had exceptions. Adam had been so tired. Maybe he drifted off without thinking about the alarm. It was another question I'd never have an answer to now.

"What did Guidry talk to you about while you were alone?" That's how I always avoided empty silences: with facts. Busywork. Things to check off the to-do list.

"She said they needed to contact my mom, since you're technically my stepmother. I guess you told her Mom still has rights to me."

"I wasn't going to lie to her, Ethan. We'll have to deal with it eventually. It's going to be okay, though." I had no way of knowing if that was true, but it was what we both needed to hear right then.

He didn't answer.

"Hey, back at Kevin's house, you looked at me for a second like maybe you wanted to say something to me in private." I tried to pull up the image of his face in that moment. If I didn't know my kid, I'd say it was rage. It was nothing I had ever seen in him before. Or were my perceptions shaped by my own sense of guilt? "Do you want to talk now? About Dad, or anything at all?"

He shook his head.

"So what exactly did Detective Guidry ask?" I realized how desperate I sounded.

"How I felt about them calling Mom."

"And?"

He shrugged. "I told her she's barely my mom. And she's, you know, a bunch of drama. So she said you guys worked it out that Mom would be called later, and was I okay with that. Honestly, I wish we didn't need to tell her at all."

"Ethan." Adam had always let Ethan believe that his mother had essentially abandoned him, but I knew the truth was more complicated.

"Whatever. I just want to go to my room and be alone."

I couldn't even give him that. The pool "house" was really just one big room with a wet bar in the corner, but it did have a tiny sleeping loft.

"There's clean sheets on the bed," I said. He was halfway up the stairs when I checked with him one more time. "And you're sure that's the only thing the detective asked you about? Nicky?"

"Yes."

Had they asked him about me? That is what I wanted to know. "Nothing else?"

"No!" he said, clearly aggravated by my cross-examination.

He was trying to be calm, I could tell, but I heard him start to cry almost immediately once he reached the bed.

If only he had done that back in the Dunhams' kitchen, I thought. Because I had seen the way Guidry looked at him. Whatever test she had in mind for how a kid should act when he hears his father's been murdered, Ethan had failed it, and now the police were going to put our family under a microscope.

10

DETECTIVE JENNIFER GUIDRY plucked another gelatinous piece of candy from the tear in the upholstery of the passenger seat of her department-issued Impala. If her count was right, it was the seventeenth one so far—not counting the one Chloe Taylor had found. She wondered how long Bowen had been stuffing them in there. If she had to guess, it probably started around the time she called him out for that weird thing he kept doing, rolling up little strips of Scotch tape and dropping them into a coffee cup. If only he were as obsessive and compulsive about police work.

She closed the car door and made her way back to the Dunham house across the street, which she had left only forty minutes earlier. Andrea Dunham was still in her robe when she answered the front door.

Andrea kept clutching at the collar to cover her chest, even though she was wearing some kind of tank top beneath it. Guidry thought about telling her to go upstairs and do whatever she needed to do to be less fidgety, but she was working on fumes and needed to get home to catch a few hours of shuteye.

Andrea gave a small laugh when Guidry asked whether she and Chloe Taylor were close.

"Sorry," Andrea said, "but you saw their house, right? And you see the one you're sitting in now. No, we don't exactly hang out. The boys have been friends for years, though. They met in sports camp when they were ten years old. But we only know Chloe and Adam to say hi to them, coordinate play dates when the kids were little, that kind of thing. I can't even believe it about Adam. She must be beside herself."

Guidry had assumed the two women weren't friends. Chloe hadn't even hugged Andrea when she left the house, just a thank-you for the coffee and for letting Ethan spend the night.

"Do you know who they're close to out here?"

Andrea was looking up at the kitchen ceiling, searching for answers, but then a worried expression crossed her face. "Chloe's not a suspect or anything, is she?"

"This is standard for an investigation," Guidry assured her. "We focus on the victim and work our way outward. Try to find sources of conflict, potential motives."

Andrea nodded. "They're summer people, you know? They hang around with the friends they know from the city. I can't really help you."

"Perhaps your son would have some names?"

"Maybe. He spends time over there."

"That would be great," Guidry said, as if Andrea had volunteered to wake her son. Andrea was about to leave the kitchen when Guidry stopped her. "It's lucky the boys were here last night instead of at Ethan's. Were they here all night, by the way?"

Andrea waved a hand as if the suggestion were silly. "Don't judge me, but I have no idea. Kevin's room is in the basement, and there's a walkout door from there, so he's always coming and going. As long as he makes curfew, I consider myself lucky."

"And what time was last night's curfew?"

"One on weekends."

"And how do you know he made it?"

She shrugged. "He's a good kid. You'll see."

SHE'D SPENT THE REQUISITE AMOUNT of small talk with Kevin—did he know Ethan's family, could he name their friends—before turning to the time line for the previous night. "Before I go, can I just confirm that Ethan was with you until this morning?"

"Yeah. We were out all night, just like driving and stuff. Got back here around 12:30, played some Fortnite. He was gone when I woke up."

"Where'd you drive?"

"Cruising is all. Went as far west as Watermill. East as far as Montauk."

Guidry remembered cruising the main drag in Boston. At sixteen years old, she wouldn't have been able to describe the details any better.

"This was all after the movie?" she asked.

"Is this like on TV? Where you make sure Ethan and I agree on what movie we saw? You can't seriously think Ethan did something to his dad, right? Because that's, like, crazy."

"Nothing like that," Guidry assured him. "It's standard to exclude members of the family first so we can move on from there."

"Okay, cool."

"Great," Guidry said, jotting down the recited movie title before tucking her pen away in the spiral notebook.

Walking to her car, she told herself she'd made the right decision going back to speak with Kevin Dunham. The name of the movie itself wasn't especially noteworthy. It was the same film Chloe had mentioned when she accounted for Ethan's whereabouts the previous night.

The problem was that, according to Ethan, there had been no movie at all.

11

I'M STANDING AT an altar, surrounded by white orchids, look-ing out at a sea of despondent faces. Everyone is wearing black. I think I'm wearing a veil, because when I look down at the pages on the lectern, I can't read the words. I fumble with the netting in front of my face until I can make out the letters clearly. I begin reading auto-matically, not even processing the sentences that are coming out of my mouth. The people in the audience glance at each other in confusion and begin to murmur. They grow so loud I can't hear my own voice. I look down at my notes and realize I brought the wrong speech. I'm thanking everyone for my award during Adam's funeral.

I was still opening my eyes when my hand grabbed for the cell phone I had tucked beneath the throw pillow. According to the screen, it was two in the afternoon. I had gotten a response to the message I had sent before finally drifting off to sleep.

You were up awfully early. How was the party last night? I'm out here, too. Let me know if you can find time.

He obviously hadn't heard the news yet.

I sat up, already feeling the crick in my neck from sleeping on the hard, narrow daybed in the pool house.

I clutched the phone to my chest and said a silent prayer of thanks that he had insisted on being so careful. He had given me the tiny black flip phone five months earlier, right before Christmas.

"What are we, spies?" I had asked.

He held up a second one that he had purchased for himself. "My regular phone's billed through the firm. Someone might recognize your number. I figured you should have one, too. Maybe I'm being paranoid, but Adam will never shake that former prosecutor bug."

"What does that mean?"

"He's organically suspicious. He notices everything—and interprets every detail in the worst light. Am I telling you something you don't already know?"

I remember pulling the sheet over my chest, pinning myself down beneath it with my elbows as I studied the burner phone. I couldn't disagree with what he was saying, but I also didn't want him talking about my husband—not like that.

He turned on his side and brushed sweat-damp hair from my brow. "Hey, where are you right now? Is it the phone? Am I being presumptuous to assume this might keep happening?"

The first time, I had insisted afterward that it was a mistake. A one-time thing that we could never allow again. Then it kept happening, and we both knew it was going to continue.

Are you home now? I typed.

Yep. My aspiration for the day is to see how long I can sit next to this pool. Unless you come over. Then I will move.

I made my way off of the daybed and looked up at the sleeping loft. Ethan was on his side, his back facing toward me. His breathing was slow and deep. I hoped he was actually sleeping and not just pretending.

I peered through the edge of the white curtains that covered the sliding doors out to the pool. Crime scene tape ran the width of the backyard, starting at the edge of the swimming pool closest to the house. I could see the movements of police personnel inside.

I slipped on a pair of old flip-flops I found under the bench that stored the beach towels and slid the door shut quietly behind me. I kept expecting an officer to catch my attention as I made the trek past the pool, down my driveway, and halfway down Pudding Hill Lane, but no one came. With my test run complete, I ventured back to the pool house and dropped both of my phones in the front pocket of the beach cover-up I was wearing. I donned my Chanel aviators as a final touch, just in case they stopped me this time and asked me why I had returned to the house so quickly.

As I stepped outside once again, I thought about the headline-of-the-moment crime stories I had covered over the years and the formula that had ensured top-of-the-hour billing on all the cable stations. White victim. Good teeth. Female preferred, but not essential. At least three photographs to suggest a seemingly perfect life. But the real kicker for a local crime story to go national? You needed a suspect. It couldn't be a slam dunk, because then the police would have an arrest, and there'd be nothing much to talk about until trial. No, you needed someone who seemed guilty enough to deserve the public's scornful attention, without quite enough evidence to back up the speculation. A chicken to stew in the pot.

A sure way to land in the Dutch oven was to fail whatever stereotypes the true-crime junkies held for family members of the victims. The stepmom who went to the gym the same day of the kidnapping. The husband who smiled during the heart-wrenching interview. Too many social media posts was always a no-no. I remembered every single name I had helped grind through the mill, based on nothing other than the failure to meet fantasy expectations.

I hated myself for even thinking about it, but the fact of the matter was that I now had a role to play. My husband's murder would be noteworthy, and I was his widow. If I had absolutely nothing to hide, what would I do?

I assured myself that a lonesome walk to Main Beach made perfect sense. If anyone were ever to ask, I could recite from memory all the reasons that the beach had been special to Adam and me.

When I reached the end of Ocean Avenue, I opted to turn left, away from the pavilion where a couple of women appeared to be setting up for some kind of party, based on the balloon bouquets they were struggling to tie to picnic tables. I walked east until I passed the lifeguard stand, and then kicked off my flip-flops and let the waves wash over my shins. When I was certain I was alone, I put my right hand in my pocket, retrieved the burner phone, and sent one final message. When I was done, I pulled out the SIM card and let it slip away with the current.

I continued to walk east, pausing to retrieve a paper bag that was caught in the brush. When I reached Egypt Beach, I placed my defunct burner in the bag and tossed it into a trash can in the parking lot for the Maidstone Club as I made my way north to Further Lane.

On the way home, I stopped by his house to tell him that I no longer had the phone he gave me. My husband had been murdered, and we couldn't see each other again. Not any time soon, at least.

AS I APPROACHED THE TURN to my house from Ocean Avenue, I noticed a small group gathered at the corner, their collective gaze focused north. They had to be watching the police activity, wondering what had brought so many cars to the house at the middle of Pudding Hill Lane.

My remaining phone—the real one—rang in my pocket. I checked the screen. It was Catherine. She'd already called once before when I was still at his house, saying goodbye. It was so like her to call the day after a party, wanting to kibitz about every moment. I hit the call-decline button and tucked the phone back into my pocket.

As I neared the intersection, I noticed a young woman in a white hoodie and black yoga pants nudge the woman next to her. I had been spotted. She raised her cell phone as if she were checking messages, but I recognized the move. I turned my face away on instinct, hoping it was fast enough to avoid her camera. I picked up my pace, but not so much that I could be described as running away from onlookers.

To my knowledge, the news of Adam's death hadn't broken yet, but it wouldn't be long. And once it did, I knew the speculation that would follow. After all, isn't the spouse always a suspect?

When I turned the corner, I saw a Porsche 911 heading in my direction. It pulled suddenly to the left side of the street and parked directly in front of my house. Catherine was at the wheel of the convertible, her cell phone in hand.

In all the years I'd known her, I had never seen her without makeup, let alone in a Pretenders T-shirt and jeans. She was all limbs as she climbed out of the tiny car and rushed toward me.

"Is it true? About Adam?"

Apparently the news was out.

I nodded, tears pricking my eyes. "Last night. I found him when I got home from your place. I couldn't bring myself to call anyone yet."

"I found out from Grace Lee." Grace Lee was a reporter with the *Daily News*. Her husband was NYPD, and she was always at least an hour ahead of the rest of the press when it came to the big crime-beat stories. "Apparently 'out of respect'"—Catherine made air quotes—"the official editorial response was to place a call to your lawyer instead of you directly."

"Bill?" I asked. I checked my phone. No other calls besides Catherine's.

"This is the problem with having such ancient friends," she said. "He's probably calling his secretary right now, trying to find your cell phone number. I can't believe that geezer didn't call me."

She stopped speaking and pulled me into a tight hug. The curls of her humidity-soaked red hair tickled my cheek. It was the first time since I'd heard the news about Adam that I'd been able to let anyone comfort me. I sank into her embrace.

"Do they know what happened?" she asked.

"They think it was a burglary. Still the off-season. But . . ." I shook my head. They didn't know a damn thing.

"Love, I know you don't want to hear this, but you need to do a press release. Through the magazine would be best."

My instinct was to hold up a hand, but I reached for hers instead and gave it a squeeze. "I really can't deal with that right now, Catherine."

"Stay ahead of this," Catherine warned, "or the true-crime crowd will make you their newest black widow by bedtime."

I looked up at the cloud cover and sighed. "Or . . . I'll put out a press release like you say, and they'll tweet about the selfish bitch who worried about burnishing her public image before her husband was in the ground. I'm not playing their game."

"Well, I told Grace I'd reach you. Let me at least get back to her. I can be an anonymous source. Someone close to the family."

"No."

Her lips—I'd never seen them without lipstick before—opened, but no words came out. I couldn't remember a time that I hadn't been grateful for her advice. The truth is that she was probably my closest friend, but it had always been about the work. She didn't know the parts of me that mattered right now.

And she must have felt that, too, because even though she had driven to my house, she didn't follow as I marched across the gravel driveway. "Call me if you change your mind," was her last attempt. She'd done enough so she could tell me—and everyone else—later that she'd tried her best.

How would it look that I was at a party without Adam when he was killed? Or that he had barely made it to the awards banquet

on Thursday night? They were only two innocuous scheduling details, but could easily be twisted into a headline-grabbing, trouble-in-
paradise narrative. And if they found out about the affair? Forget it,
I'd spend the rest of my life a tabloid villain. I wasn't going to let that
happen.

12

I HAD ALMOST reached the pool house when I heard a voice behind me, calling out my name. I turned to see Guidry on the opposite side of the pool, standing at the threshold of the main house's open sliding glass door. I resisted the urge to scold her about bugs getting inside.

"I was waiting to call you in case you had managed to fall asleep, but I see you're up."

"I walked down to the beach. It usually calms me, but . . . not enough. You're still on duty?"

"I went home for a bit, but, yes, I'm back at it." She walked to my side of the yard, closing the distance between us so we didn't need to raise our voices. "If you're up for it, we're ready for you and Ethan to do a walk-through of the house with us."

"I'm not sure that's a good idea." I looked back toward the pool house. "For Ethan to see that, I mean. Or me, for that matter."

"We don't need you to view the actual spot where your husband was found. But you know the house, and we don't. If you could help us identify anything that's missing . . . what's out of place . . . that sort of thing. And Ethan, too, I'm afraid. It's important."

————

THE HOUSE FELT LIKE A bizarre replica of the home we had once called our little slice of paradise. Same three bedrooms and 2,700 square feet. Same white-slipcovered sofas and driftwood tables. But our house had always been notoriously tidy. Both Adam and I were naturally fastidious; even when Ethan was little, we had a rule that he had to pick up his toys and put them away each night. When he started to slack off as a tween, Adam threatened to take anything that was left out and donate it to charity. Every night for the next week, I had found the talking Jar Jar Binks doll my mother had given him for his birthday posed conspicuously at the bottom of the staircase.

I had since grown accustomed to the fact that—at least for the time being—my son was a teenage Tasmanian devil, incapable of maintaining any kind of order when it came to his personal possessions. I had trained him, however, to confine his chaos to his own bedroom. The rest of the house looked ready for a real estate showing, which Adam and I considered the highest compliment.

But now, in the new, weird world in which Adam was gone, our meticulously maintained slice of paradise was a giant garbage bin. Even from the dining room at the back of the house, I could see that kitchen drawers and cabinets were open. Entire bookshelves had been emptied onto the floor in the family room. Chairs were overturned. The police had used numbered yellow cards to document the havoc.

Standing next to me, Ethan reached for my hand and gave it a squeeze. "Jesus Christ. Your OCD must be going crazy right now," he whispered.

It wasn't just the mess that had altered the house. All the light was gone. It felt like the entire house was covered with a gray filter. It even smelled different.

I walked over to my dining room table and futilely righted the three ceramic vases that had been knocked to their sides on the tabletop. At least they weren't broken.

I realized how my fussing must have looked in that moment from

Guidry's eyes. "Sorry," I muttered, wiping away a tear. "Sentimental value."

My friends James and David ran a pottery studio and had designed these especially for me as a wedding gift. Three different vessels—representing me, Adam, and Ethan—each beautiful on its own, but which fit perfectly together in a single form.

"Of course," she said.

As I moved farther into the house, I forced myself to gaze toward the living room. Adam hadn't even looked like a real person by the time I found him. More like those wax statues of celebrities at Madame Tussauds. But now the room was bare, the furniture pushed into a corner next to the fireplace.

Ethan seemed to shrink next to me. "This is where . . ."

I nodded.

"We cleared that area before you came in," Guidry explained quietly. I pictured the rug Adam had been so proud to find in the ABC clearance basement, now bloodied on a table somewhere in a crime lab.

"So what do you need to know?" I asked.

"What looks different?"

"Are you kidding?" Ethan blurted out. "Like, everything?"

"It's been ransacked," I said quietly. "You already told me at the police station." I had been so focused on Adam after I found him, I hadn't even noticed.

Guidry placed her hands on her hips. "Okay, but please try to take a closer look. What do you think they were looking for?"

I shrugged. "Valuables, I guess. Not that we have any. The only jewelry I have of any value is my wedding ring and these." I tucked my bobbed hair behind my ears to reveal the diamond studs that permanently occupied my earlobes.

"Files? I didn't see a home office."

I told her it was in the pool house—pretty much only for my use—and that she could look there if she wanted, but there was no sign of a break-in.

"What about cash?" she asked. "A lot of people out here keep a stash in a dresser drawer or closet."

I shook my head. "We're just regular wallet people."

"Speaking of which . . ." Guidry made her way back to the kitchen and gestured toward a man wearing a uniform. He handed her a Ziploc bag, which she in turn gave to me. "We already took photographs, so you can have these back for now. It might take a couple days before we're completely out of your hair."

There was something about the way she said it, like we both knew it wasn't true. She wasn't going anywhere.

I immediately recognized the bag's contents. Hermes wallet. Tag Heuer watch. Platinum wedding band. Pieces of Adam.

She also handed me a slip of paper torn from a spiral notebook. It was a list of credit cards written in big bubble letters—the style of print I associated with young girls—plus a notation of "$253."

She asked me if all our cards were there. They were the ones found inside his wallet. I did a mental count and confirmed nothing was missing.

"If it was a robbery, why didn't they take this stuff?" I asked, circling my husband's ring with my index finger through the plastic.

"The wallet and watch were on a nightstand in the bedroom." She was leading the way to the open master bedroom door. It felt odd to follow someone else in my own house. "This is how we found the room. Does anything look out of place?"

My side of the bed was still made, covered in part by the blanket that had been tossed from Adam's side.

I shook my head. "Other than the covers. It looks like he was in bed and then got up."

"That's what we're assuming, too. The intruder—or intruders—may have thought the house was empty. They hadn't reached your room yet. He heard the noise while he was sleeping, went to the living room. After the . . . confrontation, they panicked. They leave."

"I'm sorry. I know you're trying to share information," I said, "but it's a lot to process. Like you're asking us to look at things from the perspective of whoever did this. This isn't a project for us, a puzzle to be solved. Do you understand that?"

Ethan had one hand masking his eyes, the way he did when I made him uncomfortable. He wasn't groaning, which was a sign he knew I was right, but I supposed it wasn't easy to have parents who always spoke their mind, no matter the circumstances.

"You're right," Guidry said, because, of course, I was. "I have no idea what you're going through right now. But I know you want me to do my job well. So I'll stop trying to sugarcoat it for you, and ask you to do the work I can't do on my own. We need a list of anything that's missing, as well as your thoughts about anything else you might notice as you do your walk-through. Fair enough?"

I nodded, and Ethan and I began the work of conducting an inventory of a house we hadn't been to for weeks when we were still trying to process the reality of what had happened here only the previous night. Because the master bedroom was untouched, we started in the bedroom next to ours—the guest room where they'd gained access by smashing the window, and then unlocking it and sliding it open. The nightstand and dresser drawers were open, but they'd all been empty to begin with. There was nothing to steal there.

Given Ethan's slumped shoulders when he opened his bedroom door, I inferred that the intruder—or intruders, as Guidry had noted— had gone there as well, but, truth be told, I couldn't tell the ransacked version from its usual state. Guidry and I left him there while we continued the tour.

When we were finally finished, I told her that the only thing I noticed missing was the portable Bluetooth speaker that lived on the kitchen windowsill. "We take it outside sometimes to listen by the pool. It's possible it's somewhere else, but, honestly, I don't think anything else is gone. Except maybe Adam's laptop? We both carry ours back and forth. And he should have had his briefcase, too."

Guidry was already nodding. "We have both. We're hanging on to those for now."

"This seems like a lot of searching for a random burglary," I said, thinking aloud.

"We're aware of the threats that have been made against you on-line, Chloe. We're already working on a subpoena to try to identify the users who posted the most inflammatory comments."

"You should also try to find out where my husband was the last couple of days. He told me he was meeting with a client called the Gentry Group at a hotel near JFK. He was supposed to be there all day Thursday and Friday, but when I asked him for the details, he seemed a little evasive."

Guidry lowered the pad of paper she had been jotting notes in to make eye contact with me. "Do you have a theory about where he might have been other than with this client?"

I told her it was nothing that specific, just a gut instinct. "Usually when he ran late, he'd tell me more about the specifics of the work. I feel like it's something you should check. Just to be a hundred percent certain."

"Like verifying that your sister was in Cleveland?" Guidry asked. She said it like we were friendly enough for her to mock me, which we weren't. But she was right. It had been a silly request, and I knew it.

"No," I said with a sigh. "That, I admit I was being paranoid about. But I have to think it's relevant to nail down where a homicide victim spent the last two days, and I'm telling you that it was unusual for him to spend all that time at some business commuter hotel with a client without giving me any other details—like bad fish sticks for lunch, or moldy carpet, or a colorful hooker at the bar. Adam and I shared those kinds of dumb observations with each other."

She gave me a sympathetic smile and placed a gentle hand on my forearm. "Okay, I understand now. And, yes, we'll make sure we have his movements locked down. And I did check your sister's whereabouts, by the way. You can rest assured that her cell phone was pinging in Cleveland, right where she belonged."

"You still haven't called her, right?" I asked. Guidry had assured me she'd give me until "the end of the day," but that could mean anything.

"I'm just about to. Do you want to do it together? She'll probably want to talk to you right away."

"She knows my number." I heard the iciness in my own voice. It was unavoidable when the subject of Nicky arose.

Guidry stiffened as she looked over my shoulder, and I turned to see Ethan coming out of his room.

"They took my Beats and my Rayguns."

I rolled my eyes. The headphones had been his main Christmas present last year. Adam and I didn't understand why he needed the thousand-dollar iridescent version instead of the regular Beats. And the fight he and his father had had over those fucking ridiculous shoes. Of course they were gone.

"Beats meaning headphones?" Guidry asked. Ethan nodded. "And Rayguns?"

"They're tennis shoes," I explained. "Red and yellow and black, with a little cartoon guy on the side holding a ray gun."

Guidry was jotting down notes again. "And those are worth . . ."

"About a hundred dollars retail," I said. "But the kids resell them. You can apparently get more than a thousand dollars for them on the aftermarket." Guidry's eyes widened. Yes, it was a lot for a pair of sneakers, but the thought that my husband might have been killed for them made me want to break the rest of the windows. "I'll pull up a picture and email them to you," I added.

"So that's it? Headphones, a speaker, and the shoes?"

"Like I said, we didn't have anything valuable here. Unless they were going to back up a moving truck for the furniture, I don't know what they'd be looking for. Please, check on whether he was meeting with this client, the Gentry Group."

She said they'd be checking on everything, but was already asking Ethan for more details about the three items that had been stolen. I could see she was going to chalk the episode up to a residential burglary gone wrong.

"He took an Uber to and from the meetings. They should be able to tell you where they picked him up, right?"

She jotted down a few more notes and assured me she'd contact them. First I had asked her to run my loser sister's phone records. Now I sounded like a jealous wife who wanted to double-check her husband's whereabouts, even in death.

As Ethan and I exited through the sliding glass door, I considered imploring her one last time to look more carefully at Adam's work, but worried it would look like an attempt to deflect attention from myself. Because that's how guilty I felt.

WE HAD STREAMED FIFTEEN MINUTES of *Elf*, which Adam called my "Instant Chloe Happiness Movie," no matter what season, when I hit the pause button.

"A movie can't fix this," I announced.

"Bet you wish you hadn't flushed all that weed last summer," Ethan said dryly. Yet another fight with his father, even more colossal than the one regarding the shoes. "I can't believe he's not coming back."

I started to cry and then forced myself to stop. I had to be strong for Ethan. "Let's go back to the city. You okay with that?"

"Fuck yeah."

Once we were in the car, he asked if we could swing by Kevin's house to get his backpack. He'd been so tired when I picked him up that morning, he forgot all about it.

When he hopped out of the car, I tried again to remember everything Adam had told me about the work that had kept him late most of the previous week. Just an hour earlier, with my flip-flopped feet still sandy from my climb over the dunes, I had broken up with my lover, "at least for now," I told him. Under the circumstances, of course he understood. He kissed me when I left—it was a good kiss—and then said he had something he needed to tell me, even though it might hurt me: he didn't think Adam had actually met with the client he'd supposedly spent Thursday and Friday with.

I asked him how he could possibly know that.

"I checked yesterday. When you said he was late to the gala because he was meeting with the Gentry Group, it didn't sound right to me. He hadn't billed a single minute to Gentry for the last ten days."

The person I was sleeping with behind Adam's back was one of his law partners, Jake Summer. He was the one who had convinced Bill to buy a table for the Press for the People gala, so he could be there for my big night without raising any suspicions.

"Maybe he just hadn't done his time sheets yet." One of the many things Adam hated about private practice was the requirement that he account for his time in six-minute increments.

Jake had shook his head. "He filed his time sheets last night, a little before seven." It must have been during the car ride. "He had a few phone calls and emails billed to various clients—less than two hours total—but nothing for Gentry."

"*Two hours?* But he was gone all day Thursday and Friday."

"He blocked out both days as client development, Chloe." Client development. Meaning, not billed. Two full days of time in a black hole. "I'm so sorry."

So when I asked Guidry to look into Adam's schedule, I had good reason. But I couldn't exactly tell the police about that, could I?

My thoughts were so focused on why Adam might have lied about seeing a client that it took a few of Ethan's taps on the back window of the station wagon before I popped the hatchback. We rode in silence back to the city, Ethan choosing the playlist and playing games on his phone while I wondered if Adam had been having an affair, and if I would have even cared if I'd known about it.

13

BEFORE HER PARTNER opened his mouth, Guidry knew Bowen was going to say something about the wife being involved. He'd made his mind up before they'd even walked into the house the previous night.

"You said I was jumping to conclusions? Did you see the way she was fiddling with those vases? That was straight-up rain-man bullshit."

Thoughts were pinging so quickly in Guidry's head, she was having a hard time making room for Bowen's comments. "Says the man who has been stuffing Mike and Ikes in our fleet car upholstery."

She decided to walk through the house one more time.

The house was one story, exempting the basement and the pool house. Adam Macintosh had been killed in what was basically the middle of the house, near the entrance of the living room, but only a few steps in any direction from the kitchen, master, and the other two bedrooms. The house had been trashed, but the pandemonium wasn't divided equally. The master was untouched, as was the living room.

But what was bothering Guidry were the other two first-floor bedrooms: one belonging to the son, Ethan, the other the guest room, where the intruder had broken a window. The theory was that Adam had woken up and surprised the burglar. But if the burglar thought the house was empty, why save the living room and master bedroom for last?

She was standing in the hallway that connected the two smaller bedrooms, listening to Bowen psychoanalyze Chloe Taylor. "Sorry, I know it's not PC, but the bitch is an ice queen. Who the fuck marries her own sister's husband?"

Guidry held up a hand, trying to block out what she considered to be noise for the moment.

"The scene," she said. "We need to focus." Nothing was missing from the guest bedroom, according to Ethan and Chloe, and yet she couldn't pull herself from the doorway. And then she realized what she had been missing. "We've got a problem," she said.

"That's what I've been trying to tell you. We need to take a closer look at the wife."

She crooked a finger to nudge him closer. "Take a look at this room only. The glass from the window."

"It's broken. That's where they gained access."

"Yeah, but look." The duvet cover was white with tiny yellow ducks on it. Little rubber duckies. It looked high-end, crisper than any cotton Guidry had ever slept under. It was folded in thirds, accordion style, but the entire comforter had slipped sideways from the foot of the bed onto the hardwood floor. She pointed to the shards of glass that were scattered on top of it. "See that?"

It took Bowen too long to figure out the implications, confirming everything she had always thought about his intelligence.

A window broken in the wrong direction—inside to out—was the most obvious mistake she'd ever seen in a staged break-in. In this case, the glass was at least broken from the outside, but the shards of glass had fallen onto a comforter on the ground. "This is one of the ransacked rooms," she said, "but nothing is missing." The nightstand and dresser drawers were open, but, according to Chloe Taylor, they had been empty to begin with.

Bowen had now caught up to her chain of reasoning. "And look, there's some shards in this open drawer, too. We need to get CSU back in here."

The implication was obvious. The room had been mildly mussed up—drawers opened and duvet thrown to the ground—*before* the glass was broken from the outside.

Bowen shimmied his shoulders as if he were about to dance under a mirrored ball. "I knew it. Did you see how Chloe was in total robot mode just now? Like she was trying to figure out how an innocent person is supposed to act when her husband's killed. Like she was trying to replicate it perfectly for a camera."

Guidry shook her head. "She's alibied. Besides, she's way too smart to make a mistake like this."

They knew from Adam's texts that he didn't get to the house until after Chloe was already at her friend's house. Chloe said she left shortly after midnight—which they could easily confirm with other guests at the party—and the 911 call came in at 12:23. Given the drive time from Sag Harbor, she couldn't have had time to kill him and then ransack the house. And she couldn't have trashed the house before the party, or Adam surely would have mentioned it in their text conversation.

"So then she didn't do it herself," Bowen said. "She had someone do it for her, and made sure she was alibied up at her friend's house when it went down."

"Then why did she text him from the party asking him one last time if he wanted to join her? Not exactly a good way to set him up for the hit man."

She had no idea what kind of strings Bowen had pulled to be working major crime investigations. His career should have stalled out on rounding up late-night beach trespassers.

"Admit it," she said. "You don't like her or what she stands for, so you want her to be guilty." Guidry had read the entire series of articles for which Chloe Taylor was now famous, and she had wondered how long it would take for those stories to trickle their way into law enforcement.

"Then what's up with the glass being on top of the blanket? You think it just slipped to the floor at some point and she didn't notice? Did it ever dawn on you that you might have a blind spot for your feminist hero?"

She had no interest in taking Bowen's bait. "We need to take a deep dive on Ethan. Look at the things that were missing from the house: a Wi-Fi speaker, headphones, and shoes? Only a kid's going to know that a pair of kicks is worth a grand. And it would explain why the master's untouched." Guidry remembered how freaked out she felt whenever she went into her parents' bedroom as a child, even if it was just to use the phone.

"Yeah, but if Chloe spent any time reading the local crime stats, she'd know most of our burglaries are pulled off by teenagers. It's inevitable, when you think about it. All summer they're surrounded by Porsches and Teslas, city kids buying ice creams with hundred-dollar bills at the beach shack. If I had grown up like that, I might've been tempted to even the score a little myself. So Chloe hires someone to off her husband, and then tells them to take some of her kid's toys to make it look like a burglary."

His logic wasn't wrong, but Bowen hadn't been in the room when Ethan heard the news about his father. The kid had gone wooden, absolutely still like that old game of freeze tag, waiting for permission to move again. He hadn't even cried. It wasn't normal. She did her best to describe it to Bowen, knowing she sounded no more persuasive than he had when he'd deemed Chloe's responses too "robot-like" for a grieving spouse.

"There's also a problem with Ethan's alibi," she said. "He and his friend Kevin each say they were together all night, but the details don't match up. Remember how Chloe said the kids went to a movie? Well, when Ethan told me what he was doing all night, he said he and Kevin were just cruising around, hanging at different beaches. Super vague. When I talked to Kevin alone, he was equally mushy, mentioning some of the same beaches but no particular time line. And then I made a point of saying 'This was after the movie, right?' And he couldn't have confirmed that version of the story fast enough."

"So maybe they did see the movie and Ethan forgot to mention it."

She shook her head. "Nope, I specifically asked him. He said it was sold out, which I confirmed with the theater. All the tickets were sold online before the ticket counter even opened. My guess is Ethan realized we might figure that out, so he told the truth about missing the movie. But Kevin didn't know that and was trying to parrot whatever he thought Ethan said. Something's not right. You had a point about Chloe being guarded with us. But maybe she's not covering for herself. If I noticed the kid seeming off, she had to see it, too. She could have her own suspicions."

"No way you could stab someone like that and not end up with blood on your clothes," he said.

"Ethan was wearing a black T-shirt and blue jeans when we picked him up at his friend's. He's probably got ten of each lying around his bedroom floor. He strips down by the body, puts on clean clothes, sends the bloody stuff out into the ocean."

She was relieved when Bowen didn't immediately argue with her theory again. "Why would a spoiled kid like that stab his father?" He shook his head at the idea of it.

"You never know what's going on in a family behind closed doors. Speaking of which, I need to call Chloe's sister."

"The one who's also the ex-wife and the biological mother?"

"One and the same."

"I'm sorry, but that's fucking weird," Bowen said.

"My guess is she might have something to tell us about that perfect family."

14

WHEN WE GOT back to the city, I stood in front of the open refrigerator while Panda rubbed against my shin and Ethan checked out the options over my shoulder. Unexpired milk and an enviable collection of condiments, but no food except a jar of pickles, a mystery brick of tinfoil, and four pieces of string cheese.

"Good job, Betty Crocker."

"How do you even know who Betty Crocker is?" I asked.

My son smiled for the first time that day. "I actually have no idea."

"We'll get takeout."

"Just let me go downstairs." There was a Greek deli beneath our building. The owner, Kostas, continually flouted the city code "fascists" by allowing dogs inside. He also, in my opinion, flouted gender discrimination laws by only hiring his sons and women with a minimum C cup.

Ethan must have sensed my reluctance to let him leave on his own, because he added, "It might be the last time I get to go outside before everyone starts treating me like 'that poor kid.'"

So I wasn't the only one wondering what our lives would be like once the news of Adam's murder broke. All any teenager ever wanted was to blend in with the crowd, and Ethan already had a hard time fitting in.

I put in my order for a Reuben and handed him a fifty from my wallet. Once he was gone, I poured myself three fingers of scotch and downed it. No amount of the stuff was going to help. I laughed to myself as I realized that Ethan's mention of marijuana was stuck somewhere in the back of my mind.

Adam had found the bag of pot last summer when he went wading through the swamp of accumulated clothes, soda bottles, textbooks, and game controllers on Ethan's bedroom floor, in search of the tennis racket I thought Ethan had used last. We had three others in the closet, but Adam was adamant that he needed the Yonex. The summer tournament had him going up against Colin Harris, a handsome lawyer who had a way of bringing out my husband's competitive side.

We never did find that stupid tennis racket, but Adam emerged from Ethan's bedroom carrying a freezer bag of weed. He was screaming out the back door for Ethan to get out of the pool before I even registered what he was holding. I still remembered Ethan standing on the bluestone deck, water dripping from his swim shorts, while Adam threatened to drive him to the doctor right then and there for a drug test.

I finally convinced Adam to keep his cool while I gave Ethan a towel so he could come inside. The neighbors didn't need to hear every word of what was about to happen.

Ethan swore up and down he was only holding on to the pot for a friend. He said his unnamed friend worked as a cashier at a store where "they search the employees' stuff when they leave, like for shoplifting and stuff."

"Which friend?"

Ethan had never had a particularly active social life, but it was easy enough to keep track of the people he knew in the city—same private schools, same circle of parents who kept each other in the loop. But East Hampton was another story. There, he could befriend whatever group of kids he happened upon at the beach for the afternoon. Some stuck, while others washed away.

It was clear to me from Ethan's crossed arms and pursed lips that he had no intention of answering his father's question. Ethan could be more stubborn than Adam and me combined when he wanted to.

"Seriously?" Adam had asked. "You're acting like a lowlife criminal right now. Snitches get stitches? Is that it?"

When Ethan started to smile, the veins in Adam's neck flared and he balled his fists. "That was my fault," I said. "I made a face. I'm sorry, Adam."

Adam turned toward me, but his expression didn't soften. "Come on, babe," I said. "That was a little bit funny, okay?"

He told us there was nothing funny about it. That the quantity involved was serious—right around half a pound, by his estimate. He said that amount would be a felony under New York law, not to mention the penalties for distribution, which that quantity probably indicated. "Is this how you paid for those goddamn shoes?"

He disappeared into Ethan's room again, reemerging with a hightop sneaker in each hand, slamming them down on the dining room table next to the bag of weed. He was still screaming, but at least he was in something of a comfort zone at the moment—building an argument using laws that he knew and we didn't.

"I swear to you, Dad, I am not selling pot. I told my friend I didn't want him to put that in my bag, but he had to leave for work. I didn't even touch it. He stuck it in there and left. What was I supposed to do?"

"I don't believe you, Ethan. Not until you tell me the name of the friend."

"No way. You'll call the cops or whatever. Just, please, Dad. Can you just let me leave it there until I see him later? It's only pot."

I continued to hear Adam haranguing Ethan as I carried the pot, unnoticed, to the kitchen and stuffed it down the garbage disposal. Holding the empty bag open as I returned to the room, I announced that there was nothing more to discuss. I told Ethan to go to his room, and then Adam continued to take his anger out on me. He must have told me ten different times that he had been a federal prosecutor and that it was hypocritical to allow his son to wriggle out of a position that would land a poorer, darker kid in a cell. I eventually got him to see that the two of them had been at a standstill and that my approach had solved the problem. "What were you going to do?" I asked him. "Ethan's as headstrong as you . . . when he wants to be. You can't waterboard him into giving you a name."

The next day, I handed Ethan $500 to give to his friend and made him promise he'd never do anything so stupid again. No parent wants their kid around drugs, I explained, but his father was a former prosecutor. Of course he was going to be tougher than the typical dad. Ethan had no way of knowing that Adam's sensitivity about law-and-order issues might stem from his own family's history in that arena.

Now, nearly nine months later, I found that same backpack in Ethan's bedroom and unzipped that same front pocket. On the one hand, I didn't want to think he'd broken his promise to me. On the other hand, I couldn't remember a time when I would have been so happy to stumble upon a joint. The pocket was empty. As I was zipping it back up, something inside the main compartment of the backpack shifted. It was open. Without meaning to, I saw a glimmer of silver inside. I reached for it and found a flip phone.

For half a second, I felt pain in my lungs, wondering how Ethan had found the burner phone I had disposed of earlier that day. Then I realized that this was an entirely different device. I flipped it open and scrolled through the recent calls. I didn't recognize the numbers, almost all of them with 631 and 516 area codes—Long Island numbers. The contacts were stored with initials only—J, M, N, and P.

Just like I had told Adam: "Ethan's as headstrong as you . . . when he wants to be." It would have been just like him to get a second phone after his father threatened to report one of his friends to the police.

Now that he had made some connections to kids on the East End, all Ethan wanted was to keep them. I of all people knew how strident his father could be. I couldn't blame him for going behind Adam's back to have a private way of contacting people that his father might label "bad influences."

Ethan was sixteen years old and knew ten times more than I did about technology. He would find a way to talk to anyone he wanted to talk to, regardless of what I did with his secret phone. I started to return the phone to the backpack, but then I heard Adam's voice in my head, telling me that I was enabling Ethan. Giving him too much slack. Ignoring warning signs. Being one of *those* parents.

Then I heard myself arguing that Ethan was a good kid, but also stubborn. That the more we tried to control him, the more he'd do the exact opposite.

I could hear every word of a fight I'd never have with Adam again. I turned the phone off, carried it to my office, and dropped it in the top drawer. It wasn't what Adam would do, but at least it was more than nothing.

It never dawned on me to wonder why Ethan had been carrying around a backpack with nothing in it but a tiny phone.

PART II

NICKY

15

THANKS TO THE smell of bacon in the apartment, I managed to get Ethan out of his room to eat breakfast. Even though it was nearly three in the afternoon and his first meal of the day, he chewed in silence and left half his eggs on the plate.

"I wish I could make this easier for you," I said.

He shrugged. "I don't think it felt real until today. I'm getting texts from kids who have, like, never once spoken to me, saying how great Dad was and they can't believe they're not going to see him again. It's so fake, but it's also making me realize he's really gone."

"People don't know what to say when someone passes on, that's all." I told him his father would always be around as long as we remembered him, but I knew the words were no less hollow than the texts coming in on his phone.

News of Adam's murder traveled quickly once the *Daily News* published its story in the early morning hours, first online and then in the print edition in time to hit newsstands. The latest White House scandal dominated the front cover, but Adam's murder landed in the local crime headline along the bottom edge: HUSBAND OF #THEMTOO WRITER MURDERED IN EAST HAMPTON.

Of the articles I had skimmed briefly, about half reported that he had left a wife (me by name) and a teenage son. A few mentioned that his son was from a former marriage. And only one specified that the former marriage was to the sister of his current wife.

Until now, the only public interest in our family had been focused on me, not Adam. I had seen no reason to highlight the fact that Ethan was technically my stepson, let alone my biological nephew. How do you tell people that you married your sister's husband without sounding horrible? But now that one news outlet had gone in that direction, it would only be a matter of time before that juicy little tidbit was in the first paragraph of every single story about Adam's murder—or about me, for that matter. At this point, I could no longer imagine caring what strangers had to say about me.

"When's Nicky supposed to be here?" Ethan asked, pushing his uneaten scrambled eggs into a pile of ketchup.

I wondered whether my sister's imminent arrival was at least partially responsible for the shift in his mood between last night and this morning. Nicky had called right as we were turning off the television for the evening, and I made the mistake of answering. She had insisted on coming to New York, and I hadn't been able to talk her out of it.

I glanced at my watch. "Her flight got in half an hour ago. She should be here any second."

He left his plate on the table and retreated to his room without comment.

WHEN THE APARTMENT PHONE RANG, I was expecting it to be the doorman announcing Nicky's arrival, but it was Bill Braddock, calling to check in. I assured him that we were holding up as well as we could under the circumstances.

"I could sense the media hounds circling yesterday when one of them called me trying to get to you, but I took the liberty of trying to give you some time to grieve in private. I'm afraid my efforts were not successful."

I considered Bill a friend, but wasn't particularly surprised he hadn't called before now. He was the kind of person who liked to mingle at the center of the party, not necessarily hold your hand during a dark time. I told him that, if anything, maybe the media attention would bring in information that might help the police solve the case.

"Not to pry, but what do they think happened?" he asked.

The coverage, although widespread and splashy, was short on details. There were descriptions of us and our "celebrity-soaked," "sought-after" East Hampton "enclave," but little information about the crime itself other than mention of a late-night break-in and fatal stabbing.

"They seem to think it was a burglary after Adam had gone to bed. He might have heard a noise and gotten up."

Bill was making sympathetic sighs on the other end of the line. It was on his third offer to help however possible that I finally brought up the subject of Adam's hours out of the firm the previous week. "He told me he was meeting with people from the Gentry Group, but on his time sheets, he marked the hours as client development. Do you have any idea where he might have actually been?"

"Lawyers aren't exactly shift workers, as you know. You can sit in the office all day, but if you don't do something we can charge a client for, you may as well be playing golf as far as the bottom line is concerned. Client development is a bit of a catchall. It could be the real deal of putting on a dog and pony show for a potential client, but half the time I think it's socializing—lunches with a college buddy in town, that kind of thing—because you never know where the next piece of business might come from."

"And did you know of any dog and pony shows that Adam might have had?"

"No, but partners don't tend to share that kind of news until it's official. Show me the money, as we like to say. I'm very sorry not to be able to tell you more, Chloe. And forgive me for prying yet again, but I hope you're not wondering about Adam's fidelity to you. I never once saw him turn an eye toward another woman."

"I know, and I keep telling myself the same thing. But I have to wonder if this has something to do with his murder."

"Knowing Adam, he was probably planning some big surprise for you. I'm sure there's an explanation."

Maybe, but it was an explanation I would probably never have. My husband had lied to me about where he spent the last two days of his life. There was no way around it.

A beep on the phone told me that another call was coming through. It was the doorman calling from the lobby. I told Bill that I needed to go. Nicky was here.

EVERYTHING ABOUT NICKY IS ALWAYS bigger and louder than it needs to be. Normal people fly in airplanes every day and manage to make it to their ultimate destination all by themselves. I had even offered to arrange (and pay) for a car service from LaGuardia, but Nicky assured me she could find her own way. Now, nearly two hours after her flight landed, she was finally at my apartment door with two hip-high suitcases, a purse roughly the size of my wine fridge, and, most surprisingly, a man I didn't recognize.

"Chloe, meet my guardian angel, Jeremy."

Jeremy held up a sheepish hand. "Hey." His hair was thinning, and his denim shirt didn't hide a slight paunch, but he had bright green eyes and a dark beard. I could see him being Nicky's type. He was looking at Nicky expectantly.

"Oh, right, sorry. It's down that hallway. The first door on the right, as I recall."

I watched, dumbfounded, as this stranger walked past me and made his way to our powder room.

"What the hell, Nicky."

"I should have known you'd freak. He was on the shuttle bus with me and saw me struggling to get my bags off at Grand Central. He gave me a hand and we ended up sharing a cab downtown. By the time we got here, he needed to pee. It's no big deal."

I thought of all the hours I had spent around random men Nicky managed to befriend. This one sort of resembled an older version of the guy she'd brought to Asiago, where I had my first waitressing job in high school. After ordering a three-course dinner and an entire bottle of wine—he was older than her, of course—they left without paying. It was the only time I was ever fired.

Nicky insisted her date probably just forgot, but a month later, she came to my room sobbing because the same guy had used her ATM card to clear out nearly a thousand dollars from her savings account to cover a football bet. And then she kept dating the guy for another three months after that.

It was a familiar cycle with my sister. She'd complain to me about her boyfriends, alleging wrongdoings ranging from drug abuse to theft to drunken attacks of rage. You can't tell your sister that a man spit in your face and called you a stupid whore unless you're planning to leave him. But that's how it was with Nicky. She'd say too much and then accuse me of being judgmental when the relationship continued, brushing off her earlier grievances as "venting." As a result, I was skeptical about every man she brought around. They were either as bad as she said they were during the low phases, or were off-kilter enough to be drawn to a woman who seemed to thrive on histrionics. Either way, I had no interest in knowing any more than necessary. Until, of course, she met Adam.

When my unexpected bathroom guest emerged, he extended his hand for a quick shake. I was relieved when I caught a whiff of our lavender hand soap. "Jeremy Lyons. Sorry about barging in like this. And sorry about your loss."

Of course Nicky had told a total stranger why she was in town.

I thanked him for helping my sister and ushered him out the door just as Ethan emerged from his bedroom. Usually he was reluctant around Nicky, especially when a long time passed between visits. He hadn't seen her for well over a year, but rushed to greet her with a hug.

"So that *was* you," he said. "I thought I heard some dude."

"Someone helping with the bags," I said, managing to mask my annoyance.

I could tell Ethan was trying his best to seem happy to see Nicky. Of course he tried. But as we made polite conversation about whether the flight was okay and why she had opted for the shuttle ("I guess I didn't want to be alone in my thoughts in a taxi, plus it's cheaper"), I could see Ethan shrink from a sloppy second hug that lingered too long, and the way she touched his hair like he was a baby.

"I don't even know what to say about Adam," Nicky said. "I'm so sorry. For both of you," she added.

I nodded. "Thank you. I know it's a loss for you, too. Let me give you two some time to catch up together."

I had already spoken to Ethan about this in advance. Nicky would be less likely to do something rash like insist on taking custody of Ethan if she didn't feel like I was trying to control the situation. But Ethan had promised to come get me if she was too much to bear. And under no circumstances was he to trust her with a word about the details of his father's murder. Remember when that beautiful American actress married a handsome prince, and the trashy side of her family sold stories and pictures to the tabloids? I had thought of Nicky.

As I passed Ethan's bedroom, I noticed that he had straightened it since we got home the previous day. By his standards, it was almost clean. I wondered if he did it because Nicky was coming, or for the same reason I had scraped my bathroom tile grout with a bobby pin until four in the morning.

Once I was alone in my office, one look at my screen saver—a photo of Adam, Ethan, and me in front of a Louse Point sunset—had me trembling again. I wondered if I was ever going to regain control of my emotions. I forced myself to try to work, jotting down notes for a piece I would probably never publish. I had rejected Catherine's suggestion of a press release, but she had called again this morning, suggesting that I write something for next month's *Eve* about Adam's murder. "Nothing salacious," she said. "But people will want to hear from you. You're the face of the magazine. And I know you, Chloe. Writing is how you digest. How you feel. How you live. You'll know when you're ready."

After forty minutes, it was clear I wasn't even close. I woke up my computer and googled "Jeremy Lyons." The second hit was the stranger who had used my powder room. He was a research fellow at the University of Kansas. According to a recent faculty news sidebar, he would be speaking at NYU the next day about monetary policy.

So maybe he was a helpful stranger after all. Given Nicky's history, I felt no guilt about checking.

I closed my browser when I heard a tap on the office door. It was Nicky and Ethan. Seeing the two of them together, I realized how much Ethan was beginning to resemble her as his face matured. He had his father's dark hair and eyes, while Nicky was still a dark blond with only minimal help from L'Oréal. But like his mother, Ethan was long and lanky, with a thin nose and angular features.

"Kiddo here says you made a reservation at some swank hotel for me."

"The Marlton, right down Fifth Avenue." It was relatively new and nicer than the Washington Square hotel where we usually put her, but the real reason Ethan liked it was for the pastries they sold at their coffee bar. They had some fancy French name we always forgot, but they were known in our family as crack croissants.

"Thanks for the offer, but if it's okay with you, I'm fine on the couch. If I'm going to be here, I want to spend actual time with you guys." Nicky had never balked about staying in a hotel before, but apparently that was because we were living with Adam. She did a double take at the far wall of my office. "Is that a Murphy bed? I don't think I knew you had that. In fact, I don't even think I've been in here before."

"It's really uncomfortable. And the bathroom's all the way down the hall." I knew I was being obvious, but didn't care. I did not want Nicky underfoot twenty-four hours a day for however long she was planning to stay with those giant suitcases.

Before I could stop her, she had pulled the bed open. "This is perfect," she said, plopping down on the neatly tucked-in white coverlet. I noticed Ethan slip out of the room while he had the chance. "And I promise I'll stay out of your way. This room is huge. Quite a step up from your original middle-school home office."

My father had made Nicky switch bedrooms with me when I was in the eighth grade so I could have the room that was large enough to house a desk. By then, it was clear that I was the one who would actually use it, but Nicky always saw it as punishment for dropping out of college after the first semester.

I tried one more time as Nicky was rolling the first of her suitcases into the office. "Seriously, don't you want a whole room to yourself where you can unpack and spread out? Have a little privacy? And really, I don't mind paying for it at all."

"I know. You're always so generous, but really, I don't want to go to the hotel. You won't even know I'm here, I promise." She swallowed hard and then added, "Please, Chloe."

I nodded, averting my gaze. "Of course. Whatever's best for you."

"And I'm sorry again about offering your bathroom to Jeremy. I should've texted you first, but my battery was dying. And for what it's worth, I've been seeing someone anyway, so I wasn't cruising him, if that's what you thought."

"Really, Nicky, it's okay. And I'm happy for you about seeing someone." Nicky's habit of unloading the personal details of her relationships had ended once Adam left her. I had no idea whether it meant that there were no details to be had, or that she had simply figured out that I could no longer be the person with whom she shared them.

"We'll see. He's fifty-two. Divorced with two kids. I haven't even told him about Ethan yet, so—" She stopped abruptly at the sound of footsteps approaching in the hallway.

Ethan was lugging Nicky's second suitcase into my office when my cell phone rang. It was a 631 area code. Long Island. I decided to answer.

"Ms. Taylor, this is Detective Guidry. I'm sorry to bother you, but I have a few more things I'd like to go over. I have to come into the city for a district attorney thing anyway. Is it okay if we talk in person? I could come to your place, if that's okay."

I was suspicious about whether Guidry was actually planning to be in the area, but if I couldn't find a way to stop Nicky from occupying my office, I didn't know how to refuse a police officer's request to see me in person. I wondered if I had made a mistake asking Guidry to be the one to call Nicky with the news about Adam. I had no way of knowing what she might have said about me.

Because as much as Nicky said she loved me and was grateful for the life I had given her son, I knew she had never forgiven me for marrying her husband.

16

I NEVER MEANT to fall in love with him.

The first time Adam actually met me was when he came by the house to pick up Nicky for a date and ended up giving her kid sister a lift to her friend's house in Shaker Heights. But I remembered knowing about Adam when he was still in high school. I must have been in the sixth grade, and my parents would let me hang out at the mall with my friends all day on Saturdays.

Maralyn Fisher, Kristin Hoesl, and I were sitting on the bench outside Limited Express, right by the food court and movie theater. We spent the afternoon protecting our prime mall-watching territory no less seriously than gangsters fighting for turf, until Kristin's older sister and her friends decided that they were going to take our space if we all wanted a ride home at the end of the day. We stood nearby and eavesdropped as they rated the various classmates who walked by: hot or not. Their attention eventually landed on the kid with the dark wavy hair and green eyes taking movie tickets at the Regal.

"Great jawline, but he's a total dork."

"You know how grown-ups say 'she's got a good personality' about ugly girls? He's like, the *opposite* of that. Everything's blah but his face.

I tried glancing at his algebra test last year, and he nearly knocked over his desk trying to block my view."

It was Kristin's sister who reserved judgment, watching him like a collector summing up a piece of artwork. "I don't know, you guys. I think he's gonna be that stud we all regret blowing off one day when he shows up at the high school reunion with his Harvard degree and a private jet."

When he disappeared at the end of August, I wondered if he really had gone away to Harvard. I noticed him a few times around Christmas and the next few summers, but never actually talked to him. To me, he was just that smart movie theater guy that Kristin's sister had lodged in my imagination.

But then, more than ten years later, when I was the recent college graduate coming home for a visit, he showed up at my parents' to pick up Nicky. As it turned out, no one who went to Jefferson High School got into Harvard, but Adam did get a full ride to the University of Michigan. And he was the guy my sister had been talking about ever since she'd gone to her ten-year high school reunion that summer. I remember how different she looked that weekend, opting for natural makeup, a loose blowout, and simple, tasteful clothes instead of her usual hippie-dippie woo-woo outfits. Nicky never looked that good— ever. I remember feeling sorry for her, like she was pretending to be someone else to impress her former classmates.

But it must have worked—at least on Adam, who had finished his first year of law school at Case Western and was nothing like the usual guys who were sniffing around in Nicky's direction. Even in the few weeks I spent in Cleveland before starting my assistant job at *City Woman*, I could see the roles they were playing. He was the local boy done good, crushing the grading curve and landing the plum positions on the law review board. And Nicky duped him into thinking she was exactly what he needed—a fun, loyal girlfriend whose number one priority would be helping him achieve his every goal.

And then, much to everyone's surprise, especially mine, Nicky actually got her act together. Being Adam's girlfriend gave her an identity that helped guide her conduct and decisions. I wouldn't usually want to see a woman make a man her sole purpose in life, but for her, it worked. Instead of sleeping all day until her shift at the restaurant, she'd drive Adam to and from campus so he didn't need to hassle with parking. In between, she'd run not only her errands but his, so he'd have more time to study at night—often in the back booth at the restaurant where she waitressed, so he could spend time with her when it was slow. Most restaurant owners might have resented a regular lingerer, but with Adam in the picture, Nicky didn't miss work and even showed up on time. And I assumed my parents and I weren't the only ones who didn't miss the parade of horribles that would often drop in to see my sister.

Nicky held it together for more than three years—mostly. I'd learn later that there had been a couple of episodes where she got wasted at his law school parties, but it didn't stand out that much compared to other students. In her most serious early transgression, Adam threatened to break up with her when she got stopped for a DUI and then insisted the police officer call her boyfriend because he was "your boss." At the time, Adam had just finished an internship at the DA's office and had accepted an offer to work there after graduation. The episode could have derailed his career before it had even started, but the officer offered to release Nicky to a family member if she promised she'd never drive after drinking again. Then, instead of breaking up, they moved in together. Adam would tell me years later that Nicky convinced him that the only reason she'd been drinking so much was that she was worried he was going to leave her once he was a lawyer because she wasn't as educated as he was.

No one in the auditorium cheered louder at the graduation ceremony than Nicky did when Adam walked across the stage, magna cum laude. "We did it, babe!" she screamed, earning applause from the rest of the audience. For Nicky, the accomplishment was as much hers as his.

Adam started working at the DA's office, and Nicky stopped wait-ressing. Amid talk about her going back to college, he bought her a big stack of SAT prep books and even made flash cards so he could help her study at night. By my count with the calendar, it was probably right around then that Nicky got pregnant. She said she forgot to take her birth control pills a couple of times, but I had my suspicions.

Of course he married her. They told everyone they had been plan-ning to get hitched and start a family anyway, but now had a reason to skip the headache of a big ceremony.

Even then, Nicky seemed to rise to the occasion. She managed (by all appearances at least) not to drink or smoke while she was pregnant. But once she had that baby to take care of, she just couldn't keep up the charade. Nicky had never been able to look after herself, let alone another person. She was done faking it.

I could tell something was off, even when I flew back to Cleveland to meet my newborn nephew. By the time I was packing to return to New York a week later, she was pounding Bloody Marys, swearing she had enough breast milk in the freezer to get the baby through while "Mommy could finally celebrate."

Over the next two years, old Nicky gradually but assuredly con-sumed the new, improved Nicky. And then the night of the Met Gala, Nicky did something so awful that Adam had no choice. He took Ethan and left her for good.

So I know what it sounds like when people hear that I married my sister's husband, but it wasn't like that. I tried to warn her. She's the one who decided to lose it all.

17

Poppit

Thread: Who Stabbed Attorney and Father Adam Macintosh?

Latest Comments:

Posted by JamBoy

We all know it's the wife, right?

Posted by BilboB

So which one of them was cheating: him or her?

Posted by FireStarter

Two words: Chloe Taylor.

Posted by SoxSuck92

Of course, she was too good to change her last name, but we should use her full, legal name: Chloe Cunt Taylor.

Posted by KurtLoMein

We shouldn't jump to conclusions. For all we know, she's a victim, too.

Posted by FireStarter

Quoted: We shouldn't jump to conclusions.

When did you become such a pussy, KurtLoMein? You've been talking smack against that bitch for months.

Posted by BilboB

Are they sure it wasn't a suicide? Because . . . what kind of man could stay married to that?

Posted by Anonym2002

Let's see how much she hates men when she's getting passed around by the prison bulldykes.

Posted by DonkeySchlong

LOL! Can't wait to see that elitist bitch behind bars.

Posted by Bighead

Lock! Her! Up!

18

I TOLD NICKY that I needed to approve proofs for the magazine, but I really just wanted to be alone in my office. I was bouncing among Twitter, Poppit, and a Facebook group someone had started called Justice for Adam. Catherine had told me recently that my compulsive need to read the horrid things that anonymous strangers wrote about me online evidenced a subconscious desire to punish myself. She asked if I felt guilty for being a successful woman. I thought the theory was silly then, but now it was hitting closer to home.

I closed the social media windows and played yet another round of "guess Adam's email password," giving it four tries before calling it quits. I was worried the law firm's system might have a security setting that would lock me out after too many failed attempts.

Where were you last week, Adam? The police had taken his phone and laptop, and his credit card statements went to his office, so I didn't have any of those options to explore.

I pulled up our one joint credit card—the one we used for restaurants, shopping, and travel to get more points—though I assumed Adam wouldn't be careless enough to use it for anything he wanted to hide from me. Looking at our recent transactions, I realized how lazy

I had gotten about our finances since I began having more money than time.

There were no smoking guns like hotels, online dating accounts, or pickup bars, if pickup bars even existed anymore. I did, however, see a few charges from Adam: $396 for a *New York Law Journal* subscription, $25 for some court clerk's office thing, and, most recently, four Uber rides: three for $80-odd each on Thursday morning and evening and again on Friday morning, and then $320 on Friday night. The times and amounts corresponded to what he had told me about going to a hotel near JFK to meet with the people from the Gentry Group.

He had used Uber instead of the law firm's car service, and had billed the rides to our personal card instead of his business account. All of it suggested that Jake had been right. Adam hadn't been meeting with a client.

I pulled up Uber's website and logged in. We had opened a family account because Adam wanted to be able to check on Ethan's location, as if our teenage son couldn't find alternative means of traveling in New York City.

I pulled up the receipts for the four rides. The corresponding maps showed a common pickup and drop-off location: the Union Turnpike– Kew Gardens subway station. It was in Queens, right at the connection between the Jackie Robinson Parkway and Queens Boulevard, nowhere near the strip of airport hotels I'd been picturing.

I zoomed out and looked up directions from the station to JFK. The airport was more than five miles away.

I clicked on the "nearby" icon, and then clicked on "hotels." The closest option was a Comfort Lodge five blocks away, but it was hard to imagine a client like the Gentry Group using such a budget-friendly hotel. Not to mention, there were several more luxurious options located closer to the airport.

I clicked around the surrounding area in Google Maps and found a FedEx drop-off, a Starbucks, and a cemetery. Queens County Criminal Court was just a few minutes' walk from the drop-off location, but Adam had told me he was meeting the clients at a hotel. And if he'd been going to the courthouse, why wouldn't he have asked the driver to take him directly there?

I was trying to imagine Adam in a neighborhood I'd never been to, meeting someone I had never met, and I simply couldn't picture it.

I opened my contacts and pulled up the entry for Carol Mercer, the wife of the in-house counsel for the Gentry Group. I started a new email message:

> Dear Carol, I can't believe it has been three years since that epic meal at the Ledbury. At least Roger and Adam have been able to stay in touch with one another more frequently thanks to work. On that note, I have an odd favor: Can you please ask Roger if Adam was meeting with anyone from the Gentry Group last week?

"Odd" was an understatement. I tried again.

> Dear Carol, I'm sorry to write with awful news and a strange question for Roger.

My third attempt was interrupted by the phone on my desk. It was the doorman. When I hung up the phone, I closed the email message I had started and hit the print key on the Uber receipts. Detective Guidry was here.

19

I FOUND NICKY sitting cross-legged on the living room floor. Panda had twisted himself into a perfect oval to fill the space in her lap, and half of the coffee table was covered with pieces of colored ceramic and various hoops and wires.

After Mom had passed away, I had given Nicky the half that I was entitled to, and then continued to pay the property taxes and insurance so she could afford to keep our parents' house. But her day-to-day income came from the extra money she made selling jewelry on Etsy.

"Be careful with that stuff, okay?" I asked. "Panda has a way of hoovering anything he can get his paws on."

Nicky gave Panda a little rub beneath the chin. "A little reckless, are we? You like flirting with danger? You should have seen me in the nineties."

I was unlocking the front door in preparation for Guidry's imminent arrival. "Maybe cool it with the colorful humor for a second. The homicide detective's coming up."

Guidry didn't arrive alone. Detective Bowen was with her, and I wondered if he was also obligated to appear for whatever "DA thing" had brought Guidry into town on a Sunday evening.

They both declined my offer of water, tea, coffee, anything. While Guidry was asking me how Ethan and I were holding up, Bowen's eyes scoured my apartment, as if he were a contestant on the Manhattan real estate version of *The Price is Right*. If I told him we paid $4 million and had a terrace with a view of Washington Square, would that make me a murderer?

I had already asked Ethan to wait in his room. Nicky scrambled to her bare feet to introduce herself.

"I'm Nicky Macintosh," she said, shaking Guidry's hand. Nicky never changed her last name back to Taylor, and it had seemed petty to fight with her about it. "We spoke on the phone."

I offered them spots on the sofa and took a seat in Adam's favorite chair, a white leather recliner from Design Within Reach. I said nothing when Nicky decided to join us in the matching chair next to me rather than give us the room. Once we were in place, I asked the detectives if they had any leads in the investigation.

"We're looking into every possibility," Bowen said, fiddling with the piping on the sofa cushion beneath him. "But we have a few questions that might help us target our efforts."

I told them both I'd help however I could, still wishing that Nicky were somewhere else. She always had a way of saying something to make a situation even more awkward.

Guidry launched the first question with no introduction. "Why wouldn't Adam go for the gun?"

I felt my eyes blink, but couldn't get any words to come out of my mouth.

"Your gun. Or Adam's gun, at least. He has a Smith & Wesson nine-millimeter registered to the sheriff's office in Riverhead."

I remembered the weapon, that was for sure. "We don't have it anymore."

"Well, where did it go?" Guidry asked. "It wasn't on your list of items missing from the house. And yet if it had been in the house, I would have thought that Adam might have retrieved it when he heard an intruder. It's a very popular gun, precisely because it's useful for self-defense purposes."

"Adam bought it"—I paused, pretending to search my memory— "maybe a year ago. I told him I wasn't comfortable having a gun in the house and insisted that he get rid of it. My house rules are more Use Your Words than Stand Your Ground. I even went to the march after the last school shooting—well, the last one big enough for people to even notice anymore. Sorry, you can tell I feel strongly about it."

"So where is the gun now?"

I shrugged. "I have no idea. I didn't want it under our roof. I made that quite clear, and he said he understood. I assumed he took it to work or sold it or something."

The silence that followed told me nothing, but I hoped that I had checked one item off her internal list.

"That's helpful. We also want to make sure we know for certain what your habits were with respect to the security alarm at your house."

"I told you, we never set it except when we were gone or if I were out there alone."

"And when it was set, who knew the code?" Bowen asked.

I gave him what was a short list: us, the housekeeper, and her husband, who did handyman work when we needed it. "But the password is our son's birthday. In theory, it was guessable, I suppose. Speaking of which, are you able to get into Adam's emails? I'm still trying to figure out where he was on Thursday and Friday."

"His client meeting near the airport," Guidry said. "You mentioned it yesterday. We're looking into it."

I could tell from Bowen's blank expression that this was the first he had heard of the subject.

"I looked at our Uber account, and he didn't go to the airport. Or even to a hotel, from what I can tell." I handed her the ride trip receipts that I had printed out. "I asked Adam why his well-heeled client wouldn't stay at a Manhattan hotel instead of an airport crash pad. I even offered to get them dinner reservations and theater tickets, because I knew how important client development was to him as a relatively new partner. He said something about how they might need to take an emergency flight to a country that wouldn't extradite them back to the United States if things went bad. In retrospect, I think something was wrong, but I don't know why he'd get dropped off at a train station."

I could tell Guidry was unconvinced. "I appreciate that you're trying to recall anything unusual, Chloe, but that sounds like your husband was making a joke?"

I realized how random my comments sounded, and tried to offer more specific grounds for my concerns. "He was never comfortable with this client," I said. "Adam used to be a federal prosecutor—a really good one, in fact, in the Southern District. And of course he knew that when he crossed over from one side of the aisle to the other by joining Rives & Braddock, he wouldn't always be wearing a superhero's cape or the white hat, so to speak. But I could tell that the Gentry Group made him feel . . . dirty. I don't know the details, but something weird was going on. I think he was meeting with them but didn't want the law firm to know about it for some reason. Apparently he didn't even bill his time to the client, according to his time sheets. And he used Uber, which gets billed to our personal card, instead of the law firm's car service."

Guidry was nodding along as I spoke, but she chose her words carefully in response. "If he were meeting a client, wouldn't he have simply entered the name of the hotel as the destination instead of a train station? And I don't know much about lawyers, but I've never heard of one who spent two days with a client without charging them for it. Isn't it more likely that he went somewhere else and didn't want either you or the law firm to know about it?"

"I don't know. That's why I'm asking you to follow up on it."

Bowen caught Guidry's eye and then asked the next question. "Do you think your husband was cheating on you, Ms. Taylor?"

"No!" I was surprised by the certainty in my own voice. "I'm telling you: there's a reason he didn't want anyone to know where he was for two full days, and it has to be connected to his murder."

"Okay, okay," he said, scribbling notes in a spiral pad, even though there was nothing to write down. "We're going to look into this, but please understand that certain questions are routine in every homicide case. We don't enjoy asking them."

"My husband wasn't cheating."

"Got it, and to be clear, there's no third party in your life, either? We have to ask, if only to exclude that person or persons as a suspect."

"*Persons? Plural?* No, no third party. Or parties. Just a boring married monogamous couple. It does happen, detectives."

Bowen smirked as he glanced at Nicky. I wanted to take one of her earring hooks and jab it through his hand.

"And had your son and his father been getting along okay lately?" Bowen asked.

"Of course," I said. "They're very close."

I had a sudden image of Adam's face turning red, the veins bulging in his neck, as he screamed at Ethan in the car outside the school. A woman walking by heard him even through the closed windows. I had mouthed "It's okay" and implored her with a hand wave to keep going on her way. It was that stupid gun.

"Unusually so," I added, "given that Adam was his primary parent."

I looked at Nicky. She nodded and reached over to give me a supportive pat on the arm. "She's right. I wouldn't have allowed Adam to raise my son here without me if there had been any problems. I know it's not a traditional family arrangement, but Adam and Chloe have given Ethan an amazing life."

"So, then . . . no problems at all between them?" Guidry asked.

"I mean, he's sixteen years old," I said. "His room's a pigsty, and he's constantly in front of one screen or another. But no, nothing you'd call a *problem*. You can't seriously be suggesting . . ."

Guidry softened her expression. "Of course not. We just have to ask. Maybe we can speak in private with Ethan, and then we'll be all set here."

I looked up at the ceiling and blew out a long sigh. "Fine, let me get him."

I was barely out of my chair when Nicky rose to her feet. "Huh-uh. We're done here, at least as far as Ethan is concerned."

"We'll be just a few minutes," Guidry said. "Chloe—"

"No!" Nicky held up a hand, blocking my view of the detectives. "Chloe isn't his mother. I am. I have the legal documents if you need them. With Adam gone, I'm his legal guardian. And you're not talking to my kid after asking two different times if he was having problems with his murdered father, while you're obviously ignoring the evidence that my sister is trying to give you. This whole thing is disgusting."

I could hear a clock I forgot we owned ticking from a bookshelf in the hallway.

Guidry finally said, "Maybe you two could ask Ethan what he wants—"

I shook my head. "No, my sister is right. The next time you want to speak to Ethan or me, you can call my lawyer, Bill Braddock."

20

W E WAITED UNTIL we heard the ding of the elevator before saying another word.

"What the hell was that, Nicky? You're his mother, and I'm not? They're going to think we're hiding something now."

She resumed her spot in the same white chair and lowered her face into her hands. When she looked up, I could tell that she was struggling to remain calm. "With all due respect, Chloe, why do you care so fucking much about what other people think?"

I had no idea what she was talking about.

"I couldn't figure out why you were answering *any* of those questions, let alone letting them speak to Ethan. But then I realized: you were trying to please those cops, like you can keep them on your side if they just see how perfect and sweet you are."

"It's not about me being 'perfect and sweet.' But I don't want them to think we're hiding something."

"I'd say that ship has sailed, baby sister. It's obvious they're looking to solve Adam's murder inside your house. Don't you see what they were doing? They were asking about Ethan's relationship with Adam to trick you. Once they got him alone, they would have asked him about the dynamic between *you* and Adam. Who would have thought between the two of us, *you'd* be the murder suspect?" Her brows lifted in amusement.

"I'm not a suspect," I said.

"Well, tell the internet that. The reason my phone was dying on the way here is because I was refreshing Twitter so much."

"You're not taking this very seriously, Nicky. Adam's dead. It's not funny."

"'It's neither fun nor funny.' Got it, Saint Chloe. Jesus, you don't think I'm taking this seriously? I'm here, aren't I? And who's the one who told that cop to stay the fuck away from Ethan? But just because something sucks doesn't mean you can't find a glimmer of humor in it. Laughing at screwed up shit is how I've managed to stay alive after everything I've been through."

I steeled myself for a familiar round of all the ways fate had victimized Nicole Taylor, but the room fell silent instead. Nicky looked down the hall to make sure Ethan's bedroom door was still closed. When she spoke again, her voice was low.

"So how long were you cheating on Adam?"

I grimaced and shook my head. "You're unbelievable."

"I could tell you were lying when that asshole asked you about . . . 'third parties.'" She used air quotes to mark the euphemism. "Don't worry—you were always a good liar to everyone but me."

"I'm not a good liar, Nicky. Or a bad one, either. Because I wasn't lying. Some people don't lie."

"See?" she said, pointing an accusatory finger. "That's your tell right there. You get all formal and clippish: 'Persons? Plural? No third party. Or parties. It does happen.'"

I didn't appreciate the harpy, robotic tone she used for the impersonation, but it was hard to refute the point.

"I could always tell when you weren't shooting straight, Chloe. Remember when you discovered *The Muppet Show* in repeats? You'd bogart the remote control by telling Mom it was educational because it looked like *Sesame Street*. I'd tell Mom it was just puppets and that you knew all that shit anyway, and then I'd get in trouble for not being a good sister. I missed the entire last season of *Remington Steele* because of you. You couldn't even resist smiling when Mom wasn't looking, you were so proud of getting away with it. Or what about that time you got a UTI your senior year and let all your friends think it was because you finally lost your virginity? I knew it was because you worked so hard on your history paper you forgot to pee all day again, you OCD weirdo."

I felt an involuntary smile struggling to break out on my face.

"See? Things can be funny even when the world sucks."

"And it really, really sucks. I can't believe Adam . . ." My lower lip began to quiver as the enormity of it snuck up on me again. I did not want to cry, especially in front of Nicky. As much as she had deserved to lose him—and Ethan, too—she was the last person who should be expected to comfort me.

Lucky for me, Nicky never was one to give comfort. "So who's the guy?"

I shook my head. I wasn't going to confirm her suspicions, but I didn't have the energy to fight with her over it, either. Eventually, we'd need to fight about what really mattered—what was going to happen to Ethan. I wondered if she had meant it when she told the police she had brought the legal documents with her.

"Now I'm the one being serious, Chloe. Maybe you should tell the cops about whoever this guy is. I mean, you never know."

I resisted the urge to tell her that I was never the one who dated guys who might be capable of murder. "I already told them I had nothing else to say without a lawyer."

She took the statement as verification. "No wonder you've been walking around with a limp. A word of advice: if the sex is a pain in the ass, you're doing it wrong."

I couldn't help myself. It was so inappropriate, I started to laugh.

"Remember: children in the back seat cause accidents, but accidents in the back seat cause children. Hey, what's the difference between a G spot and a golf ball? A guy will actually look for a golf ball. Why did the chicken cross the basketball court? He heard the ref was blowing fowls."

How many times had I looked at Ethan, wanting to convince myself that he hadn't inherited my sister's worst traits? Yet I had to admit that one of the many things I loved about him was his take-no-prisoners sense of humor, which he certainly didn't get from Adam or me. Nicky's increasingly ridiculous jokes finally stopped when we heard Ethan's bedroom door open. "Mom. You need to see this."

We both reached for the phone in his outstretched hand, and then Nicky deferred, sinking back in her chair. I took it from him and extended the screen so she and I could read it together.

The article was only six minutes old, uploaded to the *New York Post* website: "Stab Victim's Son Brought Gun to School." According to the first sentence, "The sixteen-year-old son of slain attorney Adam Macintosh, husband of #ThemToo author Chloe Taylor, had previously brought a gun to school, sources tell the *Post*. Despite concerns from alarmed classmates and teachers, Taylor reportedly used her influence to prevent the son's expulsion, chalking the incident up to a 'misunderstanding.'"

"A gun?" Nicky was saying. "You never told me about this."

I pressed my free hand against my forehead, willing it to stop pounding. "They're blowing it out of proportion."

It had been yet another episode when Adam and I disagreed about whether and how to discipline Ethan. Most of what I'd told the police about the gun was true. Without even consulting me, Adam had bought the gun for the house in East Hampton shortly after the online threats against me became a regular part of our daily existence. Four months later, we got a phone call from Ethan's school, saying that a kid had seen it in Ethan's backpack after classes broke out. Adam acted as if Ethan was one step away from going postal on the student body. It had taken nearly an hour to get an answer from Ethan, but he finally confessed that he was trying to "seem like the cool, edgy kid" by letting another student catch a glimpse of it in his bag. It wasn't even loaded.

Had it been a public school, the hardline zero-tolerance policies would have meant certain expulsion. But I told the private school that in the shuffle of the city/East Hampton commute, the gun had ended up in Ethan's bag, and he in turn had carried the bag to school without knowledge of its contents. I hinted at a lawsuit if they didn't have grounds for rejecting our explanation. The way I saw it, if Adam hadn't gotten all macho and bought a gun, none of it would have happened in the first place. Once classes ended, I used a bandanna to tie the stupid thing to a rock and sent it out to sea on my inaugural summer kayaking trip. Adam was furious when he found out, but I did what I needed to protect Ethan. Once a kid is labeled as trouble, it becomes a self-fulfilling prophecy.

Ethan's phone buzzed in my hand. It was a text from "K."

Dude, why aren't you calling me back? Cops were here again. I had to tell them that you

I felt the phone being pulled away, and then Ethan quickly stashed it in the back pocket of his jeans.

"This isn't the time to start keeping secrets from me," I said, thinking about the flip phone I had locked in my office desk the previous day. I wondered if whoever had texted him had tried to call the burner phone first. *Cops were here again.* The contact was simply "K." Kevin Dunham, the friend he was with Friday night. "Was that from Kevin? What's he saying?"

Ethan crossed his arms and set his lips in a straight line. It was the same expression I'd seen when he would butt heads with Adam. For a

second, I understood the absolute fury Adam displayed in those moments, the recognition that the little boy who was your everything now
believed that he knew the world better than you.

I was struggling for the words that might convince him to trust
me when I registered movement in my right periphery. Nicky was out
of her seat. Ethan tried retreating toward his bedroom, but she herded
him like a border collie toward the living room wall and snatched the
device from his back pocket. He reached for it, but her stiff arm and
stern glance subdued him in a way I had never seen before.

She read the text aloud. "'Dude, why aren't you calling me back?
Cops were here again. I had to tell them that you broke off on Friday.'"

Nicky paused her reading to make eye contact with me, and I knew
that something worse was coming. "'I know you didn't hurt your dad,
but you might want to dump your bob. Sorry.'"

At that point, I didn't need to ask Ethan for an explanation. Context
was everything. I remembered the half-pound bag of pot Adam had
found in Ethan's room and how certain he was that Ethan was selling
it. I was the one who wanted to believe him when he said it belonged
to a friend.

"He's covering his own ass, Mom." I noticed Nicky look away
when he called me Mom. "I'm not a dealer, okay? The whole idea of it's
totally ludicrous."

I had to remind myself that Ethan was only sixteen. Teenagers today are so cynical and exposed to so much. But, in the end, they simply
haven't lived long enough to recognize the degree to which things are
right and wrong. A good kid knows the difference between the two—
good and bad—but still can't be expected to judge the scale of things
on either side of the line.

I played hooky once—and only once. It was in the ninth grade,
and it was an absolutely perfect day outside and my friend Maddie Lyn-
don wanted to smoke cigarettes on the giant tire swings at Coventry
PEACE Park. She smoked her unfiltered Camels while we passed be-

tween us a single bottle of Smirnoff Ice that she had pilfered from the overflow refrigerator in her garage. When I saw Coach Simon behind the wheel of a Ford pickup heading our direction, I nearly waved on instinct. But Maddie, the more experienced ditcher, grabbed me and we both dove to the ground to avoid detection. Peeking up at the last minute, we saw him lean over to plant a long, nasty kiss on our classmate, Leah Weller. I never told anyone, because, in my mind, I knew a teacher kissing a fifteen-year-old was wrong, and I knew cutting class to drink and smoke was bad. But as crazy as it would seem years later, I didn't really understand that one was bad enough to warrant exposing the other. Instead, it felt like a draw, like we had all done something forbidden that day.

I would have told Ethan that entire story so he might understand, but we didn't have the luxury of time. "I don't care about the pot," I said.

"So wait, the 'bob' we're talking about is pot and not something worse?" Nicky asked.

He shrugged. "It's just what Kevin calls it. He plays Bob Marley when he gets stoned, so he's all like, bob or whatever."

"What does Kevin mean by 'you broke off on Friday'?" I asked.

"He's trying to make it sound like I'm the one selling—"

"Ethan, stop it. I'm not your father. I'm not going to be mad at you, or disappointed. You need to tell me where you were Friday night. I told the police you were with Kevin, because that's where I believed you were. Is he saying something different now?"

Ethan scrubbed his scalp so frantically with his fingers, I was afraid he'd draw blood. "We didn't go to the movie. It was sold out."

"Okay," I said, trying to remain calm. "They asked me where you were, and I said you saw that movie based on what you told me, but that's only from my perspective. Did you tell the detective you saw the movie?" I was already spearheading a strategy to explain the discrepancy. Change of plans. Confusion of tense. A misunderstanding.

"No, of course not, because we didn't go. But I guess Kevin said we did. He told me yesterday when we went by his house to pick up my backpack. He made it sound like the cop steered him to it. Like, 'we just need to confirm you both went to the movie.' He assumed that's what I told them, so he repeated it, because what really mattered is we were together."

I wanted to build a time machine and crawl back into it. Nicky was right. I never should have let Guidry speak to Ethan without me. "But you weren't together? You broke off?"

For the first time, I felt as if Ethan were looking to Nicky for help. "Eyes on me, Ethan. I asked you a question." If he thought *I* was grilling him, there was no way he could handle Guidry and Bowen.

"We were apart for like, an hour. At most."

"Jesus, Ethan. Why didn't you tell the police that? I don't even know what to do with you right now."

"When Dad found that pot last summer? It *really* wasn't mine. I was telling the truth about holding it. It was for Kevin while he worked his shift at K-Mart. He totally freaked when you dumped it down the sink. I mean, I paid him back for the cost, but he had plans to sell that to all the city kids through the summer. And Kevin's like my magnet to everyone I know on Long Island. He was dropping by a couple of houses Friday to do some deals. And I was like, no way can I go, because I knew Dad would kill—" His eyes began to water, but then he shook his head and regained his composure. "You saw how pissed he's been lately, especially at me. I wasn't about to get caught in the middle of some drug deal. So Kevin dropped me off at Main Beach and I just hung out until he was done. That's all."

I pressed my eyes shut and rubbed them. I wanted to scream at Ethan to wake up, but I knew from experience he would only shut down. Ethan was at his best when you allowed him to make his own choices.

When I'd first noticed his stoic response to his father's death, I told myself it was because the news had been delivered by a total stranger. Since then, I had attributed his detachment to his tendency—shared with his mother—to find humor in every situation. But for the life of me, I could not understand why he would have withheld information from a police officer during his father's homicide investigation.

I had been so focused on dragging information from Ethan that I hadn't noticed that Nicky had her hands on her head and was physically trembling. It was as if her whole body was being jolted with electrical current. "Oh my god. We have to do something." Whatever humor she had been able to find when she thought the police suspected me was gone now that we were talking about Ethan. But Ethan still didn't understand the implications of his friend's text.

He slipped his hands into his pockets. "What was I supposed to do? Narc Kevin out? It's not like he hurt Dad or anything. It was totally unconnected. And if I had told her I hung out alone for an hour, she would've wanted to know why. And then Kevin would have gotten busted, and I'd look like a bad kid by association. And now that's exactly what the cops are going to think."

"Ethan, were you high on Friday?" I asked. "Is that what you didn't want to tell the police?"

His shoulders began to shake as the severity of the situation descended upon him. I stepped toward him and pulled him into my arms. To my surprise, Nicky did the same. Our kid was in trouble, and we both knew it.

NICKY WAS THE ONE TO convince Ethan to leave his phone in the living room with the two of us while we spoke in private. The last thing we needed was to have Ethan text something that one of his friends would post on Snapchat or sell to a gossip website.

Nicky was running her half-painted fingernails through a tumble of dark blond waves she had draped over one shoulder. "We have to do something. I can't believe this. My kid's going to be treated as a murder suspect because he's covering for some 90210 pot peddler?"

"He doesn't have a lot of friends," I said.

I heard Nicky mutter something about wondering where he got that from.

I didn't need her to guilt-trip me about this. That's why I had never mentioned the incident last year with the gun in his backpack. For so many years, I had been able to assure her that Ethan was happy, smart, thriving, funny—all the other adjectives that kept her content with the idea that she had basically lost her son, but that he was having a better life because of it. The few times he'd gotten in trouble, I thought I was handling the situation, protecting him from an overreaction. But now, here we were.

"I'm pretty sure the police think Ethan killed his father." It was the first time I'd been able to speak the words aloud.

"I agree," Nicky said. "It was better when I thought they were accusing you."

Totally deadpan, once again. I was starting to remember what it was like to live around my sister. "I think I need to get him a lawyer."

"Why don't you call your boyfriend? What? I mean, if I had to guess . . . that's apparently your type. Is that the Bill name you gave the cops?"

"Will you stop? He's the magazine's lawyer, and he's eighty years old."

Of course, I didn't tell her that "the boyfriend" she was asking about worked at the same firm, two offices down from Adam. The reality is that I couldn't think of a better person to give me a referral for a criminal defense attorney than Jake. And a phone call to one of my husband's law partners wouldn't look suspicious, even to Nicky, who apparently knew my tell.

"I'll call someone at Adam's firm." I made a point of looking up Jake Summer's contact information in the master contact list on my computer, then using our landline to call his phone number. The least intimate method of communication possible.

"Hey," he said. So much feeling with that one little word. His voice was tender and caring. I wanted to fall into it.

"Hi, Jake," I said, trying to sound businesslike. "I'm so sorry to call you."

"Of course you can—"

"Thanks so much for asking. Yes, we're holding up as best we can. But I have a favor that I wish I didn't need to ask."

"Chloe, stop it. Of course I'd do anything—"

In an instant, I saw a life I might be living if I had left Adam the way Jake wanted me to. Somewhere in my gut, I knew none of this would be happening now if I had simply walked away.

"We have attorney-client privilege, right?"

"Yeah, of course. As long as you're contacting me in my capacity as a legal advisor. Is that what's happening here?"

"I need to call a criminal defense attorney. Not someone like you or Bill. Someone who could potentially handle a homicide case."

"Oh, Chloe. The police can't possibly think—"

"Someone who could represent a teenager, for example."

"Oh my god. I'm coming over right now. Please. Let me help you."

I felt my eyes begin to water. I wanted to travel back in time and undo so many choices. "A phone number. And a name. Really, that's what I need right now."

The name he gave me was Olivia Randall. After a quick Google search to make sure she was legit, I made the call.

Forty minutes later, Guidry and Bowen were back. And this time, there was no call from the doorman to announce their arrival. They had six officers in uniforms with them, and a search warrant.

21

GUIDRY WATCHED OVER us in the living room while the other officers—all men—swept through the apartment as if they were expecting henchmen with machine guns to ambush them from the closets.

"You were just here. Is this all necessary?"

Guidry was silent until someone—Bowen, I thought—yelled "Clear!" from Ethan's room. "We have the right to keep you here while we execute the warrant, but to be clear, you're not under arrest."

"We have a lawyer on the way," Nicky said.

"That's all fine and well," Guidry said, "but that's not going to change anything about the search warrant. Now we're going to do a brief pat-down on all three of you just to make sure you're not holding anything that might be used to hurt us, okay?"

A uniformed officer thoroughly patted down my terrified son, checking his pockets and inside his waistband, while Guidry used a cursory back of the hand for Nicky and me.

"We've got some sharp objects over here," one of the officers noted, gesturing to the coffee table.

"It's stuff I use for jewelry," Nicky explained. "Trust me, a paper cut would be worse."

The officer inspected a pair of wire cutters and tucked them into his already-loaded belt. I couldn't believe this was happening. They were frisking us and seizing Etsy tools. Nicky rolled her eyes, and for the first time ever, I wished I had her fuck-it, this-is-bullshit attitude. I was the one who was always worried about low-probability but high-consequence outcomes. I was also the one who tended to trust authority. Even now, when I saw clickbait about police supposedly getting something wrong, something in me said "There must be more to the story." Deep down, in my fearful, rule-abiding core, I believed that if the police were in my apartment with a warrant, they knew they were going to find something.

I was picturing the burner phone in my desk when the apartment door opened. Olivia Randall was pretty with dark, straight, shoulder-length hair, angular features, and an athletic build. She wore jeans, a black T-shirt, and flats, and had probably pulled on the blazer at the last minute when I begged her to come over as soon as possible. The fact that she recognized my name as soon as I uttered it probably explained the instantaneous house call.

She immediately homed in on me. "We okay here?" she asked, taking in the activity unfolding around us.

I handed her the document that Guidry had served me. She gave it a cursory glance before focusing on Guidry. "I'm Olivia Randall, and I represent Ms. Taylor and her son, Ethan."

Guidry told her to feel free to review the warrant.

"I just did, and even from the face of it, I can tell that it's overbroad. Do you have any reason to believe that Ms. Taylor is holding evidence of a crime?"

"The warrant speaks for itself."

"It does, and it's obvious that you have treated Ms. Taylor and her son as if they were equal co-occupants of a particularly large residence for New York City, without making any attempt to discern between separate living spaces."

The tit for tat that followed was quick and technical, but I could make out the arguments. Guidry believed the whole apartment was fair game. My stranger of a lawyer was claiming that they were obligated to carve out areas of the apartment that were under the control of individual people.

"My office," I blurted out. "I'm the only person who uses it, exclusively for business. I can prove it. I took a home deduction on it and survived an audit. That's got to mean something." I had rolled Nicky's suitcases into the closet as soon as I was alone in the room. Sometimes excessive neatness comes in handy.

Olivia Randall jumped on the information and then started building the case against searching my bedroom.

"It was the victim's bedroom, too," Guidry said. "No dice."

She left us momentarily and disappeared, first into our bedroom and then into Ethan's. As she stepped back into the hallway, she paused at my open office door.

"I take it this is your workspace?" she asked.

I nodded, and Guidry pulled the door shut. "Great. Now Ms. Randall can justify the thousand dollars an hour she's going to charge you for being here."

"You don't need to have them standing here, either," Olivia said.

"No one's leaving," Guidry said.

"At least let them sit in the office until you're done."

Guidry shrugged, and we shuffled single file down the hall. Once we were alone, Olivia introduced herself.

"I didn't understand any of that," Ethan said. "Why did they need a warrant? And why is this room off-limits but the rest of the apartment isn't?"

I started to tell Ethan that they had a right to look around our apartment, as they had at the house, because Adam was a crime victim, but Olivia shot me a sharp glare. "I'm sorry, Chloe, but you're not helping right now."

When I opened my mouth to speak, Nicky shook her head.

"Ethan," Olivia continued in a firm voice, "you already know that your friend Kevin told the police you were by yourself for an hour Friday, not far from your house, after you had told them you were with Kevin all night long. Clearly they have used that information—and perhaps more—to get a search warrant. Unlike the crime scene processing they did in East Hampton, this is a search for criminal evidence based on probable cause against a specific suspect."

I doubted if anyone had ever spoken so directly to Ethan before, let alone about a subject so serious. He wouldn't stop blinking. "A suspect? But then how come they're not in here?" His question provided its own answer. He looked at me and collapsed in on himself, hunching over and crossing his arms.

Nicky and I were patting him on the back, telling him it was going to be okay, but Olivia Randall kept on lawyering. "No matter what happens here tonight, Ethan—all of you—it's only the beginning of a process, okay? It's possible that nothing will happen at all, but even if they find something that's a problem, there's an investigative process, charging, a grand jury—nothing that gets decided today is permanent."

This time, I knew exactly what she was talking about. I had been married to a prosecutor. She expected Ethan to be arrested.

"None of us is going to talk to them without Olivia present," I said. "Does everyone understand that?"

Ethan was nodding, but I could tell he was scared and going along with anything we said. Olivia was more firm. "Ethan, I need you to practice this with me. 'I'm not talking without my lawyer.'"

She made him say it ten times. By the end, he gave a small smile at the absurdity of it.

"And you remember my name?"

"Olivia Randall," he repeated. She was pretty. My son remembered the names of pretty girls.

"Great. Now, this is less than ideal, but I'm going to talk to each of you individually, if that's all right." She used the Murphy bed as a makeshift interview station, speaking to us one at a time while the two outcasts waited across the room on the built-in window bench. She spoke to Ethan first and longest, which only confirmed my suspicions about the scenario she was predicting.

Two hours in, she was speaking to Nicky when the office door opened. It was Guidry. "Can you all step outside into the living room again?"

It happened fast, as if they had choreographed each movement. The uniformed officers quickly formed a wall to separate Ethan from the rest of us. A set of handcuffs appeared at Bowen's side from nowhere.

Ethan's eyes darted between me and Nicky, imploring us to protect him. The scream that came from my throat was more pained than when I had found Adam's blood-soaked body. Nicky shouted "No!" and ran for him, provoking two uniformed officers to push her against the wall by force.

"He's a minor," Olivia bellowed over the chaos in the room. "He's represented by counsel. He's invoking all applicable rights, including the rights to silence and a lawyer."

I saw a sudden focus in Ethan's face. "I'm not talking without my lawyer." His voice was quiet but assured. My kid was so brave.

And he was under arrest for the murder of Adam Macintosh.

22

S HE HAD TO have a swimming pool.

As a starting prosecutor at the Cuyahoga County District Attorney's Office, Adam made a decent salary, at least compared to what either his parents or mine ever made. And he'd gone to both college and law school on full academic rides, so he wasn't saddled with debt the way a lot of attorneys are. But he worked for the government, not the private sector, and his wife was an ex-waitress who was supposedly planning to start college.

Yet when it was time to rent a house, Nicky insisted on having a swimming pool. She said that water calmed her, and that she knew she would study harder for the SATs if she could sit with her books by the pool when it was warm out. She claimed that having her own pool had always been her dream, even though I hadn't heard her mention it since she was fifteen years old and Mom and Dad took us to Niagara Falls and she was floating on her back in the indoor pool of the Holiday Inn, saying that when she grew up she wanted to be rich and have a swimming pool where she could lie out and tan and have drinks with paper umbrellas in them. Dad had responded by telling her that if she wanted to be rich, she should be more like me when it came to her schoolwork.

Somehow she and Adam had managed to find a place they could afford that had an in-ground swimming pool in the backyard. It even had a hot tub on the deck for the colder months—not one of the fancy ones, but those clunky plug-ins you can buy at Home Depot. The landlord had given them a break on the rent because he was so certain that a young assistant district attorney and his new bride would be perfect tenants. Adam, always a Dudley Do-Right when it came to ethics, went so far as to confirm with his office that there was nothing unethical about the situation before signing the lease.

Nicky, to her credit, did love that pool once she had it, but there was definitely no studying going on there. She would lie for hours in the sun, listening to music, painting her nails, flipping through gossip magazines. She had this prenatal aqua workout she claimed she was doing every single day. But once the baby was born, and old Nicky was back with a vengeance, she'd drink for hours, leaving her chaise only when the baby monitor alerted her that Ethan required attention.

I only went home to visit one or two times a year. Maybe that's why I could see the change in my sister more than my parents did. The proud girlfriend who had doted on Adam during law school was nowhere to be found. She'd day-drink and then try to hide it from Adam when he came home from work. She'd snap at him for the smallest questions— like whether she'd gone to the grocery store that day or what they were having for dinner. I'd tell her that I thought we should engage the baby with his blocks and other brain-building toys, but she'd leave him for hours in front of the television as long as he didn't cry. Before Adam, she used to drink a lot, but she was (usually) a fun drunk, more likely to make out with a dude in the bathroom than sulk in her bedroom or scream about old perceived slights from our childhood. But something about her had changed. She was thirty years old and seemed to have given up on her life. I wondered if there was more than alcohol at work.

I tried intervening once, about a year before it all blew up. It was probably the third or fourth time Adam had called me since the baby was born. I was her sister. He thought I might have some magic formula that would exorcise this new Nicky, who was actually more like the old Nicky, yet still different. But because I never did know what made Nicky tick, the phone calls would turn more into venting sessions where he would tell me how worried he was about her, and I would try to hold my tongue about how I always thought she was in over her head doing the wife and mother thing.

I called Nicky and warned her she was going to lose Adam if she didn't get her shit together. "Perfect Adam isn't going anywhere," she told me. "He loves the baby too much." It was so telling that she didn't say he loved *her.* He loved *the baby.* She was willing to use Ethan to keep Adam glued to her for life.

My parents, of course, took her side. They said that Adam was too "rigid" and didn't understand that "for better or worse" meant exactly that. That was choice, coming from my parents. My father had been a completely different person before he stopped drinking, and my mother paid the price for it. Why couldn't they see that Nicky was doing the same thing to Adam? Meanwhile, Adam's calls to me increased, but, as Nicky predicted, he loved the baby too much to leave.

The pattern finally stopped the night I was at the Met Gala with Catherine.

It was the fucking swimming pool.

He had come home from work but still had prep to do for a trial the next day. It was a beautiful May night, and Nicky wanted to have dinner outside. They grilled quesadillas and corn. When Adam was done eating, he went inside to go over his opening statement again. He got so engrossed in his work that he didn't realize nearly two hours had gone by without a peep from either Nicky or Ethan.

He found Nicky half floating in the pool, her shoulders against the steps, as if she'd been sitting there and then slithered down into the shallow end. The baby was in her arms, near her lap. Only the top of his head was visible.

Adam pulled Ethan out first and turned his head to the side in an attempt to drain the water from his nose and mouth, but Ethan wasn't responding. Adam did CPR, but does anyone really know how to do it until they have to? And Ethan was only two and a half years old. Adam didn't know whether to do mouth-to-mouth or to cover Ethan's entire mouth and nose, like he remembered learning for babies. And how hard could he press a little toddler's chest without crushing him?

Adam never stopped having nightmares about those uncounted minutes that passed before Ethan finally spat out a stream of chlorinated water and then coughed. Once he knew Ethan was breathing, Adam pulled Nicky out, too. He didn't tell me until after we were married that he actually thought about leaving her in the water.

By the time Adam called me, Nicky was at the Cleveland Clinic. The hospital would be checking, but he was certain she had to have drugs in her system.

"Just tell me, Adam. Tell me why you're really calling."

"I need your help."

He was trying to put her on a psych hold, and my parents were contesting it. "I can't take another chance, not with Ethan. Every day when I go to work, I wonder if she's going to leave the stove on or drop him or forget about him in the car. I don't know how she got this bad, but it has to stop. She needs to get help. The lawyer who handles civil commitments for our office says that if it's just this one incident, Nicky will probably get released tonight, and then it'll be my word against hers, plus your parents, in family court about what happens to Ethan. But if she's put on a psych hold tonight, I'd go into family court with a head start toward custody. Hopefully that will be the wake-up call for her to get some help, because she's certainly not listening to me."

He was right. There was no other way. Nicky wasn't the kind of person who cared about consequences until they actually happened. She was going to have to lose Adam and Ethan if she had any chance of getting her life back on track.

"And what do you need for a psych hold?" I asked, pressing a finger against my ear to block out the sound of the gala. By then Catherine was out of the ladies' room, glaring at me, wondering why I was on the phone when I was supposed to be soaking in every second of the experience she had bestowed on me.

"It would help if there was someone else asking for it, other than a spouse."

Someone like her only sibling.

I did it. I took his side. I signed an affidavit the next morning, swearing that I had seen a decline in my sister over the course of more than two years that was consistent with the self-destructive behavior she had exhibited as long as I could remember. And when she tried to say that Adam was lying about her, I signed another affidavit detailing the many times that she had told me horrific things about her lovers when she was mad at them, only to retract them later after they had reconciled.

Adam was a lawyer who had friends who were other lawyers who were willing to represent him for free, however long it took. And Nicky was . . . Nicky. She had no lawyer and no plan, only denials about the severity of what she had done. *I swear, Chloe. I have no idea what happened. I must have fallen asleep. You have no idea how exhausting it is to take care of a kid all day.*

They agreed to a divorce that gave Adam sole physical custody but did not permanently terminate her parental rights. I don't know whether she signed it because she didn't care anymore or because she actually believed she could work her way back into a shared custody situation.

But instead of getting better, she got worse. She would have been homeless if it weren't for my parents. I've always wondered if they both would have lived longer if they hadn't been constantly dealing with Nicky and her drama.

When Adam first moved to New York, I persuaded my mom and

dad that it would be best for Nicky to stay in Cleveland, where they could keep an eye on her. What we thought would be monthly visits became less regular as my parents got older, Nicky got worse, and Adam and Ethan got more settled in Manhattan. When I called Nicky to tell her that I was seeing Adam and that it was serious, she actually sounded grateful. "All I ever wanted was for Ethan to have a happy life. You're better at it than I am. Maybe he'll turn out to be more like you than me. But funnier. That would be good." I could tell she was wasted, but I think she meant it.

Somewhere along the way, Nicky started to clean up her act. She never told me the details of how she did it, but I think a switch was flipped after our father died. She had always been so resentful of him, blaming him for all of her troubles. It was like she refused to be who he wanted her to be, just to spite him. And then once he was gone, she leveled out. Mom swore she was getting better, and I could hear a newfound clarity in Nicky's voice when I called and the couple of times a year she'd visit. And then Mom died, too.

Nicky thought about moving closer to us, since she no longer had my parents to watch over, and vice versa. But there was no way she could afford to live in New York with no job or higher education. And besides, it was just too late. Ethan was thirteen years old by then. And he was a good, happy, stable kid. He didn't need the disruption of a biological mother he barely knew.

To this day, I really don't believe that Nicky was trying to kill her baby. She was simply never meant to have one.

PART III

PEOPLE V.
ETHAN MACINTOSH

23

THEY BROUGHT ETHAN into the crowded Suffolk County court-room through a side door. He was wearing the same striped T-shirt and navy blue sweats he'd had on when he was arrested the previous day and was still in handcuffs. Olivia was with him. So far, only she—not I, and not Nicky—had been allowed to meet with him.

I was now into my fourth day without any meaningful sleep, but Nicky was the one I felt trembling next to me when she saw him. He looked both older and younger at once. Under the fluorescent lighting of the courtroom, his skin seemed gray. His long bangs, usually swept high with product, had fallen straight across his forehead. Beneath them, he peered out like a frightened little boy pushed from behind a curtain onto a brightly lit stage.

Olivia led the way across the courtroom to the counsel table. A deputy of some kind—bald, wearing a black bulletproof vest embla-zoned with white letters reading "New York State Courts"—was at Ethan's side. Ethan's eyes bore into me, asking for help that I couldn't give him.

"Has he been in those cuffs all night?" I tried whispering to Olivia.

Nicky and I were seated in the first row behind the defense's table, but I felt so far away from my son.

Olivia brushed off my question as a court clerk called the case. Olivia and Ethan had barely stood up and sat down again before the prosecutor started reading case numbers and statutes from a folder in front of her. My son was now a file. And he was being charged with the second-degree murder of his father. His case was technically being handled in a special "youth part" of the criminal courts, but the murder charge meant there was no way to move the case to family court, which meant Ethan would be facing an adult-like trial and adult-like penalties if he was convicted. Olivia had warned us to expect it, but Nicky let out a guttural cry upon the reading of the murder charge. I may have, too. I could hear nervous movement and whispers in the galley behind us, but didn't want to turn and look.

Nicky lowered her head when the prosecutor announced that they were seeking to detain Ethan pending trial. I reached over and grabbed her hand. All these years, I had convinced myself that she was more like a semi-estranged aunt than his actual mother, but she was sharing this pain.

The only thing that gave me hope in that moment was Olivia. She was good. Really good. She took Adam's best attributes and made them Ethan's. She described Ethan moving to New York City with his father when he was four years old after his parents divorced. How Adam, who served nearly ten years as an esteemed federal prosecutor, was Ethan's role model and lifeline. How devastated Ethan was by his father's murder. She depicted the police as having treated Ethan and his stepmother as suspects from the second they responded to the 911 call.

"There is a presumption of innocence, Your Honor, and Ethan is in fact innocent of this horribly unjust accusation. I know we all get so used to defendants being marched in and out of these rooms, and we say we presume they're innocent, but do we? Really? No, we treat it as a phrase that represents the panoply of rights we afford to those that we believe are probably guilty. So, please, Your Honor, just imagine for one second that this sixteen-year-old boy, Ethan, is *actually* innocent. He has just lost the man who was his only constant parent throughout his life. And within seventy-two hours, the police snatch him out of his home and accuse him of murdering the father whose death he has only begun to mourn. Holding him in custody while I prove what an injustice this is will change him, Your Honor. It will rob him of any kind of faith he has in adults, or the legal system. I am telling you: if you allow the prosecution to do this, you won't be able to sleep when you eventually realize how mistaken the police are in this case."

I noticed that Nicky's head was down and her lips were moving. I was fairly certain she was actually praying. I closed my eyes and did the same silently, asking a God I hadn't spoken to for more than twenty years to send Ethan home today.

The prosecutor could barely hide her disdain as she dismissed Olivia's narrative as a "fairy tale."

"Your Honor, the police didn't need to jump to any conclusions. The conclusions leaped into view from the evidence." As we expected, she depicted Ethan as having lied to the police, offering as a false alibi a friend who instead told the police that Ethan had asked to be dropped off at Main Beach "for what his friend assumed was the defendant's ongoing practice of selling marijuana on the East End."

According to the prosecution's theory of the case, once Ethan was alone, he walked the three and a half blocks from the beach to our house, killed Adam, and then staged the scene to resemble an interrupted burglary.

The judge asked for more detail about the evidence of staging, and the prosecutor produced a photograph, first handing a copy to Olivia. "The evidence at trial will be more extensive, but this one photo gives you a clear idea."

The judge's expression was indifferent at first, but then he donned a set of reading glasses. "These arrows are . . ."

"Pieces of glass, Your Honor. From the broken window."

Without a view of the picture, I had no idea what they were talking about, but the tone of the judge's "Uh huh, I see" had me tighten my grip on Nicky's hand.

"Also, Your Honor, the detectives asked the defendant and his step-mother if anything was missing from what was supposed to look like an extensive exploration of the house. His stepmother noticed a wireless speaker missing, and the defendant then added that he was missing a pair of headphones and a very specific pair of tennis shoes. They were described as red, yellow, and black, with a cartoon character holding a ray gun."

The courtroom was silent. It was clear the prosecutor was building up to a big reveal. My stomach suddenly hurt. It's like my body knew what she was going to say before my brain had figured it out.

His backpack. When we left East Hampton, Ethan wanted to circle back to Kevin's for his backpack. And when we got to the city, I looked in it and found nothing but a burner phone. If the only thing Ethan had carried off to Kevin's house was a phone, why had he taken his backpack?

And then, boom, the prosecutor said it. "The same friend who said that Kevin was out of his presence for an hour the night of the murder told police that when he picked Kevin up at Main Beach afterward, he was carrying a backpack that he hadn't had with him earlier in the night. Although he did not see what was inside the backpack, when the po-lice searched the defendant's New York City bedroom yesterday, they found an empty backpack, and they found items matching the three supposedly stolen items—including the very distinctive sneakers—on the top shelf of his bedroom closet, covered by a blanket."

The judge removed his reading glasses and looked directly at Ol-ivia, waiting for an explanation that didn't come quickly enough.

"There is an explanation, Your Honor. The defendant's parents have two residences."

"So you're saying that he owned two pairs of those shoes?"

"Your Honor, a bail hearing should not be a mechanism for the government to force my client to give testimony or to trick me into previewing my entire case for them. What matters here, Your Honor, is that there is no reason why Ethan needs to be held pending trial, where he will be vindicated. He can be released, on bail if you so require. He has no prior criminal history and will remain with his stepmother—whose reputation is beyond measure. Any remote concerns you might have could be addressed with electronic monitoring."

The prosecutor jumped in without an invitation. "With all due respect to Ms. Randall, that's just offensive. Would any other defendant—who didn't have two residences, designer tennis shoes, and impeccably credentialed parents—have any chance of being released on bail in a murder case? I have only given you a few pieces from the mountain of evidence we have against this defendant, because we fear that he might tamper with potential witnesses, as when he tried to rope a friend into a false cover story. But as far as his stepmother being an appropriate safeguard for him, I will add this. She told the police multiple times that the family rarely used their home security system, but records from the alarm company show that the system was used regularly as members of the family moved in and out of the house. And on the night of the murder, it was armed shortly after a car service dropped Adam Macintosh at the home and was subsequently disarmed—in our view, by the defendant. But the important point is that we believe Ms. Taylor—despite her, quote, 'reputation beyond measure'—is motivated to protect her stepson. Quite understandably," she added as an afterthought.

I noticed the judge glance quickly in my direction. I could feel him reassessing whatever it was he thought he had known about me.

"Well, we don't need to get into any of that," he said. Despite his conciliatory tone of voice, a burn building in my throat and stomach forewarned of what was coming next. "But your point about equal treatment is well taken. You've shown that the case has merit. The consequences of a conviction for this young man would be quite severe. I don't want a situation where we release him, only to find out he's left for the Swiss Alps on a private jet."

When a snicker erupted behind us, I thought Nicky was going to break my hand. If she had eyes in the back of her head, that person would have gotten knocked to the floor after court.

"The defendant is remanded without bail."

I COULD STILL HEAR THE judge's words ringing in my ears when we walked out of the courtroom. The press was waiting for us and started yelling questions the moment they saw me emerge into the hallway. *Is it true you lied to the police? Do you think Ethan killed your husband?* And some of the questions were obviously about Nicky. *Is that your sister? Are you his actual mother?*

Olivia shuffled us through the crowd and down the hall to an unused jury room she had arranged for just this purpose. Once the door was closed, Nicky and I were talking at once. *How do we appeal? When will Ethan get home? What if we offer to hire private security to watch Ethan around the clock?*

Olivia tried to calm us down by telling us that Ethan would be housed with other juveniles, not in county jail, and that this was only the beginning of the process.

Nicky slapped the table. Hard. "Stop fucking saying that. It's the beginning of a shit show, but it's the end of everything that was good for him. The only question is how bad it's going to be from now on."

Olivia took a deep breath and nodded. "Fair enough. I just wanted you to know how many people do get cases dismissed prior to trial. Or get acquitted. Or reach some agreement that involves far less serious charges. You haven't lost him. You're not going to lose him."

I was still trying to recover from what I'd heard in the courtroom. "I don't understand. Why would he take those things from the house?"

"I'm sorry, but I have attorney-client privilege with Ethan, not you."

"So he told you why he had those things in his closet?"

She pressed her lips together. "What if, hypothetically, he just got confused. Maybe in the chaos of carrying items back and forth between your two houses, it's hard to keep track of what gets left where. And maybe you were also both still in shock when the police asked you to do the walk-through so soon after Adam died."

"So he said he was confused? But then why didn't he have his backpack with him the first half of the night with Kevin?"

"It's not for us to explain their evidence, or even to take it at face value. You have no idea how much pressure they put on his friend to get him to say what they wanted."

But Olivia didn't know what I knew about the backpack being empty that first night back in the city. And the police had discovered the items on the top shelf of his closet. It didn't take camera footage to conclude that Ethan had removed the things from his bag and put them there. No jury in the world would buy some story about his being in shock while he did it. And I knew for a fact that Ethan never put anything away.

When Adam and I decided to get married, I swore to myself that I would never treat Ethan as anything less than my own son. I researched the school districts. I went to the doctors' appointments. I met with the teachers. I did "all the things," as Adam liked to say. When Ethan had a problem, I was the one to solve it, because I was good at that. Now he was in desperate need of help, and I felt completely powerless.

"Oh my god, *why* are we having this conversation right now?" Beside me, Nicky was still standing, her breath fast and heavy. "There is no *way* Ethan did this. We have got to get him out. Like, today. *Now!* Those so-called kids he'll be held with? You can't tell me they're going to be sweet, soft kids like Ethan. Let me talk to the judge. I'll do anything to get my kid home."

Olivia nodded calmly as she allowed Nicky to rage. When she finally spoke, her voice was sympathetic but calm. "That's not going to happen, Nicky. The detention decision has been made. He will not be held with any adults during any stage of the process."

"He's sixteen years old, Olivia. I'm not a lawyer, but you can't expect me to believe that New York puts a sixteen-year-old in the same place as some little kid who went on a shoplifting spree."

Olivia pursed her lips and shook her head. "No. He'll be in a special facility for older teenagers. The official term is an 'adolescent offender.'"

"Okay, so a bunch of hard-ass criminals and sociopaths. There has to be a way to get him out of there."

I was as terrified for Ethan as Nicky was, but I was desperately trying to contain my emotions and process the evidence the prosecution had claimed to have. "Do you have that picture? The one they showed the judge?"

Olivia looked at both of us with sympathy. Two sisters: one bouncing off the walls with indignation, the other trying to pull a Sherlock Holmes and magically solve the case with her powers of observation. "Don't do this to yourselves. You two are his only family. That's your job right now, and it's not going to be easy. But let me do mine."

"I want to see the picture," I insisted.

She reached into her bag and handed it to me.

I immediately saw the problem. The glass from the broken window was on top of the guest bed duvet and inside the open nightstand drawer. Why hadn't I noticed it before? Because my husband had just been murdered. If I had seen it—if I had known I needed to protect Ethan—I wouldn't have done the walk-through. I wouldn't have answered a single question or let them speak to Ethan. They would have nothing.

I pictured Ethan telling Olivia that he had just been confused about carrying those items back to the apartment. It sounded exactly like the story I had fabricated after he took the gun to school. A person could only forget what's in his bag so many times. No jury would buy it.

And I didn't want to admit it, but I wasn't sure I was buying it, either.

"Did he really tell you he was confused?" I wanted to believe there was a rational explanation.

"Like I said, I can't reveal anything he said to me."

Nicky paced back and forth in frustration. "This is bullshit. It's obvious that's what he told you—*hypothetically*—and it sounds ridiculous, so it's not true. Just let me talk to him. I'll find out what's going on."

"This is what I meant about it only being the beginning," Olivia said. "Even if you thought you had everything sorted out today, there's nothing procedurally we could do with it right now. I know it's frustrating to be stuck in a system, but that's what this is, and I promise that I'll work the system as well and as fast as I can. But I need to be the one to do it."

I could tell that Nicky hated her, but Jake had said Olivia was one of, if not *the*, best criminal trial lawyers in the state. But she didn't know my son.

"Here's what we're trying to tell you, though, Olivia. Ethan can seem sophisticated—he's been raised around precocious kids, gone to the right schools, all of that. But he's insecure at heart. He's always looking for approval. He's terrified of abandonment. And these little episodes he's had—the pot, the gun—he's just going through a lost phase. Not to sound like the 'it's a scary time for men' crowd, but how many teenage boys are on meds, or isolated, or falling behind in school? But I swear, my only fears about Ethan have ever been about a lack of focus or drive. He would never—ever—hurt anyone, let alone his father. I know Ethan." I could feel Nicky hovering over me. "*We* know Ethan. I'm telling you he's innocent, but I'm also telling you that he *desperately* wants to please people. He will tell you what you want to hear, without regard to the consequences down the road. So you must take everything he tells you with a grain of salt, while at the same time trusting us that he did not kill his father."

The frantic expression on Nicky's face had been replaced by something else. Sadness. Sadness, and regret. I had just told this lawyer more about Ethan's real personality than I had ever shared with her.

Olivia thanked me for the insight. "And, although I of course can't break privilege," she said with a small smile, "I make it clear to my clients when I don't think the *hypotheticals* they run past me ring true."

I wanted to trust this woman, but clearly she had a callousness about her cases that was built upon years of representing guilty people. I needed her to understand that Ethan was different, even if it meant saying something negative about Adam. "Adam could be a very demanding father. He had unrealistic expectations—of everyone, to be honest, but especially his son. But Ethan was always trying to meet them. If I had to guess, Ethan had been smoking pot on Friday night, and that's why he didn't remember carrying those things from the house. And Kevin was surely smoking, too, which explains him being malleable about whether Ethan had the backpack with him all night or not. And knowing Ethan, when he found his shoes and stuff in his backpack in the city, he just put them in the closet instead of calling attention to himself by correcting the record."

For the first time since we'd entered the jury room, Olivia pulled out a notepad from her briefcase and scribbled in it. "This is helpful. Thanks. Both of you."

Nicky opened her mouth in disbelief. "That's it? She just totally explained the whole thing to you. Can't we just go to the police and clear it all up?"

"I wish we could, but no. They'll never dismiss the case this early in the process. I have investigators. We chip away and chip away, and then we use it all together at trial to create reasonable doubt."

"So Ethan's in jail now because he was too afraid to tell the police he was high? For fuck's sake. I of all people can tell him there's much greater crimes than smoking a little weed. He'll tell me. I know it. Let me talk to him."

"I'm sorry," Olivia said, "but I can't let that happen. Neither of you can speak to Ethan about anything remotely connected to the case."

As we tried to argue with her, she explained how she had done the legal research already to be absolutely certain. She couldn't guarantee that the prosecution wouldn't force either of us to testify against Ethan. "New York has a privilege for parent-child communications, but it's extremely limited. And I know you'll find this painful, but it's not clear that either of you would qualify. Chloe, you're technically a stepmother because you never formally adopted Ethan. And Nicky, you're the biological mother, but you haven't raised him, as I understand it, and the case law focuses on the unique relationship between children and their parents."

In a few quick, dry, legalistic seconds, she had laid out the dilemma of our new normal, a situation that we were still struggling to process.

"I'm sorry," Nicky said, "but, no, I can't handle this. There has to be some other way. I'm not leaving this room until we figure out how to fix this. I'll chain myself to the courthouse doors if I have to." She clenched her hands into fists and made a primal sound that resembled a growl.

"Nicky," I snapped. "You're going to get arrested, too, and then how is that going to make Ethan look?"

Even when she had come to terms with Adam taking custody of Ethan, I had never seen her this out of control. I found myself feeling resentful about her carrying on. Seeing my son dragged around by police officers made me want to yell and scream, too, but I didn't have the luxury of an outburst—not now, at least. Olivia needed to focus on Ethan's defense, not hand-holding the two of us.

"So then what are we supposed to do?" Nicky asked, collapsing into the chair next to me. "Seriously, what the fuck are we supposed to do?"

"Go home," Olivia said. "Take care of yourselves and each other. And get ready for the next steps."

Nicky reached across the table and grabbed Olivia's hand. "I need you to swear to me that you're going to get Ethan back home. Promise me, or I literally don't know how I'm going to do this."

I could see Olivia's facial muscles tighten. "I'd be lying if I made that promise—"

"No," Nicky said. "No, no, no. I need to hear you say it. I need to know for certain."

Olivia shook her head, but then gave Nicky's hand an extra squeeze. "Here's the promise I *can* give you. Right now, I am a hundred percent confident I can get a jury to send him home, based on what we heard today. Okay?"

That was more than I had expected her to be able to guarantee, but I could tell that Nicky still wasn't satisfied.

"And if that assessment ever changes," Olivia continued, "I *swear* I'll let you know. The second I don't feel good about the case, I'll tell you—no punches pulled. *That* I can promise."

Nicky shook her head and wiped her nose.

"Good," Olivia said. "When Ethan gets processed, he's going to need you both. It's going to be a while."

"Let me guess," Nicky said with a sad smirk. "It's only the beginning?"

"I'm sorry," Olivia said. "Down the road, when I hope this is all over with a good outcome, I give you permission to remind me how annoying that lecture is."

When we left the room and Nicky broke away to clean up her face in the restroom, I asked Olivia one more question. "Did you mean what you said to the judge? That you believe Ethan is actually innocent? You sounded so convinced." I had known she couldn't guarantee

Nicky a successful outcome, but I was looking for something different. I think I wanted to feel as certain as she appeared in court.

She looked around, as if she were making sure no one would hear us. "I'd like to think I always sound persuasive. But, yes, I do believe it. And I rarely do. And, as I said, I promise I'll do everything I can to prove it."

24

Six Weeks Later

I'VE ALWAYS BEEN a good student, and not only in school. If there's a task to be done, I can figure out a way to do it. And, if it's something I care about, I'll learn how to do it well. It's like Malcolm Gladwell's 10,000-hour rule. If you want to be great, you've got to work at it.

But I had come to accept that no matter how many hours I put into it, I'd never be able to host a party the way Catherine Lancaster could host a party. Her Sag Harbor home was French country, but all chic, no shabby. The food was always perfect—the flavor, presentation, timing, all of it—yet you never saw her scrambling in the kitchen the way I did if I tried to cook more than one course. For years, I was convinced she had caterers hiding in the basement, sneaking upstairs to work like ninjas while we mingled, until I finally knew her well enough to ask her point-blank. Turns out the woman who had an assistant send out her emails and do her Christmas shopping actually did her own cooking. She even curated the guest list so the conversation never faltered. Five

people you'd love to meet for a dinner party? That was Catherine's dining room table every Saturday night.

Even the playlist was carefully planned to suit her guests' desires.
When "Walkin' after Midnight" came on, Bill closed his eyes and gave
us one line—*Just like we used to do*—while his shoulders swayed. He
loved Patsy Cline so much that he had named his horse after her.

And now I was bringing Nicky to one of those perfectly curated
gatherings.

Other than the occasional pop-in by friends and coworkers offering condolences and casseroles, this was the first time since Adam was
murdered that I had accepted a social invitation. Nicky and I had decided it might be good for us to imitate normal human beings for an
evening, but now that we were there, I was still numbed by the same
shock and anxiety that hadn't faded at all after six weeks, with an extra
layer of resentment that I couldn't wallow without an audience.

It was a small shindig by Catherine's usual summer standards. Just
me, her, Nicky, Bill Braddock, and two new-to-me friends of hers:
Christof DeJong, a sixty-something-year-old Dutch artist whose large-
scale steel sculptures were regular sightings on the East End, and Liam
Ricci, who, I gathered, was a former model, now tattoo artist, hoodie
designer, and general cool guy.

"Now, Chloe, I want to know everything about where you are on
this book project of yours. You said it was two books, right?"

That's what Catherine would do at these parties—throw out little
questions like it was a cultural salon crossed with a talk show. She knew
all the details of my publishing deal, but wanted to give me a chance
to share some tidbits with the rest of the crowd. I finished swallow-
ing the bite of quail that was in my mouth before I answered. "Things
have changed a bit since I first signed the contract. It was the Them
Too series that got me a book deal, and then the memoir was sort of an
add-on. But, with recent events, I guess the demand for the memoir is
pretty high."

An awkward silence fell over the table, which never happens at a Catherine party. I should have known she'd ask me about the status of the books. I wished I'd had a better answer prepared, but I wasn't feeling up to a conversation with strangers, and even a mention of the memoir was enough to make my stomach hurt. When I pitched the idea to publishers, I was picturing an up-with-career-girls, how-I-climbed-the-ladder story. Now the editor wanted to know about Adam, Ethan, Nicky—my actual personal life. I was tempted to walk away from the contract, but I had heard rumors that a few members of the board were discussing the possibility of "changes" at *Eve* while I was "distracted" by my "family situation."

Bill held up his wineglass in my direction. "More power to you. If I wrote a memoir, I'd have a long list of enemies lined up on Montauk Highway, waiting to exact their revenge. Your book—I am confident, Chloe—will be an inspiration to millions of young women who are struggling to find their voice."

I was still forcing a smile when Catherine turned to Nicky. "Nicky, can I say how pleased I am to finally have a chance to meet you in person? Chloe talks so much about you"—I didn't—"but she never told me what a great chef you are. Watch your back, Ina Garten."

"I don't know who that is," Nicky said sheepishly. "But, 'Yeah, bitch, watch your back!'"

I tried to hide my wince and was relieved when everyone laughed.

Nicky had insisted on bringing a giant Tupperware of gazpacho even though I told her that Catherine did not like other people's food at her parties. Ever polite, Catherine had served it in cups as an amuse-bouche. At least it had been good.

Nicky had been dealing with our shared despair by cooking constantly. She was operating a full-time test kitchen, scouring my cookbooks, tinkering with recipes, and asking me which dishes I thought Ethan would enjoy most. She liked to say that when he came home, he was going to eat like a king.

"What do you do besides make delicious cold soup?" The question came from Christof the sculptor, who apparently assumed that anyone he met at a Catherine party would have an answer to the question "What do you do?"

I blurted out a nonresponse. "Nicky's visiting from Cleveland."

"I'm a jewelry designer," she said.

"Excellent," Liam the tattoo guy said. "What company?"

"Oh, just myself," she said, waving a hand. "I sell stuff online. But I get to do my own designs. Work my own hours. Keep all fifty dollars to myself."

I was mortified, but everyone pretended to laugh, which was nice. Nicky was doing a better job than I was of keeping up with the party chatter.

"Is that one of your designs that you're wearing now?" Catherine asked.

Nicky glanced down and fiddled with the necklace around her throat. The chain was some kind of blackened silver, ending in an amalgam of hammered metal jigsaw puzzle pieces. It was . . . a lot.

"Uh-huh."

"Do those pieces come apart?" Liam asked. "It looks like they're barely together."

"Nope," she said, tugging at the pendant in different directions. "All welded tight. But, yeah, that's the intended effect. Tough industrial materials, but it still looks fragile, right?"

Christof and Liam both agreed it was cool.

"You should sneak a promo for her work into *Eve*," Catherine suggested.

"Uh-uh-uh," Bill warned with a wagging index finger. "As her lawyer, I happen to know that would present a conflict of interest that would put her in breach."

"Well, *someone* should discover you," Catherine announced. "Now, who wants dessert?"

When I trailed Catherine into the kitchen to see if she needed help, she had already placed six perfectly sliced pieces of peach pie and was topping the plates with fresh whipped cream.

"So much for helping," I said.

She flashed me a quick smile. "I'm glad you're here with me, though."

I nodded. "Me, too."

"Is it okay to ask about Ethan? I just can't imagine."

"He's holding up," I said softly. "Thanks." She started a follow-up question, but I grabbed two of the prepared plates and made a dash for the dining room. "Don't want the cream to melt!"

I stopped even pretending to pay attention as the pie was consumed. Ethan wasn't "holding up" at all, not as far as I was concerned. Because of the severity of his charges, he didn't qualify for what they called "nonsecure" detention. Despite what the detention center's website claimed about providing "holistic services" for the sixteen- and seventeen-year-olds housed there, the place seemed no different to me than a jail.

Olivia had scared all three of us away from making any mention of the case whatsoever, because conversations were monitored, and Olivia seemed to think the prosecution might call Nicky and me as witnesses. So our visits were made up of small talk about how the cat was doing and whether Ethan was reading any of the books I was bringing him. The only time he mentioned his father was to ask where he was buried. When I told him Adam had been cremated, he broke down in tears, and I realized what a mistake I had made.

Not to mention that the mandatory mental health assessment he'd undergone at intake had led to a prescription for an antidepressant. I was adamantly opposed at first, but Nicky, who had more experience with that world, was open-minded. After consulting with Ethan's pediatrician, we had consented to the medication, but I was nervous about the long-term consequences. I was even more terrified that there would be no "long term" for Ethan at all—or, at least, not a normal one.

Nicky helped me clear the dishes when desserts were finished.

"That Liam is smoking hot," she said as I used the sink sprayer to rinse the plates.

"Please don't make the moves on him, Nicky. I'm begging you."

"Oh, jeez. I was just kidding." Nicky had mentioned two weeks earlier that the nameless, childless fifty-two-year-old divorcee she'd been seeing in Cleveland had finally told her that she should "do what she needed to do in New York" and wished her all the best. "You told me not to embarrass you, and I didn't, right? The soup was good. Everyone liked it, just like I said."

She was right. I knew she was. But the truth was, I still didn't want her here.

I COULDN'T SLEEP THAT NIGHT. I couldn't sleep *any* nights. From my bed, I stared in the darkness at the armoire, knowing it contained the urn that contained Adam. The medical examiner's office could only keep him so long, and then the funeral home they suggested needed a final answer, too. We couldn't even have a memorial, not without Ethan, and so I had done what sounded like the simplest thing. Adam always was practical.

Now Adam's "cremains" were in an urn, where they would stay until Ethan and I could go out together on a kayak to watch the sunset and spread them on the water. In the meantime, I couldn't even put the urn on display, because I was terrified that Panda was going to knock the container over. The cat was still getting adjusted to life in East Hampton, where we had relocated to be closer to Ethan's detention center.

It was nearly three in the morning by the time I gave up, got out of bed, and went looking for my briefcase. My assistant had forwarded a pile of mail from the office.

The fourth envelope I opened was a sympathy card from London, signed by Carol and Roger Mercer, the in-house counsel for the Gentry Group.

I picked up my iPad from my nightstand, opened my contacts, and started a new email message to Carol:

Dear Carol and Roger, thank you so much for keeping me in your thoughts. I'm sure it's proper etiquette to say I'm doing fine under the circumstances, but the truth is, it's been a struggle. I know this is an odd question, but, Roger, do you know if Adam had any meetings relating to the Gentry Group last May? I find myself trying to piece together every minute of his last days. Anything you know would help. With love, Chloe

I read the message three times, making sure it sounded like the somewhat understandable musings of a bereaved widow.

I hit the send key and tried again to find sleep.

25

Four Months Later

OLIVIA HADN'T BEEN kidding when she assured me she'd do everything she could for Ethan. It was the Thursday before Halloween, and she came by the East Hampton house because she was out for the weekend and wanted to check in on Nicky and me.

"That's quite the display out there," Olivia said as she stepped inside.

Nicky had gone to HomeGoods and bought an entire shopping cart of Halloween decorations. I had no memory of her enthusiasm for Halloween when we were younger, but apparently, she had become one of those adults who lived to answer the door all night for candy-demanding children.

Once we were settled into the family room—I still couldn't bring myself to sit in the living room, where I'd found Adam—Nicky asked Olivia if she really thought that Ethan's trial was going to start this time. In theory, it was scheduled for next week, but it had been set over twice before.

"It'll be Thanksgiving soon," Nicky said, "then Christmas. You told us at the very beginning that it would be a long process. I thought it would be next year. I want this all to be over sooner rather than later, but does that mean they're confident if they're ready now?"

"Or they don't want me to have more time to prepare? Or they have a hundred cases and will figure out on Monday that the timing doesn't work. Try not to read into it either way, okay? I still feel good about where we are."

I knew that Nicky found comfort in Olivia's original promise that she would tell us if she thought we were going to lose.

"Just think, though," I said. "If we really go to trial and it all goes our way, Ethan could be home for the holidays."

The possibility didn't even seem real. Nicky and I had each found ways of breaking out from the paralysis that had weighed on us during much of the summer, but I felt like I was living two separate lives: one where I could be a normal person doing normal things when other people were around, and one where I was in complete panic and despair the minute I was alone with the idea of having absolutely no control over what was happening to Ethan.

Nicky made the drive to Islip to see him nearly every day, but I could only visit twice a week in my status as his aunt. I could see how nearly six months of confinement had worn on him. His face still lit up when he saw me, but his affect would quickly flatten. The irreverent and persistent sense of humor that I had once tried to tame was now undetectable. It seemed as if he was ready to go back to his "room" earlier and earlier with each visit.

I was starting to worry he was going along with the visits more for us than himself at this point. It was almost as if he was resigned to his current life in the detention center, which we disrupted with reminders of the world he had lost. As far as the timing of the trial went, I didn't know whether to hope for another delay to postpone what might be an eventual conviction, or to hope for a quick disposition so we could bring him home before this experience transformed him into a stranger.

I hugged Olivia before she left, wishing her a good weekend, realizing I knew nothing about whom she'd be spending it with. I knew nothing about her at all, really, and yet she was in many ways the most important person in my life at that moment.

Once she was gone, I told Nicky I was going to a Soul Cycle class and then might drive out to Montauk to run the loop used for the Turkey Trot on Thanksgiving morning. Two years earlier, I had placed second in my age group for the 10K, which wasn't particularly competitive given that the loop was designed for a 5K, and only weirdos like me were willing to run it twice.

"Hard pass," she said. "I'm going to ginsu this here pumpkin with jewelry designs for my Etsy page. Unless, of course, you want to help me." She was at the kitchen counter with a perfectly shaped pumpkin, my best knife, and an array of jewelry parts lined up on a dish towel.

"Go to it, Holly Hobby. I'll be back for dinner."

TWO HOURS LATER, I WAS catching my breath at Jake's, the sheets piled at the foot of the bed. He used a remote control to trigger the ceiling fan.

"I remember when you didn't want me to see you completely naked," he said.

Those days were definitely over. I was lying in what the yogis called the dead man's pose, arms and legs splayed. The air circulating over me felt like magic.

He turned on his side and kissed my shoulder. "God, I've missed you."

We hadn't seen each other in ten days. I tried to keep my distance when Adam was killed, but I found myself calling him over and over again about Ethan's case. I trusted Olivia as much as I could trust someone I didn't really know, but my inner control freak needed to run her every decision by another lawyer—which turned out to be Jake.

Before Adam died, I never allowed Jake to get too close, convincing myself he was simply a periodic escape from a temporary rough patch in my marriage. But once Adam was gone, and Jake was there for me—truly *there* for me—I remembered what it was like to feel not only loved but cared for. Protected. Safe. Adam and I had become broken, for reasons only we understood. And now I was the only one left, and I wasn't going to tell anyone. It didn't matter anymore. I was free to have a second chance—with Jake.

By July 4, we were seeing each other again. Now we actually felt like a real couple, at least when we were alone.

I didn't realize I had fallen asleep until he was twitching next to me, muttering something about being wrong and that someone needed to stop. When it seemed like he was living inside a full-on nightmare, I shook his arm gently to wake him.

His head jerked from the pillow. "What?"

"You were having a bad dream." I rotated to face him and wrapped my arm around his waist. "What was it? Driving off a cliff? Teeth falling out? An exam in that math class you totally forgot you enrolled in? That's my biggie."

He rubbed a palm against his close-cropped blond hair, as if he were trying to wake himself up. "If only it were so easy. Real-world bad dreams are much worse."

I said nothing, wondering if he would tell me more. Real couples talked about real problems.

"It's about that client at the firm, Gentry."

That single word felt like a jolt of electricity up my spine. I hadn't thought about the company for months.

"See? That's why I hadn't mentioned it to you. It's a reminder of Adam."

I assured him it was okay and that I wanted him to tell me.

"The federal government's investigating them. A couple of employees—middle management, but high enough—got separate counsel, which means they're probably cutting deals with the US Attorney's Office. The hammer could drop any day with indictments of the CEO and CFO, if not the entire corporation."

"So why the bad dream? Adam had clients get investigated and charged all the time."

"But he was a criminal defense attorney, and I'm not." His index finger was tracing an invisible circle on my shoulder, a distraction as he talked to his dead law partner's widow in bed. "And we weren't working for Gentry on a criminal matter. It was strictly M&A."

Mergers and acquisitions. I remember telling Adam that he should have been happy about doing noncriminal, transactional work for once. After all, he had been the one complaining about being on the wrong side of the courtroom as a white-collar criminal defense attorney.

"So why is the government investigating?"

"Gentry was doing a lot of foreign deals. Sometimes the players in other countries have expectations that the United States government has a problem with."

"Like, what kind of expectations?"

"Paying off every person up and down the line. Some people brush it under the scope of 'cultural due diligence,' but the feds call it bribery. One of the reasons Gentry hired us was to help them get the deal closed without crossing any lines into corruption. R&B's got a ninety-eight percent satisfaction rate two years after closing of international M&As."

"And you do that by helping them walk all the way up to the line?"

"Hm-mm." His finger had stopped its rhythmic tracing. He had fallen back to sleep, just like that.

I tried to do the same, counting my breaths and timing them with his. It didn't work.

I crawled out of bed, pulled on my T-shirt and underwear, and

made my way to his kitchen. One of the many things I liked about Jake
was that he had good taste. Both his apartment in the city and house in
East Hampton were clean and modern, with a masculine touch, a mix
of neutral colors and surprising textures. As I sat on a steel barstool
and opened my laptop on his butcher countertop, I could picture myself
hosting a dinner party here.

I pulled up the map page I had bookmarked on my laptop. It was the
area surrounding the spot in Queens where Adam had been dropped
off and picked up the last two days of his life. I had already googled
every individual street address within a mile walk of the train station he
had used as his Uber location, and had still not figured out where Adam
had spent those hours. I had even driven there a few times, walking
around with his picture, not knowing who I might show it to.

If the police had ever tried to nail down this part of the story about
the ending of Adam's life, they had never told me. My guess is that
once they focused on Ethan, they stopped tracking down any leads that
weren't on the road to convicting my son.

But now Jake's bad dream about the pending criminal investigation of Gentry had me thinking again about what I'd written off as a
dead end.

I googled "FBI Kew Gardens" and knew immediately that I was
right. Up popped a map with a red icon directly across from the train
station. In addition to the map, I saw a photograph of the cube-shaped
black glass office building I had personally walked into. It was home to
a Duane Reade and a 24 Hour Fitness on the ground level, but there
had been no way for me to know what was housed on the other eleven
stories. When I googled the address, I had found a radiology practice,
a leasing office, and a medical group.

But now I knew what to look for. There, on the website for the
FBI's New York operations, was what I'd been searching for all along:
"Along with our main office in Manhattan, we have five satellite offices,
known as resident agencies, in the area." The Queens office was on
Kew Gardens Road.

If midlevel company employees had been providing information to the government, maybe Gentry's outside counsel had done the same—especially if that lawyer was a former federal prosecutor who was angry that his wife had pressured him to sell out by defending the types of people he used to put in prison. I thought about the unreturned email message I had sent to Carol and Roger Mercer, the Gentry Group's in-house lawyer. I had written it off as a sign that they were either busy or had no information to provide, but now I wondered if my question about Adam's nonexistent meeting with Gentry had struck a nerve.

I heard the slapping sound of bare feet against tile behind me. "You look good half naked in my kitchen."

I leaned my head back to accept a kiss.

"Is that your book?"

I was still on the masthead as the EIC of *Eve*, but I was on a leave of absence while Ethan's trial was pending. In retrospect, I should have forced myself to maintain a schedule at the office. After all, Olivia kept reminding me that it was her job, not mine, to prepare his defense. With him in custody, there was nothing I could do other than visit him twice a week and try to give him hope that this was all temporary.

In the meantime, I had been trying to finish the memoir. The chapters about my career were done. Jake knew I had been struggling with the more personal sections. How could I sum up twenty years of feminist publishing without talking about the love I carried for the father who used to hit my mom when he drank too much, or the resentment I had for the mother who, in my view, had not done enough to protect herself or her daughters? And now that everyone knew the backstory to my marriage, I needed to write about my relationship with Nicky as well.

"I'm starting to think the advance wasn't enough," I joked. "Hey, that thing you said about Gentry being investigated? Take a look at this."

I pushed my laptop over so he could see the map on the screen. "The FBI has an office in Queens, right next to that train station." He knew I'd been trying to figure out where Adam had been those two days.

"Are you sure? The field office is in Manhattan."

"Sorry, not the actual field office, but like a branch. I think it's called a resident agency."

He shrugged. "Shows what I know about criminal law."

"Is it possible that's the office that was investigating Gentry?"

"I don't think so. Our contacts have been with the Southern District."

I knew from Adam's prior employment there that the US Attorney's Office for the Southern District covered Manhattan and the areas north, while Queens and Brooklyn fell into the Eastern District.

"Can you find out?"

"What's this all about?"

"Maybe Adam was providing information to the FBI about Gentry."

"That would be a blatant ethical violation. He would have been disbarred."

Would Adam have cared? I was probably the only person who knew just how much Adam had been struggling since he'd taken that job at Rives & Braddock. He didn't feel like the good guy anymore. It's like he'd become another person.

"But let's say he was willing to break all the rules. Was Gentry doing something that, in Adam's mind, would have warranted it? Just how much of a threat was Adam to that company?"

"I'm really sorry, Chloe, but I can't have this conversation with you. I don't break the rules, not even for you."

"So what should I do with this information?" I gestured toward my laptop. "This could be what got Adam killed. It proves that Ethan's innocent."

He pulled me close and kissed the top of my head. "I can't be the one you talk to about this."

———

I WOKE UP IN MY own bed the following morning to the remote sound of Nicky yelling my name.

I pulled on my pajama pants and found her heading in my direction in the hallway. Behind her, I could see mountains of bagged candy on the kitchen island. "Happy Halloween," I groused, not remembering a time when Nicky had beaten me out of bed.

"I don't think so. There's a guy on the front porch who said he'll wait for you all day if he has to."

The guy was a process server, and he had a subpoena for me. I was on the prosecution's witness list for Ethan's trial.

26

THE JURY SELECTION alone consumed four days. Some of the potential jurors had the usual excuses: babies to watch, jobs to work, too much to do to sit in a courtroom for what might be weeks. A few were probably looking to get thrown out, like the guy who said defendants should have to prove they're innocent. But the biggest problem was finding people who didn't already have an opinion about the case. Almost all of them had heard some of the pretrial news coverage, and most of them walked into the courthouse with at least a glimmer of a viewpoint. And from what I could tell, those preexisting views did not cut in Ethan's favor. As one woman said, "I mean, his mom's, like, famous. I don't think they'd arrest him and put him on trial unless he really did it."

Olivia had tried to convince us that the negative first impressions were ultimately to Ethan's advantage to get all those people tossed from the jury. The ones who were left were what she called either "low-information jurors" or "very open-minded." It sounded to me like she thought only dumb people would vote to acquit, which was hardly encouraging.

For the first day of the actual trial, after jurors had been selected

and sworn, I wore slim black pants, an off-white silk blouse, and a dark
green blazer. To my surprise, the internet had a lot to say about it that
afternoon. Supporters wore dark green and posted photographs with
the hashtags #StepmotherPower and #FreeEthan. Opponents . . .
well, they were opposed.

The judge's name was Lydia Rivera. On first instinct, I was relieved it was a woman, thinking she'd be more sympathetic to a teenage
defendant, but it turned out she was a former prosecutor. Olivia told us
not to read into it one way or the other. "She's middle-of-the-road. We
could do better, but we could also do a lot worse."

The prosecutor was a man named Mike Nunzio. According to Olivia, he was less experienced than some of the ADAs who handled homicide cases in Suffolk County, but he was seen as an up-and-comer in
the office, getting promoted through the ranks at record speed.

Nunzio delivered his opening statement with elegance and confi-
dence. His demeanor reminded me of Adam's, the few times I'd seen
him do his thing in court. As a matter of professional ethics, prosecutors
were forbidden from stating their personal belief in a defendant's guilt.
But Adam used to say that it shouldn't be necessary to use the words "I
believe the defendant did it." He believed jurors could tell when a lawyer spoke with moral certainty. When Mike Nunzio spelled out the evidence he expected to introduce against Ethan, he sounded like a man
who was absolutely convinced Ethan was a coldhearted killer.

Olivia had told us to expect an objection to the fact that Nicky and
I were sitting in the courtroom. I was expressly on the witness list,
and Nicky could still potentially be called as well. Even though Nunzio
could obviously see us as he paced the courtroom, he said nothing to
object.

After the first fifteen minutes, I had stopped worrying about him
kicking us out of the room and was focused on the content of his statement. When he spoke about "the defendant," it didn't sound anything
like Ethan. It was as if he were speaking about a fictional character on a

television show. He described Ethan's transformation from a little boy without a mother to a privileged young man attending private school, shuttling between a multimillion-dollar apartment in downtown Manhattan and a luxury beach house in East Hampton. He spoke of him as a coddled teenager who refused to accept even the slightest bit of discipline.

"You've heard of affluenza? You're going to learn that Ethan Macintosh suffered from that affliction, and that his father, Adam Macintosh, was killed because he was determined to set his son on another path."

Olivia's objection was sustained, but I could tell that the depiction of my son as a pampered, entitled brat had taken hold. By my count, at least four of the jurors were visibly skeptical as Olivia portrayed Ethan as a naive, traumatized kid who got ensnared in a shoddy police investigation that had jumped to conclusions too quickly.

The first witness, as Olivia had predicted, was Detective Guidry. She was the witness who established the basic facts about Adam's murder: who he was, where he lived, how he died. I felt an entire courtroom of eyes follow me, including Ethan's, as I walked out during Nunzio's extensive PowerPoint display of Adam's injuries. I had been the one to find him. I remembered pressing sofa cushions against the wounds, hoping I could somehow save him, even as I knew he was already gone. Before I let the door close behind me, I made a point of holding Ethan's gaze, hoping he'd understand. It would not help his case to have the jury see me if I got sick again, like I had at the house that night.

I drove to the nearby Hyatt where Nicky and I had rented a room to have a place to hide as necessary during the trial, since the courthouse was nearly an hour away from East Hampton. For the next two hours, Nicky texted me updates from the remainder of Guidry's direct examination. The alarm evidence, the items found in Ethan's closet, the window that appeared to have been broken *after* the house was ransacked. No surprises, at least.

I returned to the courthouse for a quick recess before Olivia would have a chance to cross-examine Guidry.

"Nunzio still hasn't objected to us watching the trial?" I asked.

She shook her head.

"Is that unusual?"

"He's probably worried about the optics. You're a public figure. You're also a widow and the defendant's mother—mothers, really. I wouldn't read into it, for now."

It was hard to ignore the *for now* at the end of the sentence.

Olivia used her cross-examination to establish all of the evidence that the police lacked in their case against Ethan. No murder weapon, no DNA evidence, no blood found on Ethan or his clothing, and no bloody clothing found discarded near our home.

Olivia introduced a photograph of the block of knives on our kitchen counter. "Every slot here was occupied by a knife when you entered the house, correct?"

Guidry agreed.

"And the only other knives you found in the home were standard, silverware-style dinner knives?"

"That's correct."

"And certainly it wasn't a standard dinner knife that inflicted the decedent's injuries."

"Definitely not."

She repeated the same line of questioning with a photograph of the knife block in the city apartment.

The implication was clear. There was no evidence that the knife that was used to kill Adam came from either of our homes.

"In fact, Detective, you have no physical evidence whatsoever to tie Ethan to this crime, do you?"

"No, but—"

Olivia had nothing more for the witness. I thought I saw one of the jurors—the twenty-six-year-old woman who worked at the outlet mall—nod in my direction. Or maybe I imagined it because I needed something to hope for.

THE FIRST NON-LAW-ENFORCEMENT WITNESS WAS Margaret Carter, the headmaster of Casden, Ethan's high school. Margaret has an intentionally formal demeanor, but she doesn't fit the stereotype of a prep school principal. She's more Upper East Side wife material than English boarding school matron. Nunzio began by having Margaret summarize her own elite credentials (Phillips Exeter, Yale, then a master's degree in education from Columbia), followed by what sounded like an advertisement for Casden itself. For ten years straight, the small school had representation in every single Ivy League university's entering freshman class.

I remembered the two-pronged campaign I had spearheaded to get Ethan into Casden. One prong was getting him in. I pulled every string I could, including setting up a high school internship program for aspiring young writers at *Eve*. The other was convincing Adam. Public schools had been good enough for the both of us, in his view. We would have killed for the opportunities that a school like Casden could provide, and Ethan would simply take it for granted. I tried to convince him that Ethan was only indifferent to school because he wasn't sufficiently challenged. Once he was in an institution like Casden, he'd rise to the occasion. I eventually prevailed, but Adam made it clear that it was only because he wanted to pacify me, not because he agreed.

I never thought it would lead to having Margaret testify against Ethan at his murder trial.

Once Nunzio was done with background information about the school, he established that Ethan was completing his sophomore year at Casden when Adam was killed.

"Was there an incident in the fall semester of his sophomore year involving a weapon observed in the defendant's backpack during school hours?" Nunzio asked.

"That's correct."

Olivia had sought to suppress the evidence relating both to our ownership of a gun and the fact that Ethan had carried the weapon to school. Once Judge Rivera determined that the gun evidence was relevant, Olivia had stipulated that Margaret could testify to the hearsay reports of the fellow student who had caught sight of the gun in Ethan's bag. As Olivia explained it, there was nothing to gain from the jury hearing directly from one of Ethan's peers, who might be tempted to offer an exaggerated portrait of him, whether favorable or not.

"Please tell the jury what happened."

"One of our students was lingering outside my office after classes broke out. I got the sense that he wanted to speak to me, but wasn't quite certain about how to approach me, or perhaps whether to do so at all. After nearly thirty years at this, you get a sense of how teenagers operate. So I called him in and put the question to him directly: 'What is it you'd like to say?' He asked me what a student should do if he were aware of another student bringing a gun to school. I advised him of what I suspected he already knew—that it was a dangerous situation that we absolutely must know about. I asked him how he would feel if something tragic happened and he hadn't shared whatever it is he knew. At that point, he told me that Ethan Macintosh had a handgun in his school bag."

For the record, Nunzio had Margaret identify Ethan as the student in question. I felt all eyes on me again as Margaret explained how she had followed school protocol by calling me to report the problem.

It was just a mix-up. When we go between the houses, we have a laundry list of things that get carried back and forth, and sometimes I jam things wherever they fit. That's what I had told her. It was true, for the most part—an anomalous shortcoming in our usually methodical planning skills. Adam had once found a week-old banana inside a tennis shoe.

But Margaret didn't give the jury our side of the gun story. That was going to be one of the things I'd have to explain when I eventually took the stand.

"To the extent you spoke to Ethan's parents about any discipline that would be applied in response to the gun incident, with whom did you speak?"

"Initially, his stepmother, Chloe Taylor."

"Did you also speak to his father, Adam Macintosh?"

"Yes, I called her, and then both of them came to the school to meet in person."

"And how would you describe their responses?"

Olivia objected to the question as vague, and Rivera sustained the objection.

Nunzio quickly rephrased. "Did one of his parents appear more concerned about Ethan's current status with the school than the other?"

This time, Olivia's objection was overruled.

"It was my impression that his stepmother simply wanted to put the episode behind them, while Adam was genuinely worried that Ethan might be having problems."

"What types of problems?"

Olivia had barely risen from her chair before Rivera warned Nunzio to restate the question. Among the many pretrial motions was one to limit evidence relating to Ethan's academic performance and general social position at the school. The prosecution had wanted to show that Ethan's grades had been slipping and that he was known as a loner, but Olivia had convinced the judge that the evidence was irrelevant.

I assumed that Nunzio would excuse Margaret from the stand now that his attempt to bypass the judge's pretrial ruling had failed. Instead, Nunzio asked, "What makes you think that Adam Macintosh was more worried about his son than his wife was?"

"Because several months later he asked me about the process for admitting Ethan into a military school."

I stared at the back of Ethan's head, waiting for him to turn around so I could try to assure him—somehow, with my facial expression—that there was no way that would have ever happened. *Turn, Ethan. Look at me. Why aren't you turning?*

"And what specifically did he say to you about his desire to place his son in a different school."

Olivia objected that the question called for hearsay, but the judge declared that the question reflected Adam's then-existing state of mind.

"He told me that there had been other problems since the gun incident. That he didn't even recognize his son anymore. That Ethan had lost his way. I don't recall his exact words, but I distinctly remember him saying that he had always hoped that nurture would end up mattering more than nature. He was concerned that Ethan might have inherited some of the destructive traits of his mother—his biological mother, I mean, not his stepmother, Ms. Taylor."

I felt Nicky's hand grab mine for the first time that day.

"And he thought military school might be an answer?"

Ethan still hadn't turned. Olivia had probably given him the same admonishment she had delivered to us: "No matter what happens, do *not* look surprised. By anything. The jury has to believe during the entire prosecution's case that there's another side of the story that they just haven't heard yet." I was waiting to hear the other side of the story to this military school angle.

"He was quite adamant about it. Here, I do recall his exact phrasing. He said that Ethan, quote, needed to get his ass kicked. He thought one possibility was to pull him from Casden and throw him into one of the, let's say, tougher city public schools. But he was leaning toward a military school and specifically asked me which of them was the most 'unforgiving,' as he worded it."

"And did you provide him with a list?"

She shook her head, and Nunzio reminded her that she needed to state her answer in words for the court reporter.

"No, I did not. It's not my job to place our students elsewhere. And, besides, I thought—at the time at least—that Ethan was simply trying to get attention."

"Do you know whether Adam discussed his plans to switch schools with his wife, Chloe Taylor?"

"Not with certainty. But he told me that he knew Chloe would try to fight him, but that he was the father and had final say-so, since she was only his stepmother."

The word *only* hurt, no matter how many times I heard it.

"And when did this conversation take place?" Nunzio asked.

"I don't know the precise date, but it was nearing the end of the semester. My best estimate is that it was about a month before Adam was killed."

"Did you tell anyone else about Adam's intention to place his son at another school?"

"I did."

"And who was that?"

"I told the defendant, Ethan Macintosh."

A hum of whispers erupted from the trial gallery, but was quickly silenced by a bang of Judge Rivera's gavel.

"You told him that his father was considering sending him to military school?"

"I did. I thought it might get him to see the seriousness of his situation. Especially since my impression was that his stepmother was enabling him by making excuses."

Olivia objected, which only made me feel guiltier.

"And what did the defendant, Ethan Macintosh, say when you told him that his father was considering sending him away to military school?"

"He said, and I remember exactly, 'He can't do that to me. I'll find a way to stop him.'"

Even then, Ethan's head never turned.

———

NICKY AND I WALKED WITH Olivia in silence from the courthouse,
wearing the facial expressions we had practiced on Olivia's counsel—
concerned but confident, unfazed but with a touch of outrage. We didn't
actually speak to one another until we were back at Olivia's suite at the
Hyatt. Furnished with a conference table and whiteboard in addition to
a living area and bedroom, it was obviously designed for lawyers trying cases in the nearby courthouse.

"Did you know about this military school thing?" Olivia asked.
She was standing over Nicky and me, the two of us seated next to each
other at the conference table.

"Absolutely not." I grasped the edges of the table to keep my hands
from shaking. "How are they allowed to spring this on us like that?
Why didn't you know about this?"

Olivia pursed her lips, clearly tempering her response. "Mrs. Carter
was on the witness list, but she wouldn't talk to me or my investigator.
I think this is the reason they want you to testify. They're going to call
you to the stand and ask you about every single time Adam and Ethan
had a conflict. They're going to say that his motive to kill Adam was to
keep him from sending him away."

Olivia had tried to mitigate the damage on cross-examination, getting Margaret to admit that she didn't take Ethan's comment as a threat
or else she would have reported it to someone. But I could see the way
the jurors were looking at Ethan.

"I had no idea. And more importantly, I never would have allowed it."

"Don't try to play me like you played that headmaster."

"*Excuse* me? I'm not *playing* anyone."

"I should have pushed you harder about this earlier, Chloe. To be
honest, I think my judgment with you has been clouded from day one
because of who you are and what you've done in your work. But no
one's this perfect. This isn't about your perfect public image, okay?

This is real life. And I can't help Ethan if I'm getting surprises thrown at me in that courtroom."

"I'm telling you, I had no idea Adam was thinking about military school. For all I know, that woman's confused or lying."

Olivia scoffed. "You saw her in there. She's a total pro. The jury believed her. *I* believe her. And, trust me, I'll be talking to Ethan about this, too. I can't protect him from things he doesn't tell me about."

"Well, maybe Adam cooled down and changed his mind, and Ethan wrote it off as a momentary outburst. He never said one word about it to me."

"And that right there's what I'm talking about," Olivia said. "No family is as *Leave It to Beaver* as you and Ethan have made yourselves out to be. What else aren't you telling me?"

I closed my eyes. Where would I even begin? I dropped my face into my hands. I just wanted Ethan to come home. I had wanted to believe that this trial would finally be the end of the nightmare. I didn't know how I was going to go on if this jury didn't make things right. When I finally heard another voice, it was Nicky's.

"You fed me the same story," she said quietly. I dropped my hands and saw her eyes boring into me. "You and Adam both. You kept telling me how happy Ethan was. How well he was doing. You made it sound like I would be ruining everything if I showed up. Like I was a virus that was going to infect the perfect little family bubble."

They both wanted an explanation I couldn't give them.

Olivia wasn't letting up. "If the headmaster at the school knew this, we have no idea what others might say. Ethan could have spoken to other kids. Adam might have confided in friends. He could have called military schools, looking for openings. I've been talking up Adam's importance and closeness to Ethan, and this undermines that. Just how bad were the tensions between them?"

I didn't know what to believe anymore. Adam had apparently told Margaret Carter that he didn't recognize his son anymore, but that is how I had felt about my husband for the past year. He was a completely different person when he was angry.

I pictured Adam screaming at Ethan after finding Kevin's marijuana—or at least I had *thought* it was Kevin's. If I had to guess, only Ethan and I had ever seen him so enraged. And then only I had seen his animosity escalate once he and I were alone in our room later that same night.

"It was bad, okay?"

Nicky glared at me as Olivia asked, "How bad?"

"Not, like, physical or anything. But Adam said he didn't even know who Ethan was anymore, just like Margaret said. Sometimes he'd even cry at night, saying he still saw Ethan as the little boy who wouldn't talk until he was nearly four but would hand him a jar of peanut butter when he was at the kitchen table working late because he knew Adam liked to sneak a few spoonfuls as dessert. But when Ethan disappointed him, he lashed out and tried to force him to be the boy he wanted him to be, instead of who he actually was. Or is. And Ethan would dig his heels in even further. It got to where I felt like I was walking on eggshells if they were in the same room together."

"Well, I think we know now why Nunzio didn't object to having you in the courtroom. He wants you to see their case for yourself."

"What does that mean?"

"You loved your husband, didn't you?"

"Of course I did."

"Okay. So they want you to believe Ethan took him from you. They probably think of you as—quote—only the stepmom. If they can convince you that your stepson's the one who killed him, then you'll want Ethan punished for what he did. They think you'll basically become a witness for them instead of the defense."

The room fell silent.

"Can they really make me testify about that?" I asked. "About Ethan and Adam, I mean."

They were both talking at once. Olivia was trying to explain the legalities of the situation to me. My communications with Adam were covered by spousal immunity, but only as they related to our marriage. I'd have to testify to anything I observed between Adam and Ethan. And, once again, she reminded me I had no privilege with respect to Ethan, since I was merely a stepparent.

Meanwhile, Nicky was accusing me of hiding information from her about Ethan.

"I just won't testify," I announced. "If they ask me anything that will hurt Ethan, I won't answer."

"You'll be held in contempt," Olivia said.

"Fine. Let them put me in jail." Desperate times called for desperate measures. I wondered if the tweeters with the hashtags would take my side. Maybe the outlet-mall juror would, too.

"It will only make Ethan look guilty," Olivia said.

"Is that what you think?" I asked. "That Ethan is guilty?"

She said nothing. She'd told me when she first met Ethan that she truly believed he was innocent. If she was having doubts, how could I expect twelve jurors to believe us?

"I'll say I did it."

At some point, Nicky had placed her head on her stacked forearms against the tabletop. She tilted her face as she spoke, but I still almost didn't hear her.

"You'll say you did what?" I asked.

"*It*." She pulled herself upright. "I'll say I killed Adam. So I could take back Ethan."

"Jesus, Nicky. Not helpful, okay?" We had made progress the last six months, but this was quintessential Nicky. She always had to be so dramatic.

"I'm not kidding. If you're willing to go to jail for contempt, I'll take the stand and say I'm the one they want."

Olivia was shaking her head again. "Please don't even entertain that thought, okay? You're just going to ensure a conviction with a stunt like that."

"But why? All we need is reasonable doubt, right? Alternative suspect: right here." She pointed to herself with two thumbs.

I wondered if she'd actually learned something about criminal law while she was married to Adam, or had watched too many repeats of *Law & Order*.

"Do you realize how quickly Nunzio would debunk that?" I yelled. "They'd pull your phone records, for one. How are you going to explain your cell phone pinging in Cleveland if you were here killing your ex-husband?"

I could tell Nicky had no answer for that.

Olivia held up both palms. "I appreciate the enthusiasm—both of you—but if it looks like you're willing to say anything to save your son, it makes all our witnesses look like liars, which makes Ethan look guilty. And, Nicky, I can't suborn perjury. And even if I did let you take the stand and try to confess, they'd destroy you on the stand—with the phone records Chloe mentioned, for example—or they'd just argue that you and Ethan did this together, and he'd get convicted, and you'd be up next. So, forgive my bluntness, but don't be stupid."

"What about your promise?" Nicky said. "Where do things stand after today?"

Olivia had promised to be brutally honest if we were losing. "The promise stands, and we're still good, all right? We have a strategy. We just have to stick to it."

The strategy was nothing flashy. It was all about reasonable doubt. No murder weapon. No bloody clothes. No DNA.

Before Nicky and I left to head back to East Hampton, I asked Olivia if she had had a chance yet to follow up on my theory about Adam's purpose in going to Kew Gardens. My initial curiosity about his meetings with the Gentry Group had taken a back seat to Ethan's defense, but the discovery of an FBI office across the street and a pending investigation against the company had changed all that.

"I've been trying to figure out the best way to approach that, but preparing for trial has been the priority." I took that to mean she hadn't done anything at all. "Hang tough, okay? I know today didn't feel great, but we got Guidry on the record admitting they have no physical evidence. It's not splashy, but that's the kind of thing that leads to an acquittal. And there's a long way to go. Go home and try to get some rest."

I couldn't rest, not until Ethan came home. It didn't matter what the prosecution thought. I wasn't going to turn on him, no matter what.

27

FOR THE NEXT two and a half weeks, the drive between the courthouse in Riverhead and the house in East Hampton became our shared commute. I tended to drive in the mornings, while Nicky took the wheel on the way home. After a few rounds of arguing about the radio, we adopted the rule that whoever drove controlled the satellite stations. I tended to go for news, light rock, and the '90s hip-hop channel. She opted for metal, '80s new wave, and Howard Stern. I had to admit that I ended up liking everything except the metal.

We also fell into a rhythm at the house. Usually I'd pick up stuff from Blue Heron, a former side-of-the-road farm stand that had grown into a posh gourmet market. But I'd learned by now that Nicky was actually a good cook. Whoever chose the menu did the cooking, while the other helped with prep and cleanup.

On this particular Sunday night, I was keeping it simple with roast chicken, haricots verts, and baby potatoes. Less simple was the fact that we had two dinner guests who were out on the East End for the weekend: Catherine and Jake. I had introduced Jake as a friend from Adam's law firm who had been trying to schedule a time to check in on me for weeks, but I had a feeling Nicky knew precisely who he was to me the second she laid eyes on him.

My suspicions were confirmed after I asked Jake if he could trim the haricots verts while I trussed the chicken and Catherine made refills for our martinis.

"See, I remember back when Chloe called them 'green beans' like everyone else in America," Nicky said. Passing behind me with a bowl of scrubbed potatoes, she whispered in my ear. "Funny how the hot lawyer knew exactly where the cutting board was without being asked."

"Nicky," I said loudly, "maybe since I have these helpful minions in the kitchen, you could consider taking down all those Halloween decorations from the front porch."

"Party pooper." One of the items she had hung by the door was a motion-detector vampire that cackled and wiggled each time you passed. It was a week from Thanksgiving, and I was still jumping every time I walked out of my house. "I confess I'm better about putting things up than taking them down."

"You're going to be one of those crazy old ladies who has her Christmas tree up all year-round."

"Knock it off with the crazy old lady jokes," Catherine said, handing me a refreshed martini. "I consider them hate speech."

I heard a chime come from Jake's cell phone, which was faceup on the kitchen counter. The number on the screen was one of only ten or fifteen that I would have recognized from memory—the central switchboard for the *New York Times*. He must have recognized it, too, because he set down the paring knife he was using, said he had to take the call, and slipped out the sliding doors to the back deck.

"Hmm," Nicky mused, wiggling her fingers. "Take over bean duty or destroy all scary, happy things on the front of your house?"

"Removal of all the fun, please," I said, adding a sad trombone sound for effect.

Catherine watched as Nicky trudged off to the front door with the step stool from the pantry. "You two seem to actually be getting along."

I shrugged and took a big sip of gin that I knew I'd regret in the morning.

"And to think, last summer you were saying there was no way you could keep her under the same roof with you for the whole trial."

I avoided her gaze as I cut off a two-foot-long piece of cooking string and began to tie the chicken in a neat, tight tuck. "That was before I realized she's the only one who understands how scared I am."

When Jake came back inside, he allowed his arm to brush against mine as he spread the thin, bright beans in a single layer across a baking sheet. I shot him a warning look, but when my eyes connected with his, I realized how much I wanted to be able to be here with him like we were a normal couple.

"So was that the *Times*?" I asked.

"Invasion of privacy much?" he said with a smile.

I recited the number from memory. "Same number that popped up every time they called me for a quote." I spoke in the past tense because, these days, no one called except about Ethan's trial, and I referred all the media to Olivia.

"Just a reporter," he said.

"About Ethan?" No matter the context, my fears for him were always lurking just beneath the surface.

"No, of course not."

"A client then?"

Catherine coughed, a gentle nudge that my curiosity was bordering on rudeness. She, of course, had no idea that Jake was anything to me other than one of Adam's former coworkers. After that final year of secrets with Adam, I had gotten so comfortable with Jake that I almost forgot that, when push came to shove, I was still a liar.

CATHERINE AND JAKE LEFT SHORTLY after dinner to make it back to the city.

"You sure Catherine's okay to drive?" Nicky asked, closing the door, newly unadorned, behind them.

"Please, Catherine hasn't driven herself since 1986." It was only a slight exaggeration. I knew for a fact that she had her housekeeper take the Porsche around the block once a week to keep the battery from dying.

"Must be nice," Nicky said.

I began loading the dishwasher and then paused to pour another splash of Barbaresco.

"You sure you're going to be okay for court tomorrow?" she asked, eyeing the glass in my hand.

I knew I had been drinking more than usual since everything happened with Adam and Ethan, but I never thought I'd see the day that Nicole Taylor, of all people, was lecturing me on my consumption.

"Honestly? No. And I could drink an entire case of this heavenly nectar, and it wouldn't make one lick of a difference, one way or another. But, yes, I'll be able to do whatever I need to do tomorrow."

"You've always been good at handling anything thrown at you," she said. "You'll be fine."

We worked side by side in silence, me loading dishes while she cleared the counters and hand-washed the pans.

"I keep thinking about when the trial started and you told Olivia you were willing to put yourself on the stand and say you were the one who did it. Did you really mean that?"

"A hundred percent. I'd do anything for Ethan. I mean, wouldn't you?"

Of course I would. I would switch places with Ethan in a heartbeat, if it was possible. But it was Nicky who had thought of the possibility, not me.

"I'm sorry I never realized how much you cared about him." My voice was low, and I cleared a lump that had formed in my throat. "I think it was easier for me to do what I did if I believed that you didn't really want him."

When I looked up, she was staring at me. Her sudsy hands dripped over the sink as hot water ran. "Wanting him," she said, as if the words were foreign. "That's really only a question when you first get pregnant, and, yeah, Adam and I thought about it. But once Ethan was born, it was never a question of want or not want. He was there. This little person. This new, amazing, unformed, demanding little guy was there. And he needed me. He needed . . . so much. And every single day, I felt like I was giving everything I was able to give him, and it was never going to be enough." She wiped her face with the back of one of her hands, allowing the tears that were forming to blend with the dampness on her skin. "So, yes, I mean it when I say I'd do anything for Ethan. Going to prison for him would be way easier than it was to give him up so Adam could raise him without me. But . . . like you pointed out, they'd see my cell phone was in Cleveland, and it would only make Ethan's case worse."

I dropped a cleaning pod in the dishwasher, closed the door to run it, and took another sip of my wine. I knew I'd had too much, but I was past the point of caring.

"You were so quick to realize they'd be able to disprove it," Nicky said.

"Too many crime TV shows."

"No, but that's okay. I know you. You've always assumed the worst of me."

"No, I don't. What are you even talking about?"

"Just don't, Chloe. Okay? I'm fine with it. You checked my cell phone records. Or had the police do it. Or something. But it was obvious to me when you were immediately like, 'Don't be stupid. They'll pull your phone records.'"

My first instinct was to deny it, but I wanted to stop repeating the same old patterns that had kept us practically estranged for a decade and a half. "I'm sorry," I said. "Adam had just been killed. I didn't know who I could trust."

She shook her head. "Like I said, it's fine. I actually get it."

We reached the point where the kitchen could not be any cleaner short of a power wash before either of us spoke again.

"Do you even remember when we used to be close?" she asked. "And I know, you hate talking about the past. 'So much drama,'" she said, impersonating me.

"I am an emotional robot, after all." How many times had she called me that when I refused to reminisce about our childhood? I pushed past my first instinct and forced myself to answer her question. "And, yes, I remember. You used to rush home from school, ignoring the kids playing kickball in the street and Four Square on the corner, just so you could see me." I would wait for her at the window starting a few minutes after three, like a dog waiting for its owner to return. She would take me to the park and push me on the merry-go-round until I screamed for her to stop, even as I giggled wildly. And when it was raining or too cold even for a couple of Cleveland girls, she'd put price tags on a bunch of stuff in the living room and we would play store. It was her way of teaching me how to add and subtract. I wasn't sure whether I really remembered those early scenes or if the memories had been ingrained from all the times Nicky had reminded me of them.

"I was ten years old, and my best friend was a four-year-old. It was probably an early sign of stunted growth," she said dryly.

"Remember when Mom would make us say our prayers at night, and I'd get all scared?"

I had forgotten how much I loved Nicky's belly laugh. "You were terrified every single night that the Lord wouldn't give you your soul back."

Now I lay me down to sleep, I pray the Lord my soul to keep, if I should die before I wake, I pray the Lord my soul to take. Why do we force children to recite something so utterly terrifying?

I had never learned to pray until I was eight years old because my parents didn't go to church until Dad joined AA.

"I was so scared," I recalled. "But then you changed the words for me: 'If I should die before I wake, I'll wait for you at Wallace Lake.'" It was still a creepy thought, but at least Nicky and I would be together in a familiar place.

She broke out into an amused smile, as if she had a private joke. "You have the worst memory—"

"No, I don't."

"Not about everything, but it's like you've got holes in your brain when it comes to Cleveland. It was definitely Shadow Lake, because that's where my friends and I would sneak off on weekends to drink and get high. It was my way of being a wiseass about the fact we had to pray because Dad wanted to stop drinking."

"I missed the joke," I said, feeling slightly sad about her correction.

She shrugged. "Besides, you're the one who liked Wallace Lake for that fishing thing they did for little kids every year. You probably switched them in your head over the years."

I replayed both versions of the rhyme in my head and realized that she was right. It was "I'll wait for you at Shadow Lake."

"Don't look so bummed," she said. "I've seen how you like your wine. It would be a much better afterlife than sitting around waiting for your sister to die, too."

"Good point," I said. She also had a point about my childhood memory having selective gaps. "How long did the prayer phase last?"

"My whole ninth-grade year, into the summer before he fell off the wagon." Eventually sobriety took, but not on our father's first try. By the time the program worked for him, he seemed to focus more on the actual steps than making the rest of us go to church. Nicky moved into the family room and sat down on the sofa. "Do you even remember him drinking?"

Usually I would take a moment like this as my cue to turn in for the night, but I found myself wanting to continue the conversation. Carrying my wine, I joined Nicky on the couch. "Sure. Like if I came home and could hear the Stones playing from the sidewalk, I knew we'd probably find him with a beer in his hand."

"It was never one beer, Chloe. He'd go through a twelve-pack. Mom would be so embarrassed to take the cans back for the deposits that she'd make the two of us do it. Don't you remember that?"

"Maybe." Did I? The cans, yes. That they were beer? Not really.

"Mom and I hated how much you loved him."

The statement was shocking in its clarity. I set my wine on the table. "I don't even know how to process that, Nicky."

"It's fine, you were young. Way too young to understand. But you'd get so happy when he'd crank up the music and grab you and dance in circles. But Mom and I knew that his version of a party was only beginning. Don't you remember how on those nights in particular, she'd make a point of getting you into your pajamas and putting you to bed early? She and I would lower the music a little tiny bit at a time—enough so you could fall asleep, but not so Dad would notice what we were doing and get mad. I've never asked you this, but do you even remember him hitting Mom?"

I nodded. "Of course." Only a few times, always when he was drunk. I couldn't actually picture the images in my head. Did I see it? Or only hear it? Somehow, I knew it had happened.

"So why were you always so much closer to him than to her?"

I honestly didn't know. I had never even thought of it that way. "Is that even up to a kid? It was more like he was the one who decided to be close to me. She wasn't."

"Because she was always trying to manage Dad. You couldn't see that? You didn't see how miserable she was?"

"Of course I did. But at the time, I thought it couldn't be that bad, or she'd leave him. It seemed more like she was using him as an excuse for everything that was wrong with her." I had spent my whole career writing about the power imbalance between men and women and never realized what a hypocrite I was when it came to my own family.

"Like what you think about me?"

How many times had I told Nicky that she had to stop blaming her crappy childhood for her failings as an adult? "No," I said quietly. "At least, not anymore."

"You never understood that you and I basically had different parents. I remember Dad kicking the crap out of Mom while she was huddled in a ball on the floor. I remember him coming home wasted, crawling into my bed, and putting his hand in my panties, thinking I was Mom."

"Oh, Nicky." All this time, my instinct had been to silence her. "I'm sorry. I didn't know."

"You didn't want to know. But it's all right. I get it now. Believing you had a good dad who wanted all of the best things for you allowed you to be who you are now. It's what made you so ambitious. And you're probably right I used him as an excuse to fuck up a good decade and a half of my life."

I could hear the whir of the "whisper-quiet" dishwasher from the kitchen. "What happened that night in the pool with Ethan, Nicky?"

She shook her head. "It was the worst night of my life, and I don't remember any of it."

AS PROMISED, I MANAGED TO wake up and put on my trial face, despite all the wine. When I opened the pantry door to grab some bread for avocado toast, a wild, high-pitched cackle pierced the silence. The battery-activated novelty vampire shook from the overhead light, mocking my gullibility.

Nicky was smirking when she joined me a few minutes later, but the tone of her voice was serious. "Hey, I thought you might want to see this. Jake is quoted. And it's about that company you said Adam kept mentioning."

She handed me her iPad. It was open to a short article in the business section of the *New York Times*. As if reading my mind, Nicky said, "I read everything. One of the upsides of insomnia and not being a pharmaceutical garbage can anymore."

Three days earlier, according to the article, "the Gentry Group, a publicly traded powerhouse in the energy, health-care, and industry sectors, updated its SEC filings to disclose that the London-based company had reserved 400 million pounds for a potential settlement with the DOJ and SEC after receiving notice that certain conduct in countries outside the United States might violate the Federal Corrupt Practices Act or other antibribery laws."

There was a quote from Rives & Braddock attorney Jake Summer: "The Gentry Group is conducting an internal investigation and also plans to cooperate with all investigative agencies. It updated its financial reports in the interest of complete transparency but are confident that any irregularities will be limited in scale and scope in relation to the substantial business operations it oversees globally."

Nowhere in the article did it mention the name Adam Macintosh, his connection to the Gentry Group, or the fact that he had been murdered six months earlier.

28

WORD HAD GOTTEN out that I was expected to testify that day. While the number of cameras in front of the courthouse had dropped over the course of the trial to one or two on an average day, we were greeted by a thick flock of media when we pulled to the curb in front of the squat concrete building.

I was preparing myself mentally to push my way through the crowd as they yelled out questions when I felt the car suddenly accelerate again. In the driver's seat, Nicky was already on her cell phone. I heard her side of the conversation only, first reporting the crowd outside, and then a series of *yeah*s and *uh-huh*s.

"Olivia said she'll have some deputies meet us at a back entrance."

I nodded, still feeling rattled by the sight of the press frenzy. "Well done."

"See, you're not the only Taylor sister who can take care of business," she said with a small smile.

LOOK AT ME. AS NUNZIO asked question after question, all I could think was *Look at me, Ethan. Why aren't you looking at me? The jury sees you. You come off like you're ashamed. You look guilty.*

Olivia leaned over and whispered something in Ethan's ear. A few seconds later, his eyes lifted and locked with mine. I swallowed back a gasp before it could escape my mouth, and then asked Nunzio if he could please repeat the question.

"Is it fair to say that the success of your Them Too series of articles increased your public profile?"

I answered in the affirmative.

"How so?"

Olivia objected to the vagueness of the question, which was sustained.

"For example, do you now get stopped for autographs when you are out and about in public?"

"I have stopped going out into public whenever possible," I said. "For reasons that are probably obvious," I added, looking out at the reporters and miscellaneous onlookers who filled the courtroom.

"Prior to your husband's death, however, and after the success of your Them Too series: during this time, were you asked for autographs?"

The question made him look petty, and for that I was grateful. "Maybe less than a handful of times."

"*Time* magazine listed you as one of the top hundred most influential people of the year?"

"Yes, along with some other journalists. We were part of a group chosen to highlight the power of the First Amendment."

"In fact, you were also lauded by *Glamour, Cosmo, Vanity Fair*, and *Vogue* as a trailblazer last year."

"Not at my asking," I clarified. "I run a much smaller rival magazine, and I'm convinced they all did it to get under my skin."

The quiet laughter appeared to break Nunzio's rhythm momentarily. He didn't want me to be likable. I was going to prove him wrong. I needed this jury to love me so much that they couldn't possibly believe that I would raise a boy who would kill his father.

"You were interviewed by *New York* magazine for tips to your success?"

"That's correct. It's a series for The Cut called 'How I Get it Done.'"

"You did a piece with the *New York Times* about how you spend your Sundays?"

"Yes."

After I responded in the affirmative about my book deal and a few additional accolades, Judge Rivera nudged things along. "I think the jury gets the idea," she said dryly.

"Not all of the effects of the publicity have been positive, though, have they? I'm speaking specifically about your experiences on social media. How would you describe those?"

I had no idea where he was going with this line of questioning, but I tried to use it as an opportunity to connect once again with the jury. I told them how I was nervous about using social media professionally at first. "I was a bit of an old soul, I suppose, chasing a career in traditional print publishing as a very young person, only to see it transformed so quickly once I had a foot in the door. But I've gotten the hang of it. Readers like to see the person behind the written word. My most popular Instagram posts are the ones of our gigantic cat, Greedy Panda."

"You get some negative feedback as well, though." Nunzio didn't even phrase it as a question.

"Yes. Comes with the territory, I'm told."

"You've even received threats, correct?"

"Yes. In fact, when Adam was killed, I expected the police to investigate—"

Nunzio cut my answer off as nonresponsive.

"Based on a review of your social media posts, it appears that you sometimes respond to these comments?"

"Rarely. It's a new world out there. Some people think the best tactic is a good public shaming, but I usually end up ignoring them."

"But you read the feedback?"

"Not every single comment, but yes, I skim through."

Nunzio walked to his counsel table and picked up a piece of paper from a series of stacked piles. "I apologize in advance, but are these comments fairly representative of the negative end of your social media spectrum? 'She's full of herself. Totally fake.' 'Man-hating repressed dyke.' 'Someone needs to shut her mouth with a' and then they use a crude term for a man's genitals. This is part of your usual social media interactions?"

A few of the jurors winced. The woman who worked at the outlet mall gasped out loud. Olivia and I had been planning to introduce this evidence to suggest that a stranger may have targeted our house. Nunzio appeared to be putting it out there before we could.

"Yes, unfortunately," I said. "I received—and still receive—multiple rape threats on a daily basis."

"Do these comments tend to come from a wide number of users, or is it a small number of people writing multiple comments each?"

"There's no way to know, really, because one person could in theory have two hundred accounts with different user names. I'd say there are a number of account names I'd recognize as repeat offenders, but usually it's just some random person spouting off."

"How about Bilbo B? Does that sound familiar?"

"I believe so."

"Alpha3?"

"No, but that doesn't mean there haven't been posts."

"KurtLoMein?"

"Yes, that one I remember. The irony is that my husband was a big Nirvana fan—the lead singer was Kurt Cobain—so the name stuck. But I don't want to give these people any further attention, if you don't mind, Mr. Nunzio."

"Fair enough," he said, setting down the sheet of paper he'd been reading from. "And have you ever spoken to your stepson, the defendant, about his feelings regarding your work?"

Olivia objected on the basis of the state's privilege for parent-child communications. I didn't mind answering this particular question, but my guess was that she was raising the privilege now so we could learn one way or the other whether the judge was going to apply it to my relationship with Ethan.

Rivera beckoned both lawyers to the bench. A few minutes of whispering later, she directed me to answer the question. Apparently I was not, in this court's view, Ethan's parent.

Nunzio repeated the question about Ethan's feelings toward my career. "If he sees my name trending or something, he might mention it to make sure I know. He's made it clear he's proud of me. When I received an important award last May, he attended the ceremony with me. If you watch the YouTube footage of it, you can hear a couple of guys whistling and cheering. That was Ethan and Adam." I smiled sadly at the memory. It seemed like another lifetime. I remembered thinking at that moment that maybe Adam and I were going to be okay after all.

Nunzio suddenly shifted gears, turning to a series of questions about the security alarm at the house.

"Isn't it true that you and your family regularly set the alarm each time you entered and exited the house?"

"Not every time, I'm certain of that."

"More often than not?"

"I wouldn't think so."

I had practiced this subject area with Olivia and made Nunzio earn every piece of information. He was, however, eventually able to establish that I had twice told the police that we rarely used the alarm, but that records from the alarm company demonstrated routine use. He had already brought in an employee from the security company to establish that on the night of Adam's murder, the alarm had been set shortly before I left for dinner, disarmed when Adam was dropped off, rearmed shortly after 9:30 p.m., and then disarmed once again at 11:10, about twenty minutes after Kevin Dunham claimed to have dropped Ethan off at the beach.

"So despite your claim that your family rarely used the alarm except when you were in the city or sleeping out at the home alone, that very night, it was turned on and off four times in a matter of a few hours."

"Yes, apparently."

"You say that as if you're surprised, Ms. Taylor. Are you claiming not to have known that your own security alarm was used regularly?"

"Of course not. In hindsight, after seeing the records, I realize it's one of those things that has become so routine that I don't even think about it anymore."

"When you came home and found your husband murdered, and your home apparently broken into, didn't you wonder why the alarm never sounded?"

"I assumed it wasn't set."

"Isn't it true, Ms. Taylor, that you lied to the police about rarely using the alarm because you yourself wondered why an intrusion hadn't set off the alarm?"

I looked at Olivia and then the judge. "I'm not sure I even understand that question."

"I'll be more clear. Isn't it true that you suspected your stepson Ethan from the moment you first spoke to the police?"

"No, that's absolutely false."

"Let me ask you this, Ms. Taylor. Who other than you, Adam, and the defendant knew the code to your security system at the time of the murder?"

"The housekeeper and a handyman."

"And after your husband was killed, did you change the security code?"

It seemed like a silly question until I was about to answer it. No, I hadn't changed it. Someone had broken into my house, killed my husband, and disarmed the alarm, and I was still using the same code. Why hadn't I changed it? I shot a quick glance at Olivia. Her expression was blank. There was no way to avoid the question. I had to answer.

"No," I said.

Before I could figure out whether the jury would read into my failure to change the alarm code, Nunzio had shifted gears again and was asking me about Adam's intention to send Ethan away to military school.

"He never mentioned that to me," I said. "My guess is he wasn't serious about—"

Nunzio objected to my speculation, and the judge directed me to answer only the posed question.

"Is it fair to say that your husband and stepson had a tense relationship before the murder?"

Olivia objected on the basis of vagueness.

"Would you say that your husband and stepson were close?" he asked instead.

I answered affirmatively even as Olivia was objecting.

"Did they argue?" he asked.

"Of course, all kids argue with their parents. But it was normal stuff—was he doing all his homework, how late could he stay out, that kind of thing." I looked over at Ethan. He was gripping the edges of his chair's armrests.

Nunzio walked to his counsel table and picked up one of several thin stacks of paper lined in a row. I could see that some lines had been highlighted. "You're a loser, a druggie zombie." Olivia was on her feet, objecting, but Nunzio kept reading. "You're losing your mind, just like your mother. Is that what you want? To be a dysfunctional invalid?"

I didn't know the source for the phrases Nunzio was quoting, but it was obvious whom they were about. I tried not to look at Nicky as Olivia argued. I was convinced that as long as she didn't have to see my eyes right now, she'd be able to make it through this without breaking down.

"This is outrageous, Your Honor. I have no idea what the prosecutor is reading from. It has not been provided to the defense in discovery, and I see no basis for its relevance."

Judge Rivera called the lawyers to the bench again, and this time I could overhear bits and pieces of their conversation. *Said they were normal father/son. Impeach her testimony. Discovery violation. Ambush.*

When their huddle broke up, Rivera announced that the jury should ignore the material that Nunzio had read from the documents, and then Nunzio announced that he had no further questions for me. Olivia had no cross-examination, but reserved her right to call me back to the stand as a defense witness. Rivera then announced a brief recess so the lawyers could confer with her privately.

I was stepping down from the witness chair as Ethan rose from his to follow Olivia into the judge's chambers. As we passed each other, I reached out a hand, and his fingertips grazed mine. The sheriff's deputy at his side shook his head sternly, but I mouthed a silent "Thank you" for the brief moment.

Once I resumed my spot next to Nicky, she leaned close to my ear. Her whisper was intense. "What was all that loser druggie stuff he was reading?"

I shook my head. I had no idea, but it sounded exactly like something Adam would say.

NICKY AND I REMAINED IN our seats for the entire recess. We had learned that reporters who had no qualms about yelling out questions and snapping photographs in the hallways and restrooms would not approach us within the four walls of this courtroom.

Nearly forty minutes later, Nunzio, Olivia, and Ethan emerged from the judge's chambers. The bailiff headed for the courtroom exit, which I had learned was a sign that he would soon return with the jurors.

To my surprise, Olivia bypassed the counsel table and crossed the bar into our section of the courtroom. "I need poker faces from both of you right now, okay?" Neither of us flinched. "We'll only have one more witness today, and I don't want the jury here looking at the two of you when he testifies. So you're going to stand up right now, walk out calmly, and go back to the hotel and wait for me."

"Is this about the argument Nunzio seemed to be quoting between Adam and Ethan?"

She shook her head. "No, but we need to talk about that, too, so I'll meet you after court lets out."

"Olivia, what's going on?"

"Poker faces, remember?" We both nodded. "The next witness is the police department's tech guy. Ethan is KurtLoMein. Now go."

29

OLIVIA HAD ONLY one copy of the printout. I held it while Nicky and I read it together, perched side by side on the edge of the hotel bed.

It included every single message that KurtLoMein had ever posted on Poppit. The bulk of them were about video games like Fortnite and 2K, but a disturbing number hinted at feelings of isolation and resentment, both against parents who no longer seemed to understand him and girls who refused to pay attention to him. He was also a frequent participant in threads about #ThemToo and specifically about me.

It wasn't only the clever name that had made this Poppit user stand out. Instead of the typical let's-all-rape-the-man-hater posts, the person always wrote with such authority, appearing to claim some form of insider knowledge. He portrayed me as weaker and less secure than the persona I had managed to cultivate. That I was only pretending to be strong. That I was a hypocrite. Full of tough talk about the world needing to change the way it treats women, but she's a coward in her own life. Cares more about her picture-perfect image than actual reality. That one had hit particularly close to home, and now I knew why.

In fact, every one of KurtLoMein's posts about me was negative, until the final one—a reply to widespread speculation on the website that I had killed Adam: We shouldn't jump to conclusions. For all we know, she's a victim, too. The note was published only hours before Ethan was arrested for the crime.

"How can they be sure this was Ethan?" I asked.

"They can't, but they definitely know it came from his laptop, which was logged in variously at your apartment, house, and Camden Prep. We'll lose the jury if we even try to argue it's someone else."

"But maybe Ethan knows who—"

Then I realized she would have already asked him. Ethan would have already confirmed that he had written these awful things about me.

"Why did he do it?" I asked.

"That's not for me to try to explain to you. I'll argue that kids say things they don't mean when they're online. I've already got a call in to an expert witness from Yale who writes about adolescent social media use."

"Most of those jurors have kids," I said. I couldn't stop rereading the words, each one like a punch to the stomach. "They're going to know this isn't normal."

"Unfortunately, we also need to talk about this." She opened her laptop and clicked on a message near the top of the in-box. As the attachment slowly downloaded, she explained what we were about to see. "The quotes Nunzio started to read from in the courtroom? When he asked about tension between Ethan and Adam?" We both nodded to indicate we remembered. "The police found a video on Ethan's laptop. It looks like he recorded this without Adam knowing about it. It was two weeks before the murder."

We sat in silence until the file had downloaded. Olivia hit play.

WE WERE ALL THE WAY to the Montauk Highway before Nicky turned off the Howard Stern station.

"So how often was Adam like that?" she asked.

With my eyes closed and seat reclined, all I wanted was to float away until I never had to answer another question about Adam again. "Never. Not for the first ten years he was here, at least."

I tilted my head and could see Nicky running the numbers. "So the last two years?"

"Not even. And then it wasn't all the time. One or two blowups at first, and then more, and worse. It was this slow-building burn."

I had no way of knowing whether the incident on Olivia's laptop was the only time Ethan had seen his father that out of control, but the fact that he'd recorded the incident suggested that it was not. According to Olivia, Nunzio claimed not to have disclosed the video earlier because it wasn't relevant until I testified that Adam and Ethan were close and had a normal father-son relationship. Judge Rivera had lectured Nunzio for playing games with discovery, but she would nevertheless allow him to show the jury the video in the morning.

In it, Adam was even worse than he'd been when he found the bag of pot. Worse, even, than after the gun fiasco. Not as mean as he'd been with me at times, but much crueler and more heartless than I ever could have imagined him being with Ethan.

Nunzio had provided a transcript, the pages he'd begun to read from when questioning me.

ETHAN: Oh my god, Dad. You just sent me to my room and then you come in here to keep yelling at me.

ADAM: Because your room is your fucking sanctuary. Your room is where you can throw your three-hundred-dollar sweaters on the floor, pull on your thousand-dollar headphones, and disappear onto a computer that lets you ignore the real world.

ETHAN: What exactly do you want from me right now? To clean my room? Fine, I'll clean my room.

ADAM: I want you to get your act together. You're walking

through life like nothing matters. You don't focus on school. You don't have hobbies. Chloe put you in that school full of spoiled brats so you'd have all the contacts to open all the doors she thinks matter, and you don't have a single friend there.

ETHAN: That's not true—

ADAM: Instead, you hang out with losers who have you selling drugs. You're carrying around a gun.

ETHAN: Jesus, Dad, I told you a million times. It wasn't my pot, and I was just, I don't know with the gun. Like, trying to get attention or something.

ADAM: Well, you've got mine, that's for sure. I don't know when you got like this, son.

ETHAN: Like what?

ADAM: You're a loser, a druggie zombie. Don't you even see that you're losing your mind, just like your mother? Is that what you want? To be a dysfunctional invalid?

Even the harshness of the transcript wasn't as blistering as the actual video, where Adam was screaming, waving his arms around, his face red, as Ethan sat on the bed, his knees pulled to his chest. I knew what it was like to be him in that moment—to be willing to do anything, *anything*, to make the shouting stop.

I pictured Ethan walking home from the beach, stoned from hanging out with Kevin, and encountering Adam when he thought the house would be empty. If Adam had laid into him? If Ethan was maybe carrying a knife to be cool, the way he'd shown off that gun? Could the bad, dark side of Adam have brought out a bad, dark side of his son?

I had no idea how to explain to Nicky how it had all started. "I never should have pushed Adam to go to the law firm. He was so resentful. I think he felt pressured to do it because I was earning more—like, a *lot* more—and he felt like he had to keep up. Every single day, the hatred for that job kept building. And he was drinking. A lot."

"That doesn't excuse him for being a fucking asshole."

No, it didn't, and that's why I had felt entitled to start what I had with Jake. "I swear, the only time I saw him act that way with Ethan was once when he found pot, and once with the gun. And under the circumstances, I couldn't say he was completely wrong either time."

"That wasn't easy for me to watch, Chloe. Is that what you guys told Ethan about me all these years? That I was a druggie and an invalid?"

"No, of course not." We never used those words, but of course Ethan knew that Nicky's problems had led to his moving to New York with only his father.

"Because that's exactly how Adam used to talk to me," she said. "When no one was around. He'd seem like perfect, sweet Adam one minute, and then I'd make too much noise cleaning the kitchen while he was studying and suddenly he'd be screaming at me, telling me I had no idea the pressure he was under because I hadn't even gone to college. He'd belittle me and make me feel worthless. If I tried to argue with him or walk away, he'd grab me so hard, I'd see those little oval bruises on my arms for days. And then for a while, everything was fine again after I got pregnant, but once the baby was born, I just couldn't be who he needed me to be. It took me forever to realize it was probably normal postpartum, but I was inhaling booze, antidepressants, sleeping pills—anything to make it feel okay for just a little while, day by day. I remember him screaming at me like that. Telling me I was a 'loser' and didn't deserve him or the baby. He'd do these little slaps on my face"— her fingertips of one hand whipped across her cheekbone—"telling me that I wasn't listening to him."

I shook my head. "You never said anything," I muttered.

"I did. Yes, I did! When the two of you had me committed after what happened in the pool, I tried to explain."

But by then, I didn't believe her. I thought she was blaming Adam for her problems, just like she had always blamed our father. Even after

I saw how Adam had changed over the last year, I never connected his anger—not once—to what had happened between him and Nicky. Maybe I just didn't want to think of myself as being like Nicky.

"Why didn't you say anything while it was actually happening?" The tone of my voice made it clear that I wasn't blaming her. I believed her and was trying to understand.

Her knuckles were tight around the steering wheel. She was quiet when she finally answered. "Because I loved him. And I felt lucky to have him. I told myself he was under a lot of pressure and I wasn't doing a good enough job. Do you know what I used to do to try to make him happy? I'd ask myself, 'What would Chloe do?'"

My eyes welled up at how painful that must have been for her. I didn't know what to say, so I said nothing, and let her continue. "I remember you telling me how good I looked when I went to my high school reunion that summer. I was dressed like you. I *acted* like you. I wanted to show up seeming smart and successful and confident, so I was like, fuck it, I'll just impersonate Chloe for a weekend. And Adam obviously liked it. I felt like I was faking during our entire relationship."

I understood now why she had been so certain when Adam moved to New York that it was to be with me.

"And, let's face it, compared to the shit Mom went through with Dad, it didn't seem that bad. He never actually *hit* me."

I could see her looking at me even as she tried to keep her eyes on the road. Was she waiting for me to say something?

"Well, I'm still sorry." We both knew it was a lame response. She turned on the radio when it became clear I had no follow-up.

Two miles later, I was the one to turn it off. "What if we had been boys?"

"What kind of question is that?" she asked.

"Growing up in our house, with the same mom and dad. The same dysfunction. You rebelled. I became a control freak. But what if we'd been boys?" I remembered an article I had read about boys and mass shootings. It dovetailed with my research into the dark fringes of the web, where aggrieved young men raged against society—and against girls in particular—for not giving them their due. "When girls feel lost, they hurt themselves. Boys hurt others."

"Ethan's a good kid. Don't go down this road."

"What would have happened if that kid hadn't told the principal about the gun Ethan had?"

"But that was a mix-up with carrying stuff back and forth from the house."

I shook my head. "That was bullshit, Nicky. We weren't carrying a gun into the city, and we definitely weren't putting anything in Ethan's backpack. He told me he was just trying to look like a tough kid to stand out from the crowd. I should have taken it more seriously."

"So what are you saying?"

"I didn't change the alarm code, Nicky. Why didn't I change it?"

She had been living with me for nearly six months now, and we were both still using those same six digits, Ethan's birthday, every time we walked in and out of the East Hampton house. If I really thought a stranger had murdered Adam, why hadn't I changed the code? Why hadn't Nicky asked me to change it?

Neither one of us was going to say it out loud, though.

"Maybe Olivia can do something with that newspaper article," Nicky said.

I had given her this morning's *New York Times* write-up about the corruption investigation into the Gentry Group. "Like she keeps saying, we only need reasonable doubt. And only one undecided juror is enough to get a mistrial." Neither of us sounded optimistic. "So when all this is over, what are we going to do?"

"What do you mean?"

"When Ethan comes home." We both knew I was trying to give us hope. "You're his biological mother, but he's been living with me, and Adam's will put me down as the guardian. My understanding is that a judge would look at the best interests of the child if we fought each other for custody." When Adam was first killed, I had prayed that Nicky would be too dumb to realize that I wouldn't automatically be the legal guardian, but now I was the one broaching the subject.

"Why would we fight?"

"Because we're the Taylor sisters."

She let out a soft laugh and then let herself play with the hypothetical of seeing Ethan come home. "Your lawyers would probably run me over, especially since you're obviously banging one of them." This time, her laugh was louder. "And he's not a little kid anymore. He'd be eighteen by the time any court was done with us. So, we're not doing that, okay?"

"So what would we do?"

She shrugged. "We'll figure it out. But just so you know, Chloe, when the police called me about Adam, I only came to New York to make sure you and Ethan were okay. I wanted you to see me in person so you'd know I had changed and that you could rely on me for help if you needed it. But it never dawned on me—not even once—to try to take Ethan from you." I turned to face the passenger window and wiped away the tears that were forming. "I know you're kicking yourself now, but you raised my kid well. You gave him a better life than I ever would have, that's for sure. We're fine on that. I promise."

The next thing I remember is Nicky waking me up as we pulled into the driveway.

"Olivia texted us. She thinks Ethan needs to testify after all."

30

I T WAS JENNIFER Guidry's first full day off in two weeks. Between testifying and running point for the Ethan Macintosh trial
and working the arson investigation with the fire department, she had
racked up enough overtime to cover all her Christmas shopping for the
year, but she was ready for a break. Amy couldn't take a day off from
the bank, but in truth, Guidry was downright giddy about having an
entire day to herself.

She was on her third cup of coffee at Babette's, treating herself to
the salmon omelet—extra scallions—and a leisurely browse of all the
papers. Her ritual was to start local with the *East Hampton Star*, then
to *Newsday* for the rest of Long Island, then on to the *New York Times*
for the national stuff. She was relieved to see that not one of the papers
had yet figured out what she and the fire department already knew: the
blaze at the $40 million oceanfront mansion of an A-list director had
been intentional. The director himself had hired a special effects guy to
make it look like an electric fire. Absent a leak from the investigative
team, the news wouldn't become public until the director was picked up
on a warrant in Los Angeles later on tonight.

"Top off?" It was Ivy the waitress, offering even more coffee. Guidry happened to know that Ivy had originally been hired just for the season, needing a job of her own while her boyfriend had a gig doing private security for a party club out in Montauk. She didn't press charges after police responded to a Labor Day weekend 911 call at their summer rental, but she did move out. Now she had joined Guidry and countless others who had come out to the East End to hang on the beach for one young summer, only to start a whole new life.

"Better not, or I'll never make it through my beach walk without a bathroom break." Fall was Guidry's favorite time of year. The summer crowd was gone, the leaves had turned, and the waves were roaring. She knew Amy, for all her strengths as a girlfriend, never gave Cosmo a proper walk, and she was looking forward to seeing her beautiful boxer gallop unleashed along Maidstone.

While she waited for the check, she flipped through the one untouched section of the *Times*, the business section, in the interest of completeness. "Gentry Reports FBI Investigation."

Something about the company name sounded familiar. It was described as a "publicly traded powerhouse in the energy, health-care, and industry sectors," not exactly the crime and political news that Guidry tended to follow. But then she came to a quote from the company's lawyer, Jake Summer of the New York City law firm Rives & Braddock: "The Gentry Group is conducting an internal investigation and also plans to cooperate with all investigative agencies."

The Gentry Group was the company Chloe Taylor kept mentioning when she was trying to figure out where Adam Macintosh had spent the last two days of his life. Guidry had done the legwork of reaching out to Uber, but she hadn't learned anything beyond what Chloe already knew—that he'd been dropped off and picked up at the Kew Gardens train station. Once the investigation pointed to his son, Ethan, she had dropped the inquiry.

The year before, Guidry had been a small part of a big mail theft case that sprawled from Queens to Brooklyn and through Nassau and

Suffolk Counties. The defendants had washed and forged millions of dollars in checks. When Guidry drove to the FBI regional office handling the investigation, she had parked next to the Kew Gardens train station.

She was still thinking about that when she was about to start the engine of her CRV. It's one phone call, she thought. What's the harm?

She searched her old emails, trying to remember the agent's name. How could she have forgotten? He was a nice guy. Cute, too, and had asked her to dinner. She still felt a little guilty for not telling him the real reason she didn't accept the offer.

Damon Katz. There it was. She tapped the phone number in his email signature line to make the call and got his voice mail after three rings.

"Agent Katz, this is Detective Jennifer Guidry from Suffolk County Police. I think you'll remember me from that Tobin and DeLaglio investigation a couple of years ago. I'm hoping you can help me out with something. Any chance your office had any contacts with Adam Macintosh last spring? Perhaps something to do with a company called the Gentry Group—I'm wondering if he might have been at your offices on two specific days in May. Give me a call when you can."

By the time she pulled out onto Newtown, she'd told herself he'd never call back. There was no way the FBI was going to call some Long Island detective about a pending case. She didn't even know why she was curious. Ethan Macintosh was their guy. She had called it, almost from the start.

31

LOOKING AT ETHAN on the witness stand, I was able to see how much he had changed in the six months since his arrest. His chest and shoulders were broader, and his voice was lower. Now that his face was more defined, his chin and jawline were just like Adam's. He wasn't quite an adult, but nothing about him looked boyish anymore.

Nicky and I knew Olivia had spent hours with Ethan, preparing him to testify, but we had no idea what he would actually say. We wanted to believe that Olivia was putting Ethan on the stand because his innocence would be obvious to the jury once they heard his side of the story. But more likely she was doing it because she believed he'd be convicted unless he gave it a shot.

He grew more comfortable speaking in the courtroom as Olivia posed a series of basic questions about where he was born, when he moved to New York, where he lived, and other background information. Once he seemed at ease, she walked him through his time line for the night of the murder. For the most part, his version lined up with Kevin Dunham's. They were together all night except for a one-hour window. The only variation was the reason for the separation. Kevin had testified that Ethan was supposed to meet someone on the beach to sell some pot, while Ethan claimed he had asked to be left at the beach while Kevin finished a deal.

Olivia showed Ethan a list of the items we had reported stolen from the house after Adam's murder, and then showed him a matching list of the items seized from the top shelf of his bedroom closet in the city. "Now, are the three items from your closet the same things that were reported missing from your house?"

"Yes."

"And how did those items come to be on your top shelf?"

"I put them there."

"Do you remember when you put them there?"

"Yes. It was Saturday night."

"Which Saturday was that?" she asked.

"Sorry. The night after my dad was killed. Mom and I drove back to the city that afternoon."

Olivia stated the exact date in May to clarify, which Ethan confirmed.

"Were you in possession of those three items when you left East Hampton and went to the city that afternoon?" Olivia asked.

"No."

"So where were those items immediately before you put them on the top shelf in your closet?"

"In my bedroom."

"Which bedroom?"

"Sorry, my bedroom in the city."

"Please explain why you placed those items in your closet."

"Mom had gone to bed, and I knew there was no way I was going to fall asleep. I kept thinking, He's never coming back, he's never coming back. Even now, it seems hard to believe, but that first night was . . . really hard. And I was looking around my room, thinking about all the times I didn't listen to him. And disappointed him." His face wrinkled, and I could tell he was fighting back the urge to cry. "He was always telling me my room was a pigsty . . . if pigs hoarded overpriced clothes," he added with a sad smile. "So I started cleaning up my room. And I found the stuff we told the police was missing."

Olivia showed him a photograph of his bedroom, printed from a still shot of the video the jury had already seen when he was arguing with Adam. She then showed him a photograph that the police had taken of his bedroom during a search of our apartment on the day he was arrested. It was clear that his room was cleaner in the second image.

"So why did you put those items in the closet instead of, for example, telling your stepmother you had found them?"

Ethan looked down, appearing ashamed, and then gazed up again. "I figured they had already been reported stolen anyway, so I might as well keep them. It was stupid. And wrong."

"So why did you do it?"

"I was scared. I had seen how much more money we had recently, and I thought it was because Dad was working at a law firm. I was afraid we were going to be broke and figured some insurance company wouldn't miss a couple thousand dollars. I was going to sell the stuff if we ever needed money."

It was a plausible explanation. The jury didn't know, however, what I knew. Ethan had asked me to go to Kevin's on Saturday afternoon for his backpack, but later that night, the backpack was empty except for a burner phone.

He also had an explanation for secretly videotaping Adam in his room. "He was just so disappointed in me—making it sound like I was a really bad kid. I mean, I'm not perfect. I could follow every piece of advice he ever gave me, and I'd never be first in my class or the ninety-ninth percentile like him and my mom."

"Just to be clear for the jury, you mean your stepmother, Chloe Taylor, correct?"

He nodded and then said "Yes" for the court reporter. "Yeah, but

I call her Mom. I mean, she's always accepted the way I am, but Dad was really upset that I wasn't more like them. He was making it sound like I was going off the deep end. And, yes, he was even talking about sending me away to military school. So I recorded him. I was thinking it would be like an intervention or something—like when that girl put up an Insta story about her dad getting wasted all night. But I wasn't going to go public or anything. I was just going to show him that *he* was the one who was acting crazy when we argued. I was normal. I *am* normal. And now I feel like the police are treating me like I'm some horrible kid, too."

When he wiped his face with his palms, he momentarily looked like a child again.

"So did you ever show that video to your father?"

He shook his head.

"You need to answer aloud," she reminded him.

"No. I felt too bad about it. I didn't want to hurt his feelings." His face pruned again, and this time he couldn't stop the tears. He sniffed a few times and ran the sleeve of his suit jacket across his eyes, regaining his composure.

"There's one more thing I need to talk to you about, Ethan. You said before that you refer to your stepmother, Chloe Taylor, as Mom. Do you love her?"

"Yes."

"Are you proud of her?"

"Very. I mean, look at everything she's done."

"Did you write those posts on the Poppit website about her, under the name KurtLoMein?"

He looked at me with pain in his eyes as he answered quietly. "Yes."

"Why?"

"I honestly don't know. It's just . . . everything was changing. She always worked hard, but then she got sort of famous because of her magazine. Then when the Them Too stuff blew up, she was like a hero to people. She was busy all the time, and even when she was home, she was writing in her office or looking at her social. I think—"

"You mean social media?" Olivia clarified.

"Yeah. Like Twitter, Facebook, Instagram. Dad would tell her she was worse than a teenager, and she'd say he didn't understand the pressure she was under. That she had twenty-five-year-olds nipping at her heels who'd steal her job the second she fell behind the digital trend." The eyes of several jurors moved in my direction. It was clear that no sixteen-year-old would have come up with that sentence unless he'd heard it repeatedly from an adult. "I think I was hoping to get her attention, because I knew she read what people were saying about her online."

"Finally, Ethan, just to be clear: Did you go to your house any time after Kevin picked you up on Friday night, or before you returned with your mother on Saturday morning?"

"No."

"Did you kill your father, Adam Macintosh?"

"No, I swear."

"I have no further questions, Your Honor."

IF ETHAN'S DIRECT EXAMINATION HAD earned him any sympathy at all, it had not worked with ADA Nunzio. He stood only two feet from the witness chair, his voice bellowing with skepticism and indignation. He had purposely positioned himself to obscure Ethan's view of Olivia and therefore also Nicky and me, who were seated behind her.

He poked tiny holes in every aspect of Ethan's testimony. On the time line, he prodded Ethan to account for the hour he had been alone on the beach, making it sound nearly impossible that a teenage boy could spend an hour of solitude without sending a single text or social media post. On the marijuana, he asked question after question about the price of Ethan's various possessions, arguing that he, not Kevin, must have been the one selling pot. On the items seized from the top shelf of his closet, he ridiculed the idea that a kid of Ethan's means would believe that a few used luxuries could make a dent in the household budget.

Through it all, Olivia made repeated objections—hearsay, relevance, vagueness, speculation—until Nunzio finally accused her of trying to break up any rhythm he had for the cross-examination.

"I won't speculate on an attorney's motives," Judge Rivera said, "but I share his concern, Ms. Randall. You know how a trial works. It's his turn to ask questions."

As Nunzio's momentum built, so did his aggression. "Isn't it true that you took those items to falsely stage a burglary after you killed your father so he would not send you away to military school?"

"No, that is not true!"

"In fact, isn't that why you posted such hateful things about your stepmother? The woman who had always coddled you, apologized for you, made excuses for you—even after you brought a gun to school—was suddenly too busy to get your back."

Ethan was shaking his head, saying "No" over and over again, while Olivia objected that Nunzio was badgering the witness. Stop, I was thinking. Please, someone, just make it stop.

Nunzio began to read from the Poppit posts. "She's *weak*, you said. A *hypocrite*. A *coward*. *Cares more about her picture-perfect image than actual reality.* You said those things because Chloe Taylor was no longer protecting you from your father's discipline, and so you took matters into your own hands."

"Your Honor, Mr. Nunzio is *abusing* this witness."

Just as the judge was overruling the objection, Ethan slammed his hands down on the railing in front of him. "You're twisting it all around. I was just trying to get her attention. All I meant is that she was more worried about what other people thought of her than what was going on in our own house!"

"And what was going on in your own house is that your father was finally done allowing you to set your own rules, isn't that right?"

"No."

"And when you could no longer get your way, all the time, you decided to kill him, didn't you?"

"No!"

"Is that why you were carrying that gun in your backpack? Had you been planning before to shoot him?"

Olivia, the judge, and Ethan were all speaking at once. "No foundation, Your Honor." "Overruled." "What? No, are you kidding?"

"Is that why your father got rid of the gun? To protect himself from you?"

"Jesus, no! He was beating the shit out of her, okay? And she let him do it, and that's why I recorded him."

I heard someone gasp behind me as Nicky placed her hand on my knee and gave it a tight squeeze.

"Your Honor—"

The judge held up a hand and shot Olivia a stern look that sent her back into her chair.

"Is that why you stabbed your father?" Nunzio demanded. "To protect your stepmother because he was abusing her?"

Ethan leaned back in his chair and looked down at his lap. "No," he mumbled. "I swear, I didn't do it, but maybe I should have."

OLIVIA ASKED CALMLY FOR A recess, but Judge Rivera ordered her to ask her questions or waive her right to redirect. She rose as if she were completely prepared for the moment.

"Ethan, I know the prosecutor wants to make this seem like a big dramatic discovery—"

Nunzio wasn't even out of his chair before Rivera admonished Olivia to avoid unnecessary commentary.

"Very well. Just to be clear, though, when you spoke to Detective Guidry the morning after your father died, did she *ask* you whether there was any acrimony between your father and stepmother?"

"No." He was still rattled, but his voice was calm and level.

"Did she ask whether your father was violent toward your stepmother?"

"No."

"It was pretty clear that you didn't want that known, in fact. Is that right?"

He nodded, and then added "Yes" for the record.

"All right. But now that it's out there, you saw your father, Adam Macintosh, use violence against your stepmother, Chloe Taylor?" Olivia deserved an Academy Award for acting as if this was all old news to her—a mere distraction by the prosecution—but I was absolutely certain this was the first she had heard of it.

"No, I didn't actually see it happening. But I could hear it. They think when I'm in my room, all I do is listen to my Beats, and it's like I'm not there. But I could tell when there was tension. I'd listen when they were fighting. I was afraid they'd get divorced, because Chloe's basically my mom, and I didn't know what would happen if they split up. And some of the fights were . . . bad, really bad, like I could hear thuds and stuff. And then a few times, it was clear he was hurting her."

I realized I was biting my lower lip so hard I had drawn blood. The metallic taste was the same as the one time Adam punched me in the face with a closed fist. When people saw the bruise on my cheek and the cut on my mouth, I told them, "Can you believe I *actually* walked into a wall? Adam says I need a better cover story, or the police are going to come for him." And then everyone would laugh.

"How could you tell he was hurting Chloe, Ethan?"

"Because she'd literally be screaming, 'Adam, you're hurting me.' But when he got mad, you couldn't get him to stop. And that's why I taped him. I couldn't figure out a good way to tape him hurting her, so

I decided to record him yelling at me, so he'd at least see how crazy he got when he was angry."

"And to be clear, did your father ever hit you?"

"No."

"And does any of this have anything whatsoever to do with your father's murder?"

"No, because I didn't do it."

"And why didn't you tell anyone earlier about your father's violence toward your stepmother?"

"Because she obviously didn't want anyone to know, or else she would have done something."

Just like KurtLoMein said, I was weak. A coward. A hypocrite. I was just like my mother.

32

I NEED TO talk to Ethan. There has to be a way."
Olivia and Nicky had managed to get me out of the courthouse
when I was refusing to leave unless Judge Rivera permitted me to
see Ethan. Because I was a witness in the case, I was prohibited from
speaking to him until the trial was over, but I needed him to know
that I shouldn't have allowed it to happen. I should have protected him
better. Now I was pacing the length of Olivia's hotel suite like a caged
animal, trying to imagine the guilt and fear Ethan had to be struggling
with right now.

"Chloe! You have to listen to me."

"Do you want me to slap her?" Nicky said from the sofa. "I've
always wanted to."

I stopped pacing and stared at her. "Seriously, Nicky? Only you
would make that joke after what just happened in the courtroom."

"It worked, didn't it? Olivia's trying to explain something to you."

"It would be malpractice for me to let my client speak to a witness
directly in the middle of a trial, especially after a moment like that one.
But I know you, Chloe, okay? After six months, I think I know you.
I will speak to him. I promise you. And I will let him know what you

need me to tell him, short of coordinating testimony. Do you understand?"

I nodded and took a deep breath, trying to slow the pulse that I felt
throbbing against my right temple.

"So can we talk about his testimony, please? Nicky, maybe you can
wait in your room—"

"No, it's fine. I want her to stay." I took a seat on the sofa next to
Nicky. "I almost told you last night, when you were talking about you
and Adam. It was . . . exactly what the last year had been like with us.
It started out how you were saying—he grabbed my arm once when
I was walking away from one of his rants. I told him that if he ever
touched me out of anger again, I was done. But then it did happen
again. He pushed me—hard—but I told myself in the morning that
he was drunk, and I had been up in his face, yelling about something I
can't even remember now. But the line was crossed."

Adam's job as a prosecutor had served more than his identity as one
of the good guys—it had given him a feeling of power. Once it was
gone, he went searching for that sense of control under his own roof,
but nothing I did kept him satisfied for long.

"It got worse," I said, not wanting to relive the details, "but I just
kept moving the goalposts. I wanted to leave, but I couldn't. And not
the way other women say they can't leave. I really couldn't leave."

Nicky rolled her eyes.

"What was that?"

"Nothing."

"You rolled your eyes."

Olivia interrupted. "You guys. Maybe—"

"Don't you see, Chloe?" Nicky stood and moved to the conference
table, creating space between us. "You're *just* like every other woman
who didn't leave. Mom. Me. You. Same."

"Bullshit. I couldn't leave because I had no rights to Ethan. How
many times have I been reminded during this trial that I'm *only* his

stepmother? I'm the one he calls Mom. I'm the one who raised him. But I never could adopt him, which meant I couldn't leave."

"So this is *my* fault?"

"No, that's not what I said."

"But it's what you were thinking. Jesus, Chloe, why didn't you tell me any of this? I could've been there for you. We could have helped each other."

"Because it was no one's fucking business, okay?!" Nicky's eyes widened and she blew out a puff of air. Olivia was standing between us awkwardly. I was the crazy person in the room now. This was yet another reason why I didn't want anyone to know. "Fine, I'm a hypocrite, just like Ethan said. How was it going to look that Chloe Taylor, one of the queens of the movement, was letting her husband hit her every few weeks? And in the meantime, I kept telling myself it was just a phase. I didn't want to think he was actually a bad guy. It was easier for me to believe this was something recent. Situational. And I felt responsible, because I had made him feel emasculated. I felt so ashamed, but I told myself I was somehow retaining my dignity by . . . well, you know."

I saw no reason to tell Olivia about my affair with Jake.

Olivia cleared her throat. "You obviously have a lot to talk about, but I think we should focus on Ethan for now."

"What if he did this to protect me?" I blurted. "Is it too late to claim self-defense or something?"

"Well, if he did it to protect you, it would be defense of a third party, and that would only be if he stopped him from an ongoing or imminent attack. And if he tried to claim that he was defending *himself*, no one would believe it. Not after all this time."

"What about temporary insanity or emotional distress?" It felt like random words I'd read in crime novels were spilling from my mouth. "What if Ethan did go back to the house after Kevin dropped him off at the beach? Maybe they were arguing, and he was high." It was the first time I had voiced the possibility aloud.

"There's something called 'extreme emotional disturbance,' which would make it manslaughter instead of murder. I can ask for that jury instruction all the way up until closing argument, but I'm not ready to go there yet."

Nicky walked back to the sofa, sat next to me, and grabbed my hand. "Remember that night Mom and Dad went to Niagara on the Lake and we had a slumber party in my room and stayed up until three in the morning?"

That was when the big room was still hers. I was probably ten years old, and she was sixteen, just old enough to be trusted with her baby sister for a weekend. We bought frozen pizza, chips and dip, and ice cream bars and ate until our bellies hurt. Afterward, we chewed licorice and played Parcheesi and Sorry! until I finally stopped fighting sleep.

"You wanted to kill me when I set off the smoke detector trying to make pancakes when I woke up."

"Do you even remember why Dad took Mom away for the weekend?"

I shook my head.

"It was a make-up trip. He had fallen off the wagon again. I helped her cover up the black eye with concealer before they got in the car."

"I was crying, thinking they were leaving because it was our fault they fought. That's when you took me Krogering for whatever junk food we wanted." She had used the money she had stashed in the bottom of her jewelry box, saving for her dream prom dress.

"And while we were sitting on my bedroom floor, with your legs all crisscross-apple-sauce, you said, 'Nicky, I wish we were orphans.' And I said we'd be like Oliver Twist, but with all the junk food we could eat."

"I was ten."

"Yeah, but I was sixteen, and I remember thinking, yep, I'd be totally fine if Mom and Dad were . . . *poof*. But I didn't really mean it. Ethan obviously had issues with Adam. So did you, right? But you didn't kill him, and neither did Ethan. Olivia's right. Don't give up yet."

I looked into her eyes and knew she meant it. I could see the intensity of her faith in him, even in the way she was standing. She was absolutely certain that Ethan was innocent, and I was the one doubting him. Maybe it was true that biology bound her to him in an irreplicable way.

I could see some kind of idea forming behind Olivia's furrowed brow. "Chloe, you said before that you felt like you were holding on to your dignity by . . . *you know*. What were you talking about?"

I sighed. "It's nothing."

"Oh my god," Nicky said. "Go ahead and tell her."

"Let me just say this," Olivia said. "I hoped the lack of witnesses, the lack of physical evidence, the lack of a confession, would all be enough to make it obvious there's reasonable doubt here. But we've had some setbacks. Remember that promise I made after the very first court appearance?"

I nodded. She had promised to tell us when she thought we were losing.

"Okay, we're at that moment. Do you understand what I'm saying?"

I felt my throat tighten and my eyes begin to water. I heard Nicky suck in her breath.

"Reasonable doubt alone may not be enough at this point. It would help if we could give the jury an alternative explanation, another story to believe. To be honest, if you didn't have a rock-solid alibi, I'd be arguing that *you* had at least as strong of a motive to kill Adam as Ethan."

"That's just great," I said dryly.

"Ethan did a good job explaining how he found those things in his bedroom in the city. I think the jury will follow along once I get to closing. But we still have the problem of broken glass being in the wrong places, and the security system being disarmed before the murder. If it wasn't Ethan—and we don't think it's Ethan, right?"

"Of course not," I said, hoping I sounded sincere.

"Okay, so then the most sensible explanation is that Adam had gone to bed and then got up and disarmed the alarm for an unexpected visitor, perhaps someone he knew—or maybe not? There was a fight. It escalated. Then afterward, the person staged the scene. But who's the person?"

I finally saw the path she was trying to lead me to. "His name's Jake Summer."

"At Adam's law firm," she said, recognizing the name. "The one quoted in the article you gave me about Gentry's problems."

I nodded.

"How long had you been seeing him?"

I closed my eyes, trying to place the beginning of our affair. Standing closer than we needed to when he helped me squeeze more limes for margaritas at our Memorial Day croquet party. Brushing against him in the law firm suite at the Yankee game. Then an invitation to "grab lunch" when he happened to take a staycation at his house while I was taking a week-long writer's retreat alone.

"Right after Labor Day last year."

"So about eight months before Adam was killed?"

"Yes, but Jake didn't—"

Nicky didn't need me to finish the thought to disagree. "That's not what matters, Chloe. She's not going to have him arrested or anything. She just needs to give the jury something to chew on. It's confusion, chaos, distraction. If they don't know at the end of the day who did it, they have to acquit. And you just heard her. She kept her promise. We're going to lose Ethan forever if we don't do something."

"I don't know if I'd call it chaos," Olivia said, "but, like I said, it's about creating doubt."

I looked up at the ceiling, hoping that some brilliant solution would fall from the sky. Instead I saw Olivia, upside down, standing over me behind the sofa.

"I'll be honest, Chloe. I've tried more than two hundred felony cases, including thirteen homicides. Right now, I think Ethan will be convicted if we don't raise an alternative theory. I can go with EED, but that still means manslaughter. He'd get at least three years, but it would probably be more like ten. Or I can call Nunzio and start talking about a plea deal. Or we can talk more about Jake Summer. Those are the options. No other doors I can see."

I wiped my face with my hands. I didn't have a choice. "Is it too late to let Nicky take the fall?"

Nicky pressed her palms against her heart. "Hey, I've been ready and willing this whole time."

"Not gonna fly," Olivia said, adding a wink in Nicky's direction. "So let's talk about Jake."

I told her everything I knew about the man I had hoped would be the rest of my future, if I ever got there.

WE WERE HALFWAY HOME TO East Hampton when he called my cell. I looked at Nicky and steeled myself before I answered.

"Hey."

"I've been sitting by the phone, not knowing whether I should call."

"It's been a long day."

"Chloe, I read the trial coverage. Is that true? What Ethan said?"

"I have to testify again. The lawyer told me not to talk to anyone about it. I'm sorry. That's why I didn't call."

"Are you home? Can I at least see you, so I know you're okay?"

"You're in the city."

"Well, I'm about to not be in the city. Olivia Randall called me. I assumed you knew."

I swallowed, hating that I was doing this to him. I had never lied to him. All this time, even when Adam was alive, I had never once been dishonest with Jake. "She asked me for names of people who'd seen how loving Ethan and Adam could be together. You spent so much time with us—"

"Sure, I'm happy to help. She said she wants me at the courthouse in the morning, but I can come out east tonight and sleep there."

Olivia had called Nunzio while we were still at the hotel. To avoid a spat with her about a slew of discovery complaints she threatened to level in court, he had agreed to allow Olivia to add Jake as a rebuttal witness.

"It's not a good idea, Jake. If the prosecution finds out I met with a witness right before you testified. . . . We shouldn't even be on the phone."

"Yeah, you're right. This will be over soon, though, Chloe. It's going to be okay. Don't give up."

"Yeah."

"I love you."

"You, too."

When I hung up, Nicky blasted the '80s station so we could both pretend she didn't hear me cry all the way home.

33

I WAS FORTY-ONE years old and had managed to avoid even a single incident of public humiliation. Now I was under oath, before a packed courtroom, about to testify to the darkest moments in my marriage.

I had made the mistake of reading social media last night before going to sleep. The trolls were having a field day with yesterday's dual bombshells that my husband had been abusing me physically and that my son had been one of my most active online critics.

So Chloe Taylor shames men for telling ladies they look nice at work but has no problem with dudes who beat up their wives. What a bitch.

Imagine what a cunt you have to be for your own son to call you out like that.

Why hasn't she killed herself yet?

Worst person in the world.

Really? Well, it's about to get worse.

Olivia began by establishing that I had been in the courtroom previously and had seen both Ethan's testimony and the video he had made of his argument with Adam.

"So you heard Ethan testify that your husband, Adam, was—quote—'beating the shit out of' you?"

"Yes."

"Was he wrong?"

"Well, it's not how I would word it necessarily." There were a few nervous laughs. "But, yes, he was correct that we were having problems recently. And we had ferocious arguments—along the lines of how Adam appeared in that video, but outside Ethan's presence. And there was physical violence involved."

Olivia had prepped me for this. She had forced me yesterday in her suite to practice the lines—brutal and blunt—over and over again. But now that I was here, I couldn't say them. I looked at Ethan. He called me weak, a coward, a hypocrite, caring more what people thought about me than my actual reality. He needed me to be different now.

"Ethan spoke a truth that I never wanted known: my husband, Adam, was beating me."

"And why didn't you want this known?" Olivia asked.

Nunzio objected that the question was irrelevant.

"Your Honor, the prosecutor tried to make it sound as if Ethan dropped the evidentiary equivalent of a nuclear bomb in the courtroom yesterday when he finally badgered this boy into disclosing his family's deepest, most shameful secret. The jury deserves the right to understand his state of mind."

Judge Rivera agreed.

"I was embarrassed, and I blamed myself. I was probably in denial about it, too, hoping it was temporary. *He's drunk, he's stressed out, it won't happen again.* I was so in love with him. Against all the taboos—he was my sister's ex, for goodness' sake, my nephew's father—I dated him and then married him, because I truly believed we were soul mates. I had absolutely no idea that Ethan was aware of the abuse, or I'd like to think I would have made different decisions. But now I understand why he wrote those internet posts. Just like he said, he was trying to get my attention. To wake me up and make me see the situation from the outside, even as he internalized my own shame."

Nunzio rose again. "She can't read the defendant's mind, Your Honor."

"I'm going to allow it."

"Now, Mr. Nunzio here has suggested that Ethan was motivated to kill Adam because he was the stricter parent, while you were the more lenient. To be clear, did you adopt Ethan?"

"No."

"Who are his legal parents?"

"Well, it was Adam and my sister, Nicole, with Adam having sole physical custody once they divorced almost fourteen years ago."

"What is your understanding of who Ethan's legal parent is now that Adam is deceased?"

"Adam's will directed that Ethan remain with me, but he included that clause because, as a simple legal matter, his biological mother would become the presumptive guardian."

"In fact, when the state has sent legal notifications during this trial to the parent of my client, they've sent those documents to your sister, Nicole, correct?"

"Yes."

"And the detention center where he's been held pending trial permits you to visit not on a parent's schedule, but as an aunt?"

"Yes."

"How many times would you estimate that Adam Macintosh physically assaulted you?"

Another objection came from Nunzio. "Relevance, Your Honor. The victim is not on trial here."

Judge Rivera tapped her pen against a legal pad. "I'm inclined to agree. The bad acts of the victim are not relevant unless they were known to the defendant, and he testified to the extent of his knowledge yesterday."

"Your Honor, the defense offers this evidence for another purpose. I promise to tie it in quickly."

"A few questions, Ms. Randall, but be quick."

While they wrangled over the law, I was trying to count how many times Adam had hurt me. "I didn't keep a log or anything. My guess is more than eight, less than twelve. Maybe ten times?"

"Did he ever grab you?"

"Yes."

"Push you?"

"Yes."

"Slap you?"

"Yes."

"Punch you, by which I mean, a closed fist?"

"Yes."

"Choke you?"

"Yes."

"Did he ever leave bruises on you?"

"Yes."

"Draw blood?"

"Yes. My lip, once. He never punched me in the face after that, though."

Nunzio again, back on his feet. "Your Honor, this is clearly designed to—"

"Mr. Nunzio," the judge said, "can I please remind you that you are the one who injected this topic into the trial with your cross-examination of the defendant? You can't pick and choose which parts of the subject matter make you comfortable."

I took a tiny amount of pleasure in seeing Nunzio slither, chastised, into his chair.

"Did you retaliate against your husband in any way?" Olivia asked.

"Yes."

"Physically?"

"No, I tried defending myself once, and it did not go well." I looked directly at the jury for the next sentence. "I retaliated by having an affair."

My testimony was having the desired effect. Several jurors' eyes widened. They were all leaning forward.

"When did this affair start?"

"Last September. Right after Labor Day."

"So about eight months before your husband was killed?"

"Yes."

"Do you have reason to believe this man knew that Adam was abusing you?"

"He would see bruises. On my body. I told him that I bruised easily, and that they were from Pilates. He'd joke around that I should probably find a workout that didn't involve instruments of torture." I pictured him kissing the dark purple blotch on my rib cage, supposedly from arching against the equipment, and delicately tracing his fingertip across the scrape on my neck, where I said a spring-loaded handle had ricocheted.

"Do you know where this man was on the night your husband was killed?"

"Not precisely. But I saw him in East Hampton, where he owns a house, the following day." When I went to him that afternoon, he told me he had spent the previous night alone, watching Netflix. I was certain he was telling the truth. We hadn't lied to each other, not until now.

Nunzio was flipping through documents that I suspected were my cell phone records. He wasn't going to find anything.

"Did he know that Adam had been alone at your home the previous night?"

"Yes. I told him that, in fact. I spoke to him around five o'clock. He had just arrived in East Hampton. I told him that Ethan was staying at a friend's for the night and that Adam wouldn't be out until later. He asked to see me, but I told him I was leaving for a party."

"So this man you were seeing knew you were going out for the evening, Ethan was already gone for the night, as well, and Adam was on his way home?"

Nunzio, his attention still aimed at documents on his desk, muttered an objection that Olivia was testifying, which was sustained.

"Was this man aware that only the three of you resided at your home?"

Nunzio objected again, but this time was overruled.

"Yes," I answered. The implication was clear. My lover would have known that Adam would be alone once he arrived at the house.

"How far is this man's East Hampton home from yours?"

"About eight tenths of a mile." I thought about all the times I had stolen away to walk alone on the beach, only to turn left after the Maidstone Club to circle around to his house. I hated that I was doing this to him, but reminded myself that I had to for Ethan.

"Did this man ever express any animosity toward your husband?"

Another objection from Nunzio, this time on the basis of hearsay. Olivia responded with something about it being an excited utterance and state of mind, and Judge Rivera instructed me that I could answer.

"The last time I saw him before Adam was killed—about two weeks before the murder—he noticed another bruise." That part was true. Adam had worked late and came home to find me already asleep in the middle of the bed. He kicked me, saying he couldn't get me to move, but I knew it was because he was mad about getting stuck at work all night. "I finally told him that the bruises weren't from Pilates—that Adam was violent, but I was afraid to leave him. He was furious. The only thing I can think of is that he did this to protect me."

Nunzio, still searching wildly for cell phone evidence he wouldn't find, was slow to object. "Speculation."

The objection was sustained, but the damage was done. I could tell from the disgusted looks on their faces that the jurors had believed me. In their eyes, I was a slut, but not a liar.

"MR. NUNZIO. DO YOU HAVE a cross-examination or not?"

Watching Nunzio still flipping through those records, I realized how many dots Olivia had to connect to be confident about this plan.

She had predicted this very moment the night before in her suite. "We're not going to give him a name," she'd said. "He'll assume you're lying to protect Ethan. He'll look in the cell phone records for a Friday-night call, and he won't find it. So he'll have two choices: flail around in the dark and ask questions he doesn't know the answer to, or wait until closing to argue that you made up a nonexistent boyfriend to distract the jury. He won't even cross-examine you."

Now, here we were, and Nunzio had a decision to make.

"No questions, Your Honor."

34

AT OLIVIA'S REQUEST, Jake had been waiting in the courthouse. The plan she came up with the previous night worked best if he walked into the courtroom expecting to be asked his impressions of Adam's relationship with his son.

I saw a small smile cross his face as he walked past me on his way to the witness chair. I knew it was intended as a sign of optimism for me, but it only made me feel more horrible.

I kept my hands clasped in my lap and stared straight ahead as Olivia walked him through the basic questions she'd ask of a standard character witness. His name and age. His employment with Rives & Braddock for the past fifteen years. The fact that he first met Adam and his family approximately six years earlier through the law firm's head partner, Bill Braddock, who represented *Eve* magazine. The additional fact that the firm subsequently welcomed Adam in as a law partner to handle white-collar criminal cases a little more than two years before his death.

"Would you call Adam Macintosh a friend?"

"Definitely."

"You socialized together?"

"Yes. Often, in fact, once he joined the firm. Our weekend houses are within a mile of each other, so we saw each other out there quite a bit. And, of course, at work."

"You had cases together?"

He paused. "No, not per se. He was primarily a criminal defense attorney. I'm a transactional lawyer. But we were partners at the same firm, so, in that sense, all our work was shared. And a few clients had a need for both of us, in which case we'd team up."

"Did you even take trips with the Macintosh family?"

He nodded. "Yes, a couple of times."

"And what were those?"

"The firm had a big celebration for its fiftieth year. About a hundred of us went to Anguilla together last January. And then a much smaller group of us—more our social crowd from the East End—went up to Boston together for a Yankee-Sox game, if you could even call that massacre a vacation."

"And did Ethan Macintosh and Chloe Taylor go on both of those trips?"

He blinked a couple of times at the mention of my name, but I doubt anyone else noticed. "Yes."

"So you had a chance to get to know both of them?"

"Yes, I'd say so."

"And did you commence a sexual relationship with Chloe Taylor?"

It only took him a second. I could see the flicker in his eyes. Jake was probably the smartest person I had ever met. How many times had Adam and Bill said that he was the resident genius at Rives & Braddock? The lawyer part of his brain probably even admired Olivia for the move, realizing he never would have fallen for it if it weren't for his loyalty to me.

He turned calmly to the judge, his eyes moving quickly past mine. "I'm not going to answer that question."

Jake's own objection triggered one from Nunzio. "Inadequate foundation for the question, Your Honor."

Olivia was prepared with a retort. "Ms. Taylor's testimony laid a sufficient foundation, Your Honor. If necessary, I can recall her to the stand."

I had said everything except Jake's name. It wasn't our fault that Nunzio hadn't made the connection to Olivia's late addition of a family friend as a character witness.

"The objection is overruled," Rivera said. "You must answer the question, Mr. Summer. Unless there's an applicable privilege, of course. I can give you a recess to give you an opportunity to retain counsel if necessary."

He looked up at Olivia and set his mouth in a straight line before speaking. "On the advice of my *own* counsel, I refuse to answer on the grounds that it may incriminate me."

"Did Chloe Taylor tell you prior to Adam Macintosh's murder that her husband was physically abusing her?"

"On the advice of my own counsel, I refuse to answer on the grounds that it may incriminate me."

Over and over again, he repeated the same phrase, like a mantra.

"Did you provide a burner phone to Ms. Taylor so your private conversations with her would go undetected by Adam Macintosh and other members of your law firm?"

"At approximately five p.m. before the murder, did you receive a phone call from Ms. Taylor notifying you that she would be at a party and that her husband, Adam Macintosh, would be alone that night, less than a mile from your own home?"

"Where were you the night that Adam Macintosh was killed?"

"Jake Summer, did you stab Adam Macintosh?"

That was the question that finally made him flinch. I could see how badly he wanted to defend himself. Instead, he looked at me, a pained expression on his face, as he answered one last time, "On the advice of

my own counsel, I refuse to answer on the grounds that it may incriminate me."

When he left the witness chair, he used the opposite aisle through
the courtroom so he did not have to walk directly past me. As I watched
him leave, Nicky and I glared at him, just like Olivia had us practice.
After all, he was the man who must have killed my husband.

35

H AS ANYONE EVER told you you're a terrible driver?"
Technically the speed limit on this section of Abraham's Path
was thirty, but even civilians averaged a little over forty. Guidry could
see from the passenger seat that Bowen was rolling at a constant thirty-
one, and that's when he wasn't tapping the brakes for reasons known
only to him.

"Pretty much every person who's ever ridden shotgun with me. I
grew up in Queens. Went into the navy. Managed to never drive a car
once until I decided I wanted to be a cop. You haven't noticed I'm more
than happy to sit in that seat over there?"

"Thought you were overcorrecting for the fact I'm female."

"You overthink."

"Or maybe you just like sitting here to jam all your candy into the
seat cushion like a fucking squirrel preparing for winter." She slipped
two fingers into the upholstery tear, pulled out a gummy bear, and
tossed it out the window. "Seriously, what is wrong with you?"

He chuckled. "Just seemed funny at first. Then I started wondering
if you'd ever notice."

"I'm taking the car home tonight and having Amy sew this up for
good."

Guidry's cell phone buzzed in her blazer pocket. A 917 number, a city cell phone.

"Guidry."

It was Agent Damon Katz from the FBI. "I got your message asking about the Gentry Group."

"Not Gentry per se," she clarified. "Their lawyer, Adam Macintosh."

Bowen tapped the brake at the mention of Macintosh's name, sending Guidry lurching against her seat belt. She shot him an annoyed look and gestured for him to pay attention to the road.

"You probably figured out by now that I checked with the case agents and they weren't exactly forthcoming with information on an investigation that's not mine, and which I planned to share with a curious detective."

"Yup. I get it."

"Well, apparently that's changed now."

"Huh."

Another brake tap from Bowen, who was looking at her and uttering "What?" under his breath.

"Do you mind if I put you on speaker? It's just me and my partner in the car."

"No problem." Once the phone was on speaker, Katz continued. "So one of the case agents just gave me a heads-up. He said when you first called, it seemed like a fishing expedition. Then he saw the news from the kid's murder trial yesterday."

"They're trying to pin it on the wife's side piece." At Nunzio's request, Bowen and Guidry had tracked down Jake Summer the previous night to see if he had anything he wanted to share with them—like, maybe an alibi for the time of the murder. As expected, he refused to speak to them without a lawyer, so that was the end of that.

"*Supposed* side piece," Bowen whispered next to her. So far, they had found no cell phone records or any other evidence to substantiate Chloe Taylor's claim that she and Summer were having an affair. Bowen was convinced that Chloe and the kid's lawyer had fabricated the entire story to distract the jury. But if that was the case, Guidry didn't understand why Summer was lawyering up instead of burning the theory to the ground. Maybe if the affair was real, he was actually willing to let the defense do this to him to cover for the kid.

Or, maybe Olivia Randall was actually onto something about him being guilty, and that's why Katz was calling.

"Yeah, so, here's the thing," Katz said. "The prosecutor on the Gentry case is reaching out to the ADA on the murder case, but since you're the one who sort of set this thing in motion, the case agent said I could circle back to you. I don't have all the details, but you were right—Adam Macintosh was at our office those two dates you gave me. He was looking for a cooperation agreement for providing information on Gentry."

"What about attorney-client privilege?" she asked.

"Doesn't apply if the client's engaged in an ongoing crime. Or if the lawyers are coconspirators."

"Macintosh was dirty, too?"

"Nope, or that's what he claimed, at least. But his law firm was, and he was willing to give up both Gentry and the lawyers. And he definitely didn't want his partners to know. The case is being worked out of the field office in Manhattan. He arranged to meet with the agents here instead, because he didn't want anyone who knew him from his US attorney days to recognize him going in and out of the building."

"So maybe an affair with Chloe Taylor wasn't Summer's only reason to want Macintosh out of the way?" Jake Summer had been the one to provide a quote to the *New York Times* about the Gentry investigation, so he must have been one of the other lawyers working on the matter.

"Maybe," he said. "And that's why the lawyer on our case is calling the lawyer on your case, which is why I'm reaching out to you. If

I had to guess, you'll be hearing soon from one pissed-off ADA. The case agent told me that if you hadn't made that phone call asking about Macintosh, they might have made a different judgment call on whether to share the information with local law enforcement."

"Let me deal with that. But do you know for a fact that Macintosh was offering to flip on Jake Summer? Is it possible Summer found out?"

"He hadn't actually given up the information yet, but obviously Summer's one of the lead lawyers for the client, at least as of now. Apparently Macintosh was looking for guarantees not only that he wouldn't be charged but that he could come back to work at the US Attorney's Office. Obviously something like that's not easy to work out. Then he was killed. Seemed like you had a decent-enough case against the kid—you probably still do—but the department didn't want this blowing up on us down the road when it all becomes public. And with that, you now know everything I know."

"Got it. Thanks for the heads-up, Katz."

"No problemo."

She hit the end-call button.

"You called the feds about that Gentry thing?" Bowen asked.

The company name hadn't come up between them since the early days of the investigation, after Chloe mentioned that she wasn't sure where Adam had been the last two days of his life.

"I saw this article in the *Times* the other day about Gentry being investigated, and I realized the FBI has an office right at Kew Gardens. I got curious," she said with a shrug. She was the one who had narrowed in on Ethan. It had been her call to make the arrest, even as Chloe Taylor had been pushing her to figure out where Adam had spent the last two days of his life.

"And now you've managed to dig up *Brady* material that Nunzio's going to have to share with the defense." As a prosecutor, Nunzio was required to notify the defense of potentially exculpatory evidence, even if it came to light as the trial was coming to a close.

They were pulling into the police department parking lot when Guidry's cell phone rang again. It was Nunzio, and, as Agent Katz had predicted, he was not happy. "Do you know what a lawyer like Olivia Randall is going to do with this? You just bought me two straight days of getting splinters wedged under my fingernails."

Even without the phone on speaker, Bowen had heard enough to grasp the situation. "You don't even seem upset. That kid could get off because of this."

Guidry could live with that. Maybe that kid never would have been arrested if she had seen the full picture to begin with. If she were on that jury, she knew how she'd vote.

36

I T HAD BEEN so long since I'd spent a night in the apartment that
I opened the wrong kitchen cabinet when I went for a water glass,
envisioning the layout of the East Hampton house instead. I realized I
had literally never been alone in the apartment. Even Panda was out in
East Hampton now.

After three and a half weeks of Ethan's trial, I finally had to come
back to the city for a day to meet with the board of directors that over-
saw the magazine. In theory, the company was standing solid on Team
Chloe since Ethan's arrest, but the personal information that had come
out during the trial was taking its toll.

If social media was any indication, many of the people who had already respected me now admired me even more, while the people who
already hated me now despised me more. But there was definitely a
vocal group of "dead to me" former supporters who saw me as a phony
figurehead who needed to go for the sake of the movement. And thanks
to widespread cable news coverage of Ethan's trial, whole swaths of the
population who had never heard of me before now thought of me as
that trashy woman who used her husband's abuse as an excuse to have
an affair that got her husband murdered and her stepson sent to jail.

The me of a year earlier would have spent days preparing for to-morrow morning's meeting, weaving together digital analytics data and powerful story pitches to convince the board of my value. Instead, I had memorized a one-page statement about how committed I was to *Eve*, along with a promise to respect whatever decision they made about the future of the magazine. Either way, my publisher was plan-ning a half-million-copy print run of my memoir (thank you, cable news), and my contract with *Eve* guaranteed me a seven-figure buyout if they gave me the heave-ho. So, as Nicky had said as I got in the car to drive into the city, fuck 'em.

I taped another cardboard box of books shut, and then gave myself a break to stretch my back. I reached for the cell phone on my office desk and sent Olivia a text. No word?

It was the third day of jury deliberations.

No. I'll call you immediately. I promise. And remember: This is good for us.

According to Olivia, the jury would have convicted Ethan by now if they thought the case was as cut-and-dried as Nunzio had presented it to be. Three days in the jury room meant they couldn't agree, which meant at least one of the jurors was on our side.

I had decided to use my night in the apartment to start packing up my home office. If Ethan got acquitted, he'd be allowed to walk out of the courthouse with us that very moment. Nicky and I were choos-ing to be optimists and were planning for that to happen. Once he was home, Nicky wouldn't be able to sleep in his bedroom anymore.

Mrs. Schwartz on the twelfth floor was moving to Florida in four months. I had already signed a contract to rent her apartment for Nicky for a year with an option to buy. In the meantime, I had found the per-fect little Lucite desk for my bedroom, and I would turn my office into a nice space for Nicky until her apartment was ready.

I opened the pencil drawer of my desk, removed a key from the back corner, and crawled onto the floor with a newly popped-open box to begin the process of sorting through the files I keep at home. Half of it—old bank statements and receipts—went into the shredder. The rest of it would fit on the floor of my closet for the time being.

I reached what I thought would be the final folder—Wells Fargo—to find an unlabeled brown Redweld pocket file. I removed it from the drawer, released the elastic cord, and flipped it open. I immediately recognized Adam's chicken-scratch handwriting on the wrinkled Post-it notes jutting out from the margins of some of the pages.

Flipping through the pages, I remembered the angry look on Adam's face when I made a bitchy comment about finding his whiskey glass in here one day. He never did tell me why he'd been in my office without me, but I took it as yet another meaningless battle of wills. I assumed at the time he had simply been looking something up on my desktop instead of powering up his laptop, but didn't like the idea of owing me an explanation.

He was killed eight days later.

Looking at this file, I realized he had been working on something he didn't want stored at the law firm.

There had to be at least two hundred pages of documents. Financial statements. A flowchart of wholly owned subsidiaries and other affiliated corporations. Memoranda of agreements for various mergers and acquisitions. Some portions were highlighted. Others were flagged with Post-it notes and arrow stickers. Most of them were related to the Gentry Group, but some of the company names seemed to be unrelated. I didn't have the legal or financial expertise to understand what most of it meant.

But when I reached the end of the file, I found eight pages of yellow legal-pad paper covered with Adam's handwriting in blue ink. I was probably the only person in the world who could make out every word without effort.

It was an eight-page outline, perfectly organized in three parts, with asterisked bullet points beneath each section: (I) How I Knew—Gentry; (II) R&B Pattern; (III) What I Need.

I pieced together enough of part I to see the connection to the on-going investigation into Gentry. Olivia had even managed to get an FBI agent on the stand in Ethan's trial to give the broad strokes to the jury. As Jake had told me, Gentry was on a buying and merging spree, purchasing foreign factories, energy providers, and distributors to expand its global operations. But where he said that Rives & Brad-dock kept clients happy by steering them to the right side of the legal line, Adam believed that Gentry was crossing it—repeatedly. They set up a complicated network of sham shell companies to hide the fact that they were doing exactly what Jake had described as the forbidden temptation—paying off every player up and down the line.

Part III was crystal clear. Adam wanted complete immunity; he wanted an opinion letter from the Department of Justice that he had committed no crimes, was not violating attorney-client privilege, and was acting within the bounds of professional ethics; and he wanted his old job at the US Attorney's Office back.

It was part II that was hardest for me to digest. The first few bul-let points were about R&B's skyrocketing client-satisfaction rates after international transactions compared to other law firms, and the number of new multinational corporate clients retained in the last three years. But it was the final two notes that had the sound of my own blood rush-ing in my ears.

• R&B not going along with clients; R&B is initiating, recruiting, and planning.

• Bill Braddock: Goes to in-house counsel directly after initial docs drafts, he's "good cop" v. bad cops of assigned team, undermines compliance. Takes piece of resulting deals for PC LLC in exchange.

I flipped backward through the deal pages and found accounting entries for payments to "PC LLC." Patsy Cline, Bill's favorite singer, for whom he had named his horse.

In an instant, I realized how many things I had chalked up to Bill's old age in the last six months. Pretending not to have heard of the Gentry Group at the Press for the People gala. Not returning press phone calls after Adam's murder. Not even reaching out to me for two days. And through it all, I was so convinced he was supporting me, proving himself to be not just my lawyer but a true friend.

The Press for the People gala. I replayed the conversation in my head. When I had mentioned that Adam was meeting with people from Gentry near JFK, I didn't know that the FBI had offices in the area, but Bill probably did. I was the one who had tipped him off to Adam's extracurricular activities. It was my fault that he figured out Adam was cooperating with the FBI.

Would Bill kill someone to protect himself? I thought about all the times I had told him he was my octogenarian soul mate. *You're an assassin, Bill Braddock. Take no prisoners.*

I reached for my cell and pulled up Olivia's number. I was about to hit the call button when I stopped myself.

She and I didn't have attorney-client privilege. She had made that clear to me repeatedly. If I gave her these notes, would she have to share them with Nunzio, the way he had been forced to tell her what he knew about the FBI investigation into Rives & Braddock? I knew from Adam's trial days how a case could be upended by newly discovered evidence. The prosecution could ask for a mistrial, right when the jury deliberations seemed to be going Ethan's way. If that happened, we'd have to start all over again, and the second trial could be even worse for Ethan.

I stuffed the documents back into the Redweld, rested the file against the back of the desk drawer, and then stacked the remaining folders from the cardboard box in front of it. I locked the file drawer and walked to the kitchen to find my purse. After adding the file key to my keychain, I poured myself a glass of wine. The movers weren't hauling the stuff to storage until the next week. If the jury didn't come back with the right verdict, I could always say I found the file later, and we would live to fight another day.

I was almost done with my wine when my cell phone rang. It was Olivia. Sometimes I wondered if she had wired me with surveillance equipment.

"Did something happen?" I asked.

"The judge's clerk called. She wants me there tomorrow at nine thirty."

"The jury's back?"

"They never say, because they don't want it to leak. But, yeah, that's my expectation."

"Okay, I'll be there." I would cancel my meeting with the board and instead email the statement I had prepared for the occasion. If they couldn't understand my decision, I didn't want the damn job anymore.

"Are you all right?" Olivia asked.

I paused, thinking about those eight yellow lined pages of Adam's notes. I was the one who had introduced Adam to Bill Braddock. I was the one who pushed him to work for that firm. I was the one who said we were *lucky* to have someone like him on our side.

Bill had had Adam killed, and it was all my fault. And if I told Olivia, maybe the police could actually prove it. Adam, with his white-hat ways and meticulous record-keeping, would solve his own murder from the grave.

But all that mattered now was Ethan.

"Yeah, I'm fine."

"Do you want to ride out with me in the morning?"

"No, I'm good."

I got into my car five minutes later. I wanted to be with Nicky.

JUDGE RIVERA MAY HAVE TRIED to keep the fact of the jury's decision a secret, but her efforts had failed. There were more film trucks outside the courthouse than any other day of the trial, and courthouse security was operating the elevators to cut off access to the third floor. The courtroom was officially full.

When Ethan walked out through the side door and saw the scene, he froze for a moment. He hadn't seemed so scared since he was first arrested. This was the juncture when we'd find out whether this was the end of a temporary nightmare or the beginning of a future that would be even worse.

Olivia whispered something to the deputy who walked them to counsel table, and the deputy nodded. She turned to Nicky and me and waved us forward, allowing each of us to give Ethan a quick hug.

The courtroom silenced as the bailiff announced that the Honorable Judge Rivera was presiding. She then announced what we had all anticipated—that she was bringing in the jury to read the verdict.

Once they were seated, Judge Rivera asked the foreperson to stand.

I recognized the man who rose from his chair as the retired owner of a masonry shop on the North Fork. I thought he had scowled a few times when I was testifying, but I hadn't been sure about it. I had been rooting for the outlet-mall woman, but tried not to read into the decision.

The judge asked him if the jury had reached a unanimous decision.

"We have, Your Honor."

"Will the defendant please rise?"

As Olivia and Ethan stood, Nicky reached for my hand and grabbed it. It was finally happening.

"Will the foreperson please read the verdict?"

"On count one, murder in the second degree, we the jury find the defendant not guilty."

Ethan said something to Olivia that I couldn't hear. She answered, and then he turned to look at me and Nicky. I reached across the bar and hugged him, then felt Nicky's arms around me, too. This time, we didn't need the deputy's permission. We would stay like that as long as we wanted.

When our huddle finally broke up, Ethan looked toward the judge's bench expectantly. "What happens to me now?"

"We're going home," I said. "Let's get out of here and never come back."

37

NICKY AND I decided to drive Ethan straight to the city, despite the Friday traffic. It would be a while before he'd want to see the East Hampton house again.

He slept—or at least pretended to—until nearly one in the afternoon the next day. By then, I was already back from Bloomingdale's with a mix of size-large T-shirts, hoodies, and track pants. He seemed to have filled out in the last six months.

"I thought you should have some fresh clothes."

"You just wanted to shop," he mumbled with a grin as I handed him the shopping bags.

Panda appeared from under the sofa, buzzed past him three times at lightning speed, and then circled back to brush gently against his ankles. The sound of his purrs filled the room.

"Greedy Boy!" Ethan cried out, dropping the shopping bags to pull him into his arms.

It had been Nicky's idea to give the East Hampton housekeeper two days off in exchange for driving the cat to the city this morning.

In addition to sleeping, Ethan needed to eat. Nicky and I cooked breakfast, lunch, and dinner the entire weekend, and were happy to see him snack in between. We binge-watched the entire season of *Bosch* that he had missed while in custody. We did a jigsaw puzzle. We marveled as Panda followed Ethan everywhere he went, even the bathroom.

The one thing we did not do was talk about Adam. Or the verdict. Or the really important revelations that had come out during Ethan's trial. Or Bill Braddock, his law firm, and the documents that were locked in the file drawer of the desk that the movers would be coming for on Wednesday.

Finally, on Tuesday morning, I knocked on the door of his room when I heard signs of movement inside and asked him if we could talk. He was in the same exact spot on his bed where he'd curled up while Adam screamed at him. Dropping onto the corner of his bed and folding one leg beneath me, I started by asking him what he wanted to do about school. His detention center had supposedly been educating him while he was in custody, but I had no idea whether that work would translate into graduating on schedule. "I'm pretty sure I could shame Headmistress Carter into giving you extra assignments to catch up with your class—"

"I'm not going back there."

I nodded. It was the response I expected. He never did like Casden. I had forced it on him.

"Okay, we have time to figure it out."

"I want to go to Harvest Collegiate."

It was a public school on Fourteenth Street.

"Fine, I'll call and make the arrangements."

"Thanks."

"Also, I've been seeing a grief counselor, about losing your dad. Her name's Anna, but she knows some men who do the same kind of work, both in the city and Long Island. I thought maybe it would be helpful for you, too."

He looked down at his hands. "You think I need a shrink."

"Nope, not at all. But you've lost your primary parent to a horrible crime of violence, not to mention what you went through the last six months. I'd be a total chode"—he smiled at the use of the word—"if I didn't make it an option for you to talk to someone about that."

"I wasn't going to use the gun, you know."

"I know." Did I know?

"I really was just trying to show off. Those kids are, like, I don't know. They're like adults. I just wanted to be different. It was stupid."

"It's okay, Ethan. It's all behind us."

"And I'm sorry about those posts on Poppit."

The guilt in his eyes made my chest hurt. "Really, it's all right. I know you were trying to give me a wake-up call."

"I didn't know you couldn't leave—without leaving me, too, I mean. That's why you put up with it, right? So you'd still be my mom?"

I reached out and patted his arm. "It's complicated, Ethan, but everything's all right now."

"I took that stuff from the house, Mom—the Beats and the shoes and the speaker."

"None of it matters now." Don't tell me, I thought. I don't want to know. I was still trying to figure out what to do with the evidence Adam had gathered against Bill.

"Kevin was meeting up with someone for a deal, just like I said. And I didn't want to get in trouble, so he dropped me at the beach. But then I was cold, and bored, and so I walked back to the house to get a hoodie."

"Ethan—" There was nothing I could say. If I told him to stop, he'd never trust me again. I needed to hear him out, whatever was going to come next.

"I found Dad."

My face felt hot. I had to stop my hands from shaking. "Was he already—"

He nodded. "Yeah. It was . . . bad."

I had no idea what to say. I sat in silence, waiting for him to explain.

"I'm the one who trashed the house and broke the window and put those things in my backpack. But I swear, he was already gone when I got home." His face was red, and his lower lip began to tremble.

"Ethan, I don't understand—"

"I thought you did it."

My lips parted, but no words came out.

"I saw how he was treating you. And I knew what an important moment you were having in your job. You didn't want anyone to know what was happening. You were trapped. And so when I found him like that, I thought it had to have something to do with what was going on between the two of you. Like maybe he was hurting you again, and you were protecting yourself."

It's always the spouse. Even Ethan thought so.

"I didn't hurt your father, Ethan. You know that now, don't you?"

He nodded. "I didn't, either."

"I know," I said, wrapping an arm around his shoulder.

"So are the police even going to keep looking?"

"Of course," I said, even though I knew they wouldn't. I shifted the conversation to something more hopeful. "You're okay with staying with me? With Nicky around, too?"

When he smiled, he actually looked happy. "Yeah. It's gonna be good. I kind of like her."

"You don't have to say 'kind of.' It's not going to hurt my feelings that the two of you have grown closer." I was struggling for words to explain how much had changed while he was gone, and then realized there was no rush. He'd see for himself that things would be different now that he was home. "In fact, I'm sorry you didn't have more of a relationship with her sooner. She's changed a lot since you were little, and I don't think I realized that until all this happened."

"I wanted to know her better—even before. But Dad wouldn't let me, and I didn't want you to think I was, like, rejecting you or something. But, Mom, I did—"

"Ethan, you don't need to explain anything." I gave him a hug. "It's all going to be okay now. And Nicky's going to be around for a long time. All right?"

He paused, as if he wanted to say something else, but then the worry fell from his face. "I still can't believe you're sisters, though."

"Tell me about it."

I FOUND NICKY IN WHAT would be her bedroom for the next four months. My desk and boxes were pushed into the corner next to the window bench to make room for a dresser for her clothes. She had her iPad propped open on the dresser to stream an episode of *Real Housewives* and was sitting cross-legged on the unfolded Murphy bed, cussing to herself as she tried to weave a string of leather through an impossibly small ring of wire.

"That's going to look cool." She had shown us the sketch of the leather collar-necklace the previous night.

"If I ever finish it," she said, tossing the pieces onto the bed. "If I had all my tools, I would have been done last night."

"I was thinking about that. If you need to bring more stuff from Cleveland before your apartment's done, that would be okay."

She looked genuinely surprised. "Yeah, sure."

"I should have offered before, but—" We had been preoccupied by other things. "I'm second-guessing what we talked about regarding Bill." I found a spot on the bed next to her to sit, being careful not to jostle her jewelry-making setup.

"I know you hate leaving anything in limbo, especially something this serious," she said. "But it's not your job to run around solving crimes right now, Chloe—not even Adam's murder. Your job is taking care of Ethan."

I had shown Nicky the documents I found in my file drawer, and she had convinced me not to take them to the police for now. The way she saw it, Ethan had finally gotten home, and the last thing we needed to do was call attention to our family again. The government was already investigating the Gentry Group and had been worried enough about the potential connection to Adam's murder to notify Nunzio of Adam's contacts with the FBI. The day Olivia called an FBI agent to the stand to testify that Adam had offered to turn over incriminating evidence against not only the Gentry Group but other lawyers at Rives & Braddock, Gentry's stock had dropped nearly 20 percent, and three major R&B clients had announced they were parting ways with their law firm.

Nicky seemed convinced that the FBI would get to the truth, whether I gave them Adam's notes or not.

"But what if Adam's murder is never officially solved? Ethan will spend the rest of his life under a cloud of suspicion. People are always going to wonder."

Nicky gave my forearm a small squeeze. "We talked about this, Chloe. Just lay low for a while. You know the DA's pissed about getting their asses handed to them at trial. If you embarrass them again, they could start investigating *you*."

As far as we knew, Jake didn't have an alibi for the night of Adam's murder. There was nothing to stop the police from arguing that Jake killed Adam, and I was the one who put him up to it.

Nicky could tell that I was still torn. "The documents will be safe and sound in your desk. If the FBI doesn't connect the dots on their own, you can always come forward later."

She was right. I let myself push the thought away. For six months, I had focused on nothing except Adam's murder. I needed to think about the future.

PART IV

CHLOE

38

Three Weeks Later

THE SMELL OF fresh pine greeted me when I opened the apartment door.

It was the first time we'd gotten an honest-to-God Christmas tree in three years, and this year, we did it up right. Ethan and Nicky had lugged back a six-foot balsam fir from the Union Square Greenmarket while I served as the sidewalk lookout. And we had an even bigger blue spruce for the house in East Hampton, where we planned to spend Christmas Day.

I tossed my briefcase and the mail on the bench in the foyer, kicked off my boots, and hung my coat in the front closet. As I turned the corner into the living room, I noticed a strand of garland draped on the hardwood floor next to two ornaments that had come loose.

"Panda," I called out as I tucked the decorations back into place. "Greedy Boy!"

He appeared from beneath the sofa, buzzing past the tree like a ninja, only to circle the room and disappear under the sofa again.

"You're silly, baby."

The rest of the apartment was unoccupied, even the kitchen, despite Nicky's text to me that morning about a recipe she was excited to make. She'd promised an "epic dinner" when I got home from work.

I pulled my cell phone from my briefcase and composed a text. Where's my dinner, woman?

I waited as dots appeared on the screen, followed by Sorry. We ran late Christmas shopping and are getting groceries now. Eataly! Epic, I promise.

I grabbed the mail from the bench and made my way back to the kitchen. I reached for a bottle of wine beneath the island and then opted for a martini instead. I had reason to celebrate. It was Friday night, and the bonus check I got that day made it clear my job at *Eve* was more than safe.

The first sip of gin burned, but the second went down smooth. I hit the remote control to watch the news on the little TV next to the fridge, and then turned my attention to the pile of mail. There had been so many last-minute holiday-shopping catalogs that the mailman had to leave a rubber-banded heap with the doorman.

When I reached the bottom of the stack, I found a brown mailing envelope addressed to Ethan. It was from the Cuyahoga County Clerk of Courts.

What could Ethan need from the court system in Cleveland? I told myself it was probably something Olivia had asked for in the course of the trial and that, regardless, I'd find out for certain once Ethan came home.

I made it through half my martini and two department-store catalogs before I opened the envelope. The cover document was a form letter, indicating the date of the request, the number of pages, and the amount charged. It showed a deposit of $25 in April to initiate an archive search, and then a recent charge for the balance owed for copying the resulting pages, forty-two in all.

The case was *Adam Macintosh v. Nicole Taylor Macintosh*. These were the records from Adam's custody fight with Nicky before they settled. I vaguely recalled a $25 court system charge I had found on our credit card after Adam died. I had assumed he had once again used our personal card for a work expense, but the transaction had been Ethan's. He was looking into the circumstances that had taken him away from Nicky.

I had read the file and was stashing the envelope into my briefcase when I heard keys in the door. I was still standing in the foyer when they entered, all four arms loaded down with bags.

"Hey," Nicky said, nearly bumping me with the door.

"Hey," I said, reaching for a few of the bags and setting them down on the bench. "I'm sorry. I forgot something at work that I need to do tonight. I just need to grab it, and I'll be right back."

Nicky threw Ethan a skeptical look. "I think someone's trying to get out of cooking."

"You're the one with the epic recipe. We're cool with takeout."

"Fine. I'll do everything. But *you*," she said to me, "better be back fast. And *you*," she said to Ethan, "are gonna DJ while I prep."

MY STORAGE UNIT WAS BY Hudson Yards. On the side of the brick building, the gigantic banner that carried the pithy ad of the month read "You'll finally have enough space to pretend to do yoga at home."

The movers had followed my instructions and left the desk so that the drawers were directly next to the unit's entrance and could be opened without rearranging anything. I opened the pencil drawer and felt around until I found what I was looking for—Ethan's burner phone. I tried powering it up, but the battery was dead.

I was halfway to the elevator when I turned around. I opened my desk file drawer and pulled out Adam's file on Rives & Braddock while I was at it.

By the time I got home, the pine of the Christmas tree had been replaced by the smell of butter and garlic. I found Nicky and Ethan in the kitchen. She was pulling stems from a pile of peppers while he read off songs from his iPad, asking what she wanted to hear next.

"Oh god, I'm scared," I said, eyeing her handiwork. I did not share Nicky's tolerance for spicy foods.

"Don't worry. They're shishitos. Not hot at all, I promise. Wait, where are you going?"

"Just changing into chill clothes. I'll be right back. I'll even chop something."

I closed my door, threw my briefcase on the bed, and opened my nightstand drawer. I still had the charging cord for the burner phone Jake had given me. I plugged it into the phone I had found in Ethan's backpack. It fit.

I already knew what number I was going to find, but I needed to be sure. The screen lit up. It wouldn't be long.

39

I WAITED UNTIL the following day, after Ethan left for a bowling party one of the kids from Casden was having for his birthday. I was surprised Ethan was on the invitation list, and even more surprised that he had accepted.

I unplugged the burner phone that was still charging in my bedroom, pulled the envelope from the Cuyahoga County Clerk of Courts, and made my way down the hall to Nicky's room. She told me to come in after a quick tap on the door. She was carrying a bundle of clothes from the window bench. "Sorry, I was just straightening up."

"Nicky, you don't need to clean your room for me. It's your room."

"I'm cleaning for myself. I'll never be as OCD as you, but I'm not a *total* pig." She dropped the items on top of her dresser. "What's up?" she said, gesturing to the envelope in my hand as she took a seat on the edge of her bed. She must have sensed from my expression that I wanted to talk to her about something.

I flipped open the phone and read the number I had already pulled up on the screen. It was stored under "N." A 440 area code. I thought nothing of it when I first found the burner in Ethan's backpack—just another one of Ethan's friends he didn't want us to know about, I assumed. Cleveland had been 216 when I lived there. Apparently 440 had been added after I left.

I had already tried calling the number the night before. The woman who answered told me she'd only had the number for a month.

Nicky's brow furrowed, and she bit her lip.

"He was calling you a lot," I said. "For months." He had started to tell me when he finally opened up about what happened the night Adam was killed, but I had cut him off, assuring him that the tensions between Nicky and me were in the past.

I had expected her to lie, because in my mind, Nicky always lied when backed into a corner. Instead, she admitted it. "He started reaching out to me about a year ago, saying he wanted to know me better. I'm the one who told him to get a burner phone, and I did the same. I was terrified that you and Adam would see he was calling me, and find a way to cut me out even more than you already had."

It wasn't an irrational fear. Adam had had their custody agreement written with ironclad provisions that punished Nicky for any type of unauthorized contact with Ethan.

I remembered Ethan coming into the living room and showing us the *Post* article about his bringing a gun to Casden. "A gun?" Nicky had said. "You never told me about this."

Her comment seemed strange at the time. I never told her anything about Ethan, because we hardly ever spoke. But the comment hadn't been directed at me. It was for Ethan. Whatever information he was sharing with her, he hadn't told her everything.

"He talked to you about us?" I asked, sitting next to her on the bed.

"Not initially. Honestly, I don't think he knew at first what to say to me, but I could tell he wanted a connection. So I'd just talk about my life instead. The jewelry I make. The tomatoes I was trying to grow, even though it was obvious I was never going to make it work. I told him funny memories of you growing up. Old Tessa next door became a bit of a character in the stories—the way I'd always find her going through neighborhood trash, searching for hidden treasure." My parents' neighbor Tessa had been the local crazy old lady even when I was little. She had probably only been my age at the time. "Over time, he opened up. It was clear he was having problems with Adam."

I shook my head. "I don't understand why you didn't tell me."

"And I didn't understand why you weren't telling *me*. We're obviously in a different place now. I figured Ethan was almost an adult and could start making his own choices about what role I'd play in his life. He slowly started sharing more about what was going on—Adam struggling for power, trying to control everyone and everything. It brought back all those old memories. He said ever since Adam found out about the pot, he'd been spot-checking Ethan's room. Treating him like a criminal. I believe him about not selling, by the way, but he was smoking—a lot. Too much. It sounded so much like me before I got sober. He swore he wasn't addicted, but said it made him feel better. And then Adam would try to tell Ethan that he'd done all these bad things when he was high."

"What do you mean, 'bad things'?"

"So I guess if he smokes too much, he crashes. Like a sleep you can't wake up from." I thought of all the times Ethan had come up and fallen into a coma on the sofa. I didn't even realize he was high. "Adam would go yell at him and try to wake him up, and Ethan would be out cold. And then Adam would tell him later that Ethan had screamed at him for coming into his room. And then he told him that he had nearly hurt Panda, throwing him off his bed."

"Adam never told me any of this."

"Exactly. It was always when you weren't home, apparently. After the thing with Panda, Ethan started wondering if Adam was just making it all up."

"But why?"

"To make him feel bad. To control him. That's what abusers do, Chloe. They gaslight their victims. Adam was telling Ethan that he was starting to go crazy like his mother—just like in that video. And that was why Ethan had the webcam set up in his room—he wanted to know if those things were true. He didn't think so, but he didn't understand why Adam would lie to him."

"And what were you doing in response to all this?"

"Just listening to him. He needed someone to talk to."

I started to say that he should have come to me, but obviously he didn't think he could. If I couldn't stand up for myself, how was I going to protect him?

"Did he tell you what Adam was doing to me?" I still couldn't bring myself to say the words. I would never think of myself that way.

"Yes. And it was killing me to know that he was hurting you. I thought so many times about calling you, but I didn't want to betray Ethan's trust. And I was scared it would backfire on me if you guys knew I was talking to him. And then one day—sometime in April, I think—he suddenly throws it out there that Adam could have lied about what happened at the pool when Ethan was little. I mean, I don't remember anything from that night. I just assumed Adam was telling the truth. I was horrified. I was certain there was no way I was actually trying to hurt Ethan, but I took the basic facts as a given. But the reality is: Adam could have just pushed me into the water and dragged me back out. I never would have known."

I finally pulled the documents from the mailing envelope on my lap. "The blood tests at the hospital put you at a point-one-eight BAC, mixed with flu-ox-e-tine—" I sounded out the syllables.

"Prozac," she said. "It does a body good, but not with all the booze in the house."

"Plus zolpidem."

"Ambien."

"That much, Adam told me. But the records also show that you had contusions on your arms. Adam said it must have happened when he was pulling you from the water. When you came to, he said you started resisting him, trying to go back in." Adam was one of the most admired young prosecutors at the county DA's office. No one would have questioned his version of events. He was the heroic dad who had saved his baby from a disturbed wife.

"Maybe. Like I said, I don't remember anything. Or maybe it happened because he threw me in while I was passed out. Honestly, I want to believe that's what occurred, but I can't know for sure. But Ethan was really starting to question whether Adam lied about what went down that night. He accused him during an argument, and that's when Adam started talking about sending him to military school."

"Except I think maybe there *is* a way to know, Nicky." I handed her a page of the police report from the night Adam rescued Ethan from the swimming pool. I had already highlighted the paragraph I wanted her to read.

> Macintosh says wife appeared to be unconscious. As he tried to pull her out of the water, she began to resist him. She kept saying "I'll be an angel over Wallace Lake." Per Macintosh, it's a memory from wife's childhood. He explained it's a reference to family version of the prayer, "Now I lay me down to sleep." He took it to be an expression of his wife's desire to end her life.

"You never saw this before?" I asked.

She shook her head. "It doesn't make any sense. I never told him about that. And that's not even the right line. It was 'I'll wait for you at Shadow Lake.' We were talking about that right when the trial started, remember?"

And then she made the connection. *She* remembered the actual phrase, but *I* hadn't. I had changed it in my head over the years. And during one of those phone calls Adam made to tell me how worried he was about Nicky, I had told him what a good big sister she used to be to me when I was little. I told him how I used to get scared when saying my prayers, and she made up a version about us being angels together. And then I told him my altered version, including the name of the wrong lake.

"He was lying, Nicky. You weren't trying to kill yourself."

"Which means I wasn't trying to hurt Ethan."

"You *didn't* hurt Ethan. He couldn't even talk then. He was breathing perfectly fine by the time paramedics arrived. Adam made the whole thing up—so he could leave you and take Ethan."

"When did you get these?" she asked.

"Yesterday. Ethan ordered them back in April. It must have taken this long for the clerk to get around to the archive search."

She reached over and took the rest of the documents from me and began flipping through them.

"Is that why you killed Adam?" I finally asked. "Because he stole Ethan? You wanted custody again?"

She shook her head. I'd spent my whole life thinking she was a liar, and this time, I really wanted to believe her denial.

But she wasn't denying it, at least not the part about killing Adam. "It was because Adam was starting to hurt you, and I could see how it was destroying Ethan. He was *breaking* that sweet little boy. Sending him away? Throwing him out like that? Take a look at the newspapers, filled with headlines about monstrous men who were once boys unloved by their fathers."

Just as I had asked: *What if we had been boys?*

"It's not what I wanted, Chloe, but Ethan called me Thursday night—it was after you won that First Amendment prize. He said he spent the whole time scared shitless that Adam wouldn't show up and that it was going to set him off if you got upset about it. I guess it all worked out that night, but I could tell Ethan felt like he was living in a tinderbox. He said you were heading to East Hampton for the weekend, and he was going to spend the night with his friend so he wouldn't have to deal with Adam. So I jumped in the car first thing the next morning and was, like, fuck it, I'm going to call Adam out on this myself if I have to. Then I got to your house and had no idea what to do next. I actually saw you leave for your party. You looked so pretty."

I let her keep talking. There was nothing for me to say.

"Then I just waited, and Adam came home. I finally got up the nerve to knock on the door. He let me in." That had to have been when the alarm was turned off. "I told him Ethan saw through him better than I ever could, and that I wasn't going to let him do to him what he'd done to me. I wasn't going to let him break our son. And then that dark side came out, and I felt so powerless again. I have worked *so hard* to improve myself. To be a different person. And in a matter of minutes, it was all gone. I felt small. Meek. And then, I wasn't."

"Were you defending yourself? Did he try to hurt you?"

She shook her head. "I could say that, but it wouldn't be true. I remember his face when he realized what I had done. He was so shocked. And he looked at me, like, Oh, you are going to regret this. But then I pulled the knife out and did it again." I knew she had stabbed him a total of five times. "I'm so sorry, Chloe. I know you loved him."

"Your cell phone. You knew to leave it in Cleveland. And the knife. We weren't missing one."

"I still carry Dad's old Buck knife everywhere I go—or at least I did until that night." He had loved that thing. I had tried buying him fancier ones over the years, but he remained loyal to that twenty-five-dollar blade. "And I left my phone at home because I was terrified that he was going to haul me into court for showing up at the house unannounced. I figured I'd just lie and deny, deny, deny, and then produce my phone records showing I was getting a signal in good ol' Cleveland all weekend."

She had been planning to gaslight the gaslighter, but had ended up killing him instead.

"You're going to turn me in, aren't you? At this point, I don't even care what happens to me anymore. I wanted Ethan to be okay, and I know he's going to be all right with you—now that Adam is gone."

I wasn't going to turn her in. It would destroy my son—our son.

"Do you still have the knife?"

She said she had it hidden at the house in Cleveland.

"Well, I think it's about time you moved some more of your things to New York."

40

BILL WELCOMED ME at his front door with one of those big, warm bear hugs I used to savor. His bright blue eyes twinkled as he stepped back and flashed a contented smile. "I was beginning to wonder if I was ever going to see you again, Miss Chloe."

We had exchanged a few phone calls, but I hadn't seen him in person since the week before Ethan's trial had started. Now it was the day after Christmas, and he was spending the week at his house in Amagansett. It was only fifteen minutes away from our place in East Hampton.

I handed him a gift box from Thomas Pink, tied with a black silk ribbon. "Spoiler alert. I meant to wrap it in proper paper, but I'm afraid all my usual standards have gone out the window this year."

"Well, that's a very polite way of saving an eighty-one-year-old man from embarrassing himself in a battle with wrapping paper." He led the way to his living room, where a fire was roaring. "I'm having a hot toddy. I think you need one, too."

He disappeared into the kitchen and returned with a glass mug, complete with a cinnamon stick, to match the one waiting on the coffee table, and a bright blue gift box tied with a white ribbon. "Merry Christmas, my dear. We do know each other's favorite stores."

A navy cashmere scarf for him. A lead crystal and sterling silver martini shaker for me. "Oh, I will be putting this to excellent use," I said.

"If I'd gone through the year you've had, I'd be drunk until the next presidential election."

I exchanged the empty shaker for my current toddy and took a sip of the warm, honey-touched whiskey. "I'm not the only one who's had a few surprises thrown my way," I said, arching a brow in his direction. "I had no idea that Adam was talking to the FBI. You know that, don't you?"

He waved away my apology. "If he had just come to me, I could have explained he had nothing to be concerned about. Adam was new to M&A, and probably jumped in too fast. He was used to being on the other side of the aisle and didn't understand how deals get done, let alone the big international ones."

"But the FBI *is* investigating Gentry. And the agent who testified at Ethan's trial made it sound like they were looking at your firm, too."

"The feds are always trying to drag lawyers into their clients' scandals. It's a scare tactic—to keep us from doing our jobs. The long and the short of it is, they don't believe in the Sixth Amendment."

"But why would Adam have been trying to work out a cooperation agreement if there was nothing to worry about?"

"That husband of yours—with all due respect—was always a bit too sanctimonious for the private sector. He thought he was above the work, but your loyalty is always to the client. End of story. You know what I mean by that, certainly."

I shrugged. "I'm not a lawyer."

"No, but you just survived a monthlong trial where the government was accusing Ethan of murder. And I saw how you went to bat for him. You never believed Jake was a killer, did you?"

He was staring at me with those charming blue eyes so intensely. I looked away. "No."

"I'm sorry," he said, his voice softening. "That must have been hard for you. My point is that you did what you needed to do to help Ethan. I will never breathe a word of this to anyone else, mind you, but I don't believe for one moment that you told Jake that Adam had raised his hands to you. If you had, the police would have found Adam very much alive, but with two black eyes and a broken nose he'd have to explain. You said what you had to say to protect your son."

I took another sip of my drink.

"I know, I know," he said, waving his free hand. "Don't say anything, one way or another. I'm just an old man running my trap. But I do want to say one more thing: even Jake understands the situation you were in. He loves you, you know."

I looked down. This was going to be even harder than I had thought. "That's not possible," I said. "Not anymore."

"I can see it. He's different now. The light I saw in him—I realize now it was because of what he had with you. And it's gone now. He misses you. You should call him, down the road, when the time is right."

I reminded myself he was only pretending to care about Jake's happiness. Just like I had allowed a jury to wonder if Jake was a killer, Bill had allowed Olivia and the press to suggest that Jake was the one responsible for the wrongdoing at the Gentry Group. I knew otherwise.

"That might be a little awkward if Jake ends up getting arrested for whatever Adam was reporting to the government. I don't need a white-collar criminal in my life right now."

Bill smiled, and his gaze drifted into the distance.

"I'm not kidding, Bill. Ethan's defense lawyer said the FBI made it sound like arrests were imminent and that they're definitely targeting your firm. What if it's not just Jake? What if they come after you, too?"

"I have absolutely no plans to go to prison."

"Of course not. I'm just saying, you should be prepared. Maybe you should go ahead and get your own lawyer, in case it happens."

"I'm eighty-one years old, my dear. Any kind of federal sentence would be a death sentence. Hypothetically, if I thought that was going to happen, it would be lights out. I've had a good run." This clearly wasn't the first time he had pondered the question, and his answer did not sound hypothetical. "Now, enough with all this paranoid talk about court cases and overzealous FBI agents. Tell me everything you're doing now that Ethan's back home."

For nearly an hour we talked about Nicky and Ethan and the draft of my memoir and even a call from a film agent who was interested in our story. It almost felt like old times with my favorite octogenarian boyfriend.

After our second round of toddies, he headed to the kitchen to open a bottle of wine, but I held up a hand to stop him. "If I go down that road, I won't be able to drive home. But thank you so much for having me over. You've been so wonderful through all of this. I won't forget it."

I stood to leave, tucking my fancy martini shaker into my handbag. As he walked to the front closet for my coat, I patted his arm. "You know, I think I need the little girl's room before I hit the road. Do you mind?"

"Of course not. You know your way around."

I opted for the en suite bathroom in the guest room. It seemed like a natural enough choice. I had stayed in this room for two nights a couple of years before, when we lost power over New Year's at our place.

As I ran the water to wash my hands, I pulled the latex glove from my purse and snapped it on. I slid the middle gray wicker bin from the lower shelf of the vanity, the one filled with fresh hand towels. I unwrapped a white, waffle-textured dishcloth from around my father's Buck knife. I tried not to look at the brick-brown stains at the base of the blade. I placed it at the bottom of the bin and restacked the guest towels on top of it.

I pulled off the glove, stuffed it in my bag, and gave my hands a quick rinse.

When I returned to the foyer, Bill was waiting with my coat, wearing his new cashmere scarf. "What do you think?" he said, tossing one end across his shoulder.

"You've still got it, my friend," I said, stepping into my coat. "That's what the girls at work call a smoke show."

"Love it. And I love you."

"Love you, too," I said, giving him a final hug.

I drove straight from his house to the police station. I asked if I could leave something for Detective Jennifer Guidry. To my surprise, the clerk made a phone call, and Guidry appeared a few moments later.

I handed her the Redweld file that Adam had hidden in my desk. "I found these when I was cleaning out our home office. They're about the Gentry Group and Adam's law firm. I thought you could get them to your FBI contact."

Olivia had told me that we probably never would have known about Adam cooperating with the FBI if it hadn't been for Guidry. She opened the file and began flipping through the pages.

"I still don't know who killed Adam. But there's enough there to put Bill Braddock away in prison for years. And, oh, you should make sure the FBI knows that Bill keeps files at his house in Amagansett. He works there all the time."

41

Four Months Later

"YOU GUYS SURE you want to sell this place?" Ethan was standing in the backyard with his hands on his hips, gazing out at the two acres of woods behind my parents' old house. "This lot is pretty sick. You could, like, camp back there."

"Tried it once," I said. "Got a spider bite the size of a softball."

"Can I take that Razor trike down the hill again?" Ethan had been delighted to find a neon-yellow adult-size tricycle in Nicky's garage, apparently a birthday gift she'd reclaimed from a boyfriend who cheated on her three years earlier.

"Knock yourself out," she said. "That thing's going to Goodwill when we leave."

"No way, man. I'm going to find a way to jam it in my suitcase."

We watched him pedal away like a giant five-year-old. "I can't remember the last time I saw him this happy," I said.

"Um . . . that day he wasn't convicted of murder?" Nicky said. "That was definitely a high point."

"He seems okay, right? It's not just me?" He was doing well at the public school, both with his grades and friends. His therapist had even cut him back to once-a-week visits. The FBI's discovery of the knife that had killed Adam, followed by Bill Braddock's invocation of his right to counsel, had probably helped. Ethan now believed that his father had died trying to reclaim his white hat, not because of anything to do with our family. Public opinion had shifted, too. Even if Bill was never convicted, my son wouldn't have to live the rest of his life under a cloud of suspicion.

"Not just you," Nicky confirmed. "He's good. Really good."

We headed back inside to continue packing up the things she wanted to take to New York.

"I've got to say, I can't even believe this is the same house, Nicky. You've done a great job."

My parents' old house was barely recognizable. She'd pulled up the carpet and refinished the floors herself. Peeled the wallpaper a room at a time. Painted the dark-brown kitchen cabinets light gray. She told me she had welded the funky fireplace cover herself. It was light and modern and artsy.

"Thanks. I thought I'd be sadder about saying goodbye, but I'm ready." The house was going on the market next week, and the realtor said she thought she might have already found a buyer. Nicky had offered to split the proceeds with me, since I had given her my half of the house when our mother died, but I assured her the house had been all hers for a long time now. She was going to move to New York, at least until Ethan went to college. I promised to keep helping her with the rent on her apartment, but she had gotten a job at the David Yurman store in SoHo. She was hoping to parlay the position into actually designing the jewelry instead of selling it, but either way, I was proud of her for finding work in New York on her own.

My phone buzzed. It was a text from Olivia Randall. I knew she had been trying to find out once and for all what the Suffolk County

DA was going to do about the knife the FBI found at Bill Braddock's house while executing a search warrant related to the Gentry investigation. The crime lab had confirmed that it was the weapon that killed Adam, but so far, Bill had only been charged by the federal government for crimes he had committed through the law firm. It turned out that the bribes the Gentry Group was paying around the globe were just one part of the massive corruption that Bill was overseeing on behalf of his clients.

I could see from a glance that Olivia's message was long:

I'm sorry to text, but I'm in trial this week. I finally got Nunzio on the phone, and he hasn't changed his mind. Having already lost one trial, they don't think that the murder weapon itself is sufficient to prove the case without other evidence to connect the knife to Braddock. But I do have some good news. My contact in the US Attorney's Office says Braddock has taken a deal to serve four years. The government agreed that he didn't have to turn himself in to start serving the time until the Tuesday after Labor Day, but at least he will be serving real prison time. I hope this gives you some peace. I'll call you when my trial's done, but please reach out if you need anything else before then. Best, Olivia

Nunzio's decision was exactly what I expected. I knew from Adam how hard it was to charge a second suspect after the prosecution had already pulled out all the stops against someone else. Without charges to defend himself against, Bill was standing on his right to silence, not sharing any thoughts he might have about how an old Buck knife ended up beneath his guest towels.

Bill always said that of all the places he'd traveled—Venice, Kyoto, Iceland, Belize, the South of France—no place was as beautiful as the East End on Long Island. He had agreed to plead guilty but wanted to spend the summer in Amagansett. I couldn't stop thinking about what Bill had said the last time I saw him. *Any kind of federal sentence would be a death sentence. Hypothetically, if I thought that was going to happen, it would be lights out. I've had a good run.* I had a feeling I knew how Bill was planning to spend Labor Day.

I typed a reply: Are they charging Jake also? When I looked at his name on the screen, he didn't even feel real anymore. I deleted the message and sent a Thanks instead.

Nicky waved a hand in my face, trying to get my attention.

"Sorry."

She held up a blue-green vase shaped like a bird. "Keep or toss?"

"A little bohemian for my taste," I said.

"You're right. *Keep!*"

She was smiling, one eye on me, as she swaddled it in one of her white, waffle-textured dish towels. It was the same kind of towel she had used to wrap up Dad's old Buck knife.

"Why did you keep that knife?"

She continued wrapping the knickknacks from the mantel, avoiding my eyes. "I don't remember how many times I pulled over on the way back to Cleveland, looking for a place to dump it. Every time I started to get out of the car, I got terrified that someone would see me. So I just kept driving."

"You could've gotten rid of it afterward."

"Maybe in the back of my mind, I thought I might need it—as a last resort. I even considered trying to plant it on Jake toward the end of the trial, but I couldn't bring myself to do it. I could see how much you cared about him."

I was having a hard time believing her. She had never even asked me where Jake lived, which would have been innocuous enough.

"Or maybe it was your 'Send Chloe to the clink' card in case I gave you too much trouble?"

"Wow, you never were good at being funny. Don't quit your day job, sis." As our eyes met, her expression turned serious. So did her tone. "You have to know by now that I would never do anything to hurt you, right? The only reason I ever went to see Adam was to protect you and Ethan."

"I know. And you're right, I'm not funny." When the box was full, I found the nearest roll of packing tape, sealed it shut, and wrote NICKY'S HIPPIE SHIT on the side in all caps with a Sharpie.

Of course, I'd never really know when precisely Nicky made the decision to kill Adam, or what she had planned to do once he was dead. All I knew was that she had changed since the night I chose Adam over her. I had, too.

And we were both continuing to change, but now we would be doing it together.

Author's Note

I KNOW READERS OFTEN WANT to learn more about the originating idea behind a novel. Believe it or not, I sometimes have a hard time recalling the inchoate conception of a book by the time it is finished. That's not the case with *The Better Sister*, which, following *The Ex* and *The Wife*, completes what I see as a thematic trilogy of novels that explore the complexity of female relationships and the diverse roles that women play in contemporary society.

As we juggle busy lives, we often show different faces to our spouses, exes, children, parents, siblings, and coworkers, all while trying to know and be true to ourselves. *The Better Sister*, specifically, is about sometimes conflicting connections between adult siblings. I hope it might also provoke some thoughts about the often gendered nature of threats, abuse, and violence in our culture. Mostly, I hope you enjoy it (and that my own beloved sisters, Andree and Pamala, know that it's not about us!).

Acknowledgments

LIKE ANY OF MY BOOKS, this one was assisted and improved along the way by a village of friends, former students, colleagues, and nieces and nephews who generously lent their respective areas of expertise: Bennett Capers, Kaitlyn Flynn, Joanna Grossman, Damon Katz, Michael Koryta, Lucas Miller, Isaac Samuels, Michael Siebecker, David Smith, Jonathan Streeter, Emma Walsh, and Jack Walsh.

I am so fortunate to be surrounded by smart, hardworking publishing professionals: my editor, Jennifer Barth, to whom this book is dedicated (thirteen books and counting!), Amy Baker, Marissa Benedetto, Jonathan Burnham, Heather Drucker, Caitlin Hurst, Doug Jones, Jennifer Murphy, Kate O'Callaghan, Sarah Ried, Mary Sasso, Virginia Stanley, Leah Wasielewski, and Lydia Weaver at Harper-Collins; Angus Cargill, Lauren Nicoll, and Sophie Portas at Faber & Faber; Giulia De Biase at Edizioni Piemme; Philip Spitzer, Anne-Lise Spitzer, Lukas Ortiz, and Kim Lombardini at the Spitzer Agency; Jody Hotchkiss and Sean Daily at Hotchkiss & Associates; and Jimmy Iacobelli, who nailed yet another book jacket.

As always, I want to thank you—the reader—for bringing the story to life with your own imagination. A special shout-out to the dedicated "kitchen cabinet" who stay in touch online and in real life.

And, finally, thank you to my incredible world of friends and family, especially my remarkable husband, Sean. I got lucky, babe, when I found you.

About the Author

ALAFAIR BURKE is the *New York Times* bestselling author of thirteen novels, including *The Wife* and *The Ex*, which was nominated for the Edgar Award for best novel. She also coauthors the bestselling Under Suspicion series with Mary Higgins Clark. A former prosecutor, she now teaches criminal law and lives in Manhattan and East Hampton.

A Note on the Type

THIS BOOK WAS SET IN Fournier, one of the earliest examples of a transitional font based on the type cut Augustin Ordinaire, by the innovative French engraver and typefounder Pierre Simon Fournier, circa 1742. Transitional-style faces were the inspiration for the modern style made popular by Giambattista Bodoni later in the century.

Fournier (September 15, 1712–October 8, 1768) made numerous contributions to the field of type design—notably his creation of initials and ornaments; his standardization of type sizes; and his development of a new musical-type style, with elegant, rounded notes that made reading music easier.

The Fournier font is a distinguished roman face—almost modern in character—with an elegant French-inspired italic that produces an open, pristine setting that is both stylish and friendly.